DOYLE'S DÉJÀ VU

by

Rodney Houston

ISBN: 978-1-916732-33-9

Copyright 2024

All rights reserved. No part of this publication may be reproduced, stored in a retrieval system, or transmitted in any form or by any means, electronic, mechanical, photocopy, recording or otherwise, without prior written consent of the copyright owner. Nor can it be circulated in any form of binding or cover other than that in which it is published and without similar condition including this condition being imposed on a subsequent purchaser. The right of Rodney Houston to be identified as the author of this work has been asserted in accordance with the Copyright Designs and Patents Act 1988. A copy of this book is deposited with the British Library.

i2i Publishing. Manchester

www.i2ipublishing.co.uk

Contents

Foreword 6
The Players 7
Prologue 9
Chapter 1. Home at Hillsborough 11
Chapter 2. Regret for a past misdeed 12
Chapter 3. The reformed terrorist 13
Chapter 4. The mole 16
Chapter 5. Lawrence takes the bait 19
Chapter 6. Old acquaintances 23
Chapter 7. The hammer drops 27
Chapter 8. The P.I.R.A. revenge plot 29
Chapter 9. Falls Park revisited 32
Chapter 10. Treachery at Trostan 37
Chapter 11. The French connection 42
Chapter 12. Fealty or infidelity 44
Chapter 13. Darius 49
Chapter 14. Off the rails 53
Chapter 15. For those in peril upon the sea 57
Chapter 16. Dunwoody from Dunmurry 68
Chapter 17. The Good Friday fight 70
Chapter 18. Hypnosis at Harley Street 73
Part 2. Rome's Tentacles of Terror 77
Chapter 19. Ezekiel Ben David 77
Chapter 20. The way of sorrows 84

Chapter 21. The first Easter Sunday 90

Chapter 22. Barabbas and blackmail 94

Chapter 23. Trouble at tavern 98

Chapter 24. Suspense under starlight 101

Chapter 25. Barabbas in a bag 104

Chapter 26. In from the cold 111

Chapter 27. Pilate's pragmatism 113

Chapter 28. Ezekiel Ben David soldier of Rome 117

Chapter 29. The Tenth Legion leaves for war 121

Chapter 30. The Pass of Elija 123

Chapter 31. Elija's fire 127

Chapter 32. Promotion and provocation 130

Chapter 33. Decimation but with a difference 133

Chapter 34. Jericho 140

Chapter 35. Saul of Tarsus 143

Chapter 36. Damascus - the good, the bad, and the ugly 147

Chapter 37. The serpent in the sand 156

Chapter 38. The River Euphrates and the Silk Road 159

Chapter 39. The dream of Ezekiel 163

Chapter 40. Vasillis the good Greek 165

Chapter 41. Palmyra – the jewel in the sand 169

Chapter 42. A divided dynasty 172

Chapter 43. Entrapment 174

Chapter 44. King Nambed's nasty predicament 178

Chapter 45. The Mare of Steel 181

Chapter 46. Diplomacy but it ends in death...... 188
Chapter 47. The fatuousness of Governor Flaccus 196
Chapter 48. Purple Haze 202
Part 3. A New Beginning 206
Chapter 49. Melancholy at the museum 206
Chapter 50. Libertad springs a horrible surprise 209
Chapter 51. Palace Barracks Hollywood Co Down 211
Chapter 52. Synthesis – Provos and Prods united 212
Chapter 53. The Sting 214
Chapter 54. Boxing amongst the drumlins 219
Chapter 55. A star is born 222
Chapter 56. Timeless love 227
Epilogue 229

Foreword

This book is dedicated to those of my friends, who like me, have had to endure their own journey with cancer.

The Players

Doctor Richard Aldermatt	Hypnotherapist
Tribune Marcus Acilli	Ezekiel's first kill
Amar	Satin
Tribune Carius Aquillas	An enigma
Aketas	A Greek gladiator of few words
Batya	Ezekiel's Beautiful wife
Eamon Cousins	A reformed terrorist
James Carter	Paddy Doyle's 2nd in command
Col. Robert Conway	Mi5 known as 'Basildon Bond'
Sgt. Les Cooper	One man and his dog
Major Patrick Doyle D.S.M.	Our hero and alter ego of Ezekiel Ben David
Major Ronald Duff	Expert in chemical warfare
Seaman William Dunwoody	Provides 'light entertainment'
Chaplain Jamie Dougan	Paddy's confidant and friend.
Ezekiel Ben David	Paddy's alter ego
David Ben Efron	A sword for hire
Tribune Faisal	A traitor turned good
Governor Flaccus	Syrian Governor, a stupid man
Sean Gallagher	Former friend chose a bad path
Gabriel	God's messenger
Sam Greer	Inn keeper in the glens
Joseph Ben Gideon	A rogue
Publius Galeria	Pilate's evil advisor
General Valerii Gratus	Roman commander and a reasonable man
Miguel Gomez	Paddy's eldest son
Peter Gomez	Paddy's younger son
Sean Goldmann	A boxing superstar
Family Goldmann	Ari & Nina, good people
Commander Thomas Heron	R.U.C. Special branch
Hacerlo	Gladiator, the sprightly Spaniard
Prince Haman	A Parthian prince
Roger 'hacker' Hamilton	Nickname 'pink' a bad bastard
Ismael	Childhood friend now a bitter enemy
Zayin Krass	A sadistic Syrian
Madam Kayla	A high class prostitute
Libertad	Paddy's wife – too good to be true
Lawrence Lennon	A plant in Thiepval
Kirsty Lee	Read and you will see
Longinus	The good Centurion
William John Lavery	Another persona for Paddy
Noel Murphy	P.I.R.A. (now deceased)

Inspector James McKinney	A R.U.C. Inspector
Sgt. Major Michael Maguire	Friend & mentor
Bosco 'bloody' McLernon	Another bad bastard
Niamh	Ben Gidon's wife
King Nambed	Parthian King with troubles
Princess Nazanin	Evil personified
Pontius Pilate	Prefect (the job from hell)
Prince Ramin	Parthian prince (clever)
Batya Rosenshine	Read and see!
Captain Paul Shires	Sniper
Rauri Savage	Dedicated terrorist
Didier Serusier	An evil French dwarf
Samson	Zealot and foster father Simon of Cyrene
Help in troubled times	
Louis Sanchez	Fortunate not to lose his head
Saul of Tarsus	St. Paul
General Titus	Commander Legion Flavia Firma Vasilis
A good Greek and a hero	
Yeshua	Jesus

Prologue

My name is Major Patrick Doyle, D.S.M. I have been a professional soldier for twenty years having seen active service in Ulster and Iraq. Indeed, it was during Operation Desert Storm, in the so-called liberation of Iraq that I took a bullet to my chest. I am told that it was a close call as my vital signs almost ceased. For a full year I was in a deep coma, being kept alive on a ventilator.

I have had an eventful life. To those that I know and trust I have confided to having had two lives: a previous existence in Israel at the time of Jesus when Rome's power was the dominant force in the world. Some friends, those of a cynical disposition, roll their eyes in disbelief; I sometimes remind them that I had taken a bullet in the chest, not my brain. Others, including my wife and children, listen with enthusiasm during the few occasions when I relate my tale of my past. I have been advised not to share my story with those in authority if I wish to remain a serving officer in the British army.

And, I now find myself back at home in my native province of Northern Ireland. My rank of Major has been retained, although it has been decided that I am not yet sufficiently recovered to be placed in a 'fighting position.' Instead, high command decided my knowledge of the province would be invaluable to military intelligence. I have been offered, and accepted, the chief of military intelligence for NI. In the business the position is known as G2. Success would offer the prospect of promotion, but more importantly I would have the opportunity to help thwart the terrorists on both sides, who have blighted my homeland with sorrow for far too many years.

Of course, there are reservations about returning to the province, having been forced to leave when in 1972 I was inadvertently drawn into the conflict between the provisional Irish republican army and the Royal Ulster Constabulary. I had saved the life of a young British soldier during an IRA ambush, it was the last straw: I had to leave Belfast. Fortunately, I had attained a good standard of education, that combined with my athletic prowess gained me entrance to Sandhurst, the British army officer training academy. The rest, as they say, is history.

Chapter 1. Home at Hillsborough

Hillsborough village, eleven miles from Belfast city centre is small and pretty and has some very expensive property. Hillsborough Castle is the official residence of British Royalty and V.I.Ps when they visit the province. In days gone by when Northern Ireland had a governor, this was his official home. It's an attractive Georgian building and is in private grounds, complete with a lake and a lime tree walk. The castle is located atop a steep hill, which is lined with boutique shops, restaurants and pubs. Dare I say it, Hillsborough is very English in its appearance.

Of course, the army is not going to provide me with luxury accommodation at taxpayer's expense. Moss Cottage, located on the village outskirts, would be home to me, my Spanish wife Libertad and our two adult children. It is quaint and named appropriately as the overgrown lawns are full of the stuff. Indeed, all species of weeds known to mankind flourish in the damp gardens. Warm and comfortable and located within easy travelling distance from Thiepval Army Barracks in Lisburn it was a practical location. Thiepval is the home to British army intelligence H.Q. in the province.

We easily adapted to the regular R.U.C. patrols which passed by on a regular basis in unmarked cars, no doubt checking that the home of G2 was secure. P.I.R.A. have long memories and are not known for forget and forgive.

I quickly adapted to my new role in leading teams of analysts in intelligence gathering; in doing so we prevented numerous bombings and assassinations. My role involves active liaison with senior R.U.C. command at Knock Rd. Belfast. It was satisfying to know that my work helped to save people, but there was a fly in the ointment which could have proven to be fatal.

Chapter 2. Regret for a past misdeed

My physical strength was returning fast, after all, I was only forty-two years old and had always been athletic and very active. However, something dark haunted me in my dreams, something that I did wrong in the past. I would awake sweating profoundly; I was in a dark woodland and a man screeched in agony as I fired a revolver shot into the back of his kneecap. That man was a terrorist called Eamon Cousins.

The fact that Cousins had been part of a P.I.R.A. assassination squad sent to eliminate me for having saved a soldier's life did not lessen my sense of guilt and remorse. I had been fortunate to survive, but in doing so I had killed my erstwhile best friends Sean Gallagher and Noel Murphy, both of whom had been part of a killer squad. Their passing did not unduly worry me; Cousins had pleaded for his life and I granted his wish, but it was a life as a cripple consumed with pain. It was this act of cruelty inflicted by me that now kept me awake at night.

Thiepval Barracks at Lisburn has a fully equipped gym. This enabled me to still practice the sport of my life, boxing. I still can move fast for a big guy and deliver a devastating right hook which had sent many an opponent crashing to the canvas. As it happens the medical officer at Thiepval is a keen amateur boxer and proved to be an able sparring partner. It was after one session that I told him the story of what happened to Eamon Cousins. My friend acknowledged that this was the root of my mental health issues and suggested a way in which it might be resolved. I resolved to do so, not knowing that I was about to open a Pandora's box of trouble for my family and myself.

Chapter 3. The reformed terrorist

My post as G2 made it easy to locate Eamon Cousins. It's part of my job to keep watch on those with previous form. As far as could be ascertained Cousins had kept his nose clean. He walked with a bad limp and could just about manage with the aid of a stick. Hardly the picture of an active P.I.R.A. terrorist. Moreover, Cousins was now promoting peace, speaking at fledgeling peace rallies attempting to persuade fellow republicans that the way to bring about reforms was through the ballot box, not the muzzle of an assault rifle. It was reported that he had forsaken Sinn Fein for the more moderate Social Democratic Labour Party; was he a man ahead of his time? I would soon find out.

Nula Street, just off the Falls Road in west Belfast, is a row of newly built single-story dwellings, part of an extensive rebuild of sub-standard housing in the west of the city. It was just after three on a dull November afternoon that promised rain from the thickening clouds overhanging Belfast. I stood unaccompanied and shivered outside number 14. The chill was not just because of the temperature and rain. Although I'm not superstitious, I was slightly pleased that he didn't live in number 13!

I was aware that my actions may put my family and me in danger. Should I do this or simply walk away? The door opened; a woman with greying hair stood in the doorway. She beckoned me to come over.

"You've been watching our home. Would you like to come in?"

"My name is-------."

She interrupted, "Patrick Doyle, I know who you are, you're the bastard that crippled my Eamon!"

I went indoors and she closed the door. The die was cast.

The parlour was warm, tidy and clean. The man slouching in the chair by the fire was frail and grey.

"Hello Doyle, you'll forgive me if I don't stand and hug you!"

I suppressed a smile at the sarcasm, but Cousins grinned from ear to ear.

"Well, I never! Paddy Doyle my old sparring partner and R.U.C. informant in the flesh. I never thought I would ever see you again and now you appear like the proverbial bad penny. Not only that but alone in the Falls, amongst former friends who would now gladly slit your throat after a little bit of torture. I hope you were careful Paddy, some of the boys watch this house; you see since I turned the other cheek, they don't trust me."

"Eamon, I didn't make an announcement that I was coming to visit."

The man sitting opposite gave a wry smile. "I still have my contacts who keep me informed of what's going down. P.I.R.A. know you're back in town!"

The words sent a shiver down my spine.

"Paddy, what the hell are you doing' here and what do you want from me?"

I hesitated before replying, "Eamon, to be truthful I don't really know why I'm here. Sufficient to say that I'm greatly troubled by what I did to you. It was cruel and unnecessary. I certainly don't expect you to be my father confessor and absolve me."

Eamon certainly knew that I was not a member of his faith. I continued, "I want to apologise to you personally and to ask if there is anything which I can do to help with your circumstances?"

Cousins's tone became formal. "Patrick, you know that I was a member of a squad sent to assassinate you. It was war. Do you feel remorse for killing your former friends Gallagher and Murphy?

I thought before answering. "As you just said, it was war. They took their chances, and they got what they deserved."

Eamon coughed; it didn't sound good. "Then you will also remember that I begged you for my life. You spared me, though I had sought to kill you. You blew my knee cap off and I got what I deserved, but I didn't die. You gave me another chance and I have taken full advantage to live a better life. I am indebted to you."

Then, to my surprise Eamon Cousins rose and took both my hands in his. I was pleased that his hands still had the firm grip of a former boxer.

"Patrick, now it's my turn to be a priest. Go from here in peace."

I left the warmth and went out into the drizzle, but with mixed emotions. Lightness in my heart that I had been forgiven and worry that P.I.R.A. knew I was in town and they were not known for forgiveness. I was aware of two shady characters in an old Volkswagen watch me depart. My shivers returned.

Chapter 4. The mole

The bastards knew that I was back in Belfast. But how? Eamon Cousins had known of my return before I contacted him. There could be only one conclusion. We must have a mole within our ranks who was passing information to P.I.R.A. I knew that their army command would now decide as to whether to take me out. My concern was for my wife Libertad and the two boys. Upon my return to Moss Cottage that evening I took her aside and broke the bad news. As always Liber was fully supportive as she had been throughout my turbulent army career. I then phoned my second in command and gave instructions for an emergency team meeting to be convened. The meeting would also involve senior R.U.C. officers from special branch.

The secure room at Thiepval was soundproof and bug proof and on the severe side of being austere. My 'opo' James Carter and four of his most trusted men awaited my arrival. Commander Thomas Herron from special branch had a glum expression at being summoned at this late hour. I entered and all stood, their chairs scraping on the tiled floor.

No sooner had I motioned for them to be seated when a 'James Bond' look-alike with an attaché case in hand strode in. The guy was tall, slightly tanned and immaculately dressed in a tailored grey suit, white shirt and what appeared to be an 'old school' tie. As he took his seat, I got a waft of expensive aftershave. The man exuded confidence and someone who was used to privilege. I took an immediate dislike to him. I knew I was being unfair, perhaps even being influenced by jealously, but I had met many cocky bastards like him during my army career. Commander Herron took the floor, "Gentlemen, this is Colonel Robert Conway from MI6. I believe he will make a valuable contribution to resolving the issue in hand."

Now it was my turn and after apologising for the summons at this late hour I related the story of my visit to Eamon Cousins. I disclosed my wounding of the terrorist in

1972, which was illegal. I told of my compulsion to meet with Cousins again. As I spoke Commander Herron made an audible sucking sound through his teeth. It was obvious that the senior R.U.C. officer thought I had taken leave of my senses by my foolhardy actions. He held his peace but the expression on his face said it all. 'Bond' took copious notes as I spoke. I concluded, "It would appear that we have got a mole in our midst, some bugger is passing info to P.I.R.A. I want all of you to put forward options as to how to proceed."

Once again it was Commander Herron who stood. "Our priority G2 is to consider your personal safety and that of your family. If it is deemed appropriate it will be arranged for you to take up a new position based on the mainland. That, of course, will be your decision after discussion with your wife. We would be sorry to lose you as during the short time you have been here you have made an invaluable contribution to our intelligence network." The Commander wanted to exert his authority, however my opo, James Carter, was not prepared to let the policeman have it all his own way. He spoke up.

"It's the boss's decision, but he has my full support whatever he decides to do. I think that it may be prudent for Libertad and the family to return to England until we catch the buggers. We continually face threats, it's part of life in the province and the high price which we all pay in order to protect the public. I have given orders that a total security review takes place on all operatives based at Thiepval. Profiling of everyone's activities and contacts will begin immediately."

The man from MI6 didn't bother to get to his feet. His plummy tones, typical of the English aristocracy resounded through the room. I decided to give him the moniker of 'Basildon Bond'.

"Good evening one and all. My name is Colonel Robert Conway, Bob, to my many friends. I think I can save Mr. Carter the task of profiling everyone on base. I know who the bugger is!" All eyes in the room now focused on the posh spook.

"There's a guy working here as an assistant analyst. We've been suspicious of him for some time and have been tapping his phone and those of his contacts. We allowed him to continue operating thus far because he has been passing on false information supplied by us. On occasion P.I.R.A have taken our bait and a reception committee awaited their assassins."

Basildon smiled broadly, "The assassins became the assassinated. As you say in Belfast, slap it up them. None of us shed any tears at their demise. P.I.R.A. may have become suspicious of the quality of their plant's information, but I think there is one more job left in him. They will not be able to resist an opportunity to kill G2 and we are going to help them!"

I stared at Basildon, "What's the mole's name?"

"Lawrence Lennon, a nephew of Sean Gallagher with whom you were acquainted in 1972.

I grimaced this was becoming worse with every passing day.

Chapter 5. Lawrence takes the bait

All the team had an opportunity to put forward ideas before Basildon once again took centre stage.

"I propose we use Lawrence to bait a trap. G2, we know that you are scheduled to be the guest speaker at the forthcoming Interpol conference in Glasgow in one week's time. Of course, the conference is genuine, it's already been announced in the media. But you will not be travelling to Glasgow. However, to make Lawrence think it's genuine your travel tickets will be purchased for the early morning flight from Belfast International. I will ensure that he is privy to this information and that you will be travelling unaccompanied in order to attract less attention. Both your driver and your bodyguard will leave you alone at the set-down point at the airport. It's at this point you will be at your most vulnerable. Lennon will pass this guff to P.I.R.A. The buggers will want to hit you at the point at which you are most vulnerable, which will be the terminal entrance. We will, of course, be waiting for them. My team will always have your back; we will hit them fast and hard. Every effort will be made to avoid civilian casualties. G2 are you game?" All eyes turned to me in expectation.

Once again, I experienced the surge of adrenalin and the excitement of anticipated action. Sometimes old ways die hard. "Yes," was all I said.

Basildon made sure that the said Lawrence Lennon received details of my travel arrangements. We knew that he in turn would fully brief P.I.R.A; this would be their golden opportunity to have their pound of flesh. We would not be disappointed.

The Monday morning of my supposed travel dawned damp and dreary. That was a misnomer, it was seven am and dawn was still over an hour away. The windscreen wipers on my Jaguar worked with a hypnotic rhythm. Peter, my driver, handled the large car through the dark and dazzle of headlights on our route out of Belfast to the international airport. I sat in the back seat alongside Bruno, my armed guard. No one spoke and the atmosphere was heavy with anticipation. I felt the comforting bulge of my Glock pistol in its shoulder holster under the left side of my jacket, placed there for a smooth fast draw should it be needed. I had no wish to kill anyone but if need be, I would do so without hesitation.

All too soon the bright lights of Belfast International Airport cut through the darkness. After we entered the final roundabout, the road ran parallel with runway 25, the main southwest facing take-off and landing route. It at this point that the 'what ifs' began to run through my brain, accompanied by a tingling feeling at the base of my spine.

'What if Lennon hadn't taken the bait?'
'What if P.I.R.A. hit us on the approach road?'
'What if there's too many of the bastards?'
'What if one of my team is in the wrong place?'

The palms of my hands began to feel cold and clammy. So much for Mr. Cool, veteran of Ulster, Iraq and other theatres of war. Stop it! I reprimanded myself. The car park light complexes glowed on our right as we entered the airport. I took a deep calming breath as my hand gripped the butt of my pistol. The barrier at set-down rose and the Jaguar purred to the kerb side entrance. As normal Bruno exited first and opened my door. Both of us scanned our surroundings; nothing appeared to be unusual. Commuters wheeled their luggage; wheels click clacked on the pavement joints. People hugged their departing loved ones, all seemed to be normal; but I had learned never to accept things at face value. Bruno got back into the car and Peter drove them to the exit barrier. To all appearances it looked as though I was on my own, I certainly felt that way as the entrance doors automatically opened.

Passengers scanned overhead monitors, seeking the appropriate check-in desk, as others formed orderly lines, pushing cases forward, tickets and passports in hand. I flushed with guilt; what if our plans led to some of these innocents being killed? Some military top brass gave it the ridiculous term, 'collateral damage' which is disgusting as it degrades human life.

I shuffled forward, trying to delay my approach to the check-in desk for as long as possible without arousing suspicion. There was no sign of either terrorists or security forces, this was beginning to feel like a farce, at some point soon I would need to radio my driver to take me out. It was then that the screams started.

Two men, both wearing balaclavas, burst out into the departure hall from behind the outsize baggage department. Both held automatic AK rifles which they waved threateningly as they made a beeline for me. The crowd parted like the waves of the Red Sea under the command of Moses. Husbands pushed their wives and children out of harm's way, years of living in Belfast had taught them when it was time to get down!

The terrorists were now only ten feet away and had a clear shot at me; I knew I was about to be blasted to oblivion.

As though by magic the Glock pistol appeared in my right hand, but I knew it to be useless against AKs at this range. A sharp retort echoed around the building; Basildon stood alongside me; his baggage forgotten. His shot had taken one of the buggers in the right eye, blood and brains flowed through his balaclava eye piece. The terrorist's head jerked back, his knees buckled, and he spilt the rest of his brains when he hit the floor.

The other one tried to get a shot off, my luck was in, the AK jammed. In desperation he swung the rifle at me like a club. I froze, my pistol was almost touching his head, but something stopped me from squeezing the trigger. Bang! My would-be killer fell stone dead. Basildon, smoking pistol in hand cursed, "Sir, do you want to be feffing dead?" Strangely the plummy voice no longer irritated me.

If something, or someone, from my past had prevented me from pulling the trigger, then perhaps it was time for me to resign my commission. Had the terrorist's gun not jammed then several passengers and I would have died. Bruno and several other MI5 men bundled me back to the Jaguar.

We had all been fortunate, including the two baggage handlers who had been tied to the outsize baggage machine rails. They were now released, shaken but otherwise unharmed.

The two dead assassins were known to us. The one that drew my attention was Connor Murphy, son of Noel Murphy. Noel had died by my hand. Now his son, aged only twenty-one lay in the mortuary. This vendetta was far from over, I had disturbed a P.I.R.A wasp nest of hatred. I had to decide, stay in Belfast or take my family to the greater safety of the English mainland.

Chapter 6. Old acquaintances

My mentor in the British Army was Sergeant Major Michael McGuire, a man who had devoted his whole life to the British Army. When I took up my position with the Irish Guards, known as the Micks, I was a raw young second Lieutenant, it was the Sergeant Major who took me under his wing. He addressed me as Sir because of my commission, but in reality, it should have been the other way round. This man taught me skills which would save my life on many occasions. Michael was my best man when Libertad had consented to marry me. Now aged about seventy, he was retired and living in Dalkey in his native Dublin.

The other friend and comrade was Inspector James McKinney of the Royal Ulster Constabulary. For this man I had mixed feelings. He had sought to exploit my friendship with Sean Gallagher in order to penetrate P.I.R.A. Fair play to him, James had to use all the weapons at his disposal. When the time came and I had to leave Belfast, it was he who had secured my entrance to Sandhurst. For this I will always be grateful to him. James McKinney now lives in a comfortable dwelling in peaceful north down. Since my return to the province, we had kept in regular contact by telephone. It was as though the years had melted away and as before he proved to be a mine of information and valuable advice.

We decided that Liber would accompany James and myself to visit Sergeant Major Michael in Dublin. We would travel by the enterprise express train which links Belfast Central with Dublin Connolly, a journey of approximately ninety miles. The train stops but a few times, in Portadown, Newry and Dundalk and completes the cross-border journey in about two hours. We met the Inspector at Belfast Central. He looked well for his years, and he kissed Liber on both cheeks in Spanish style!

Travelling by enterprise is to use Ireland's premier train service and we settled into our comfortable first-class seats. Our 'heavies' were seated just across the carriage. These guys were 'carrying' which caused their well-tailored jackets to bulge slightly around their shoulder holsters. The train glided to its first stop at Portadown, a town, which like most in the province had been scarred by the P.I.R.A. bombing campaign.

Our hot Irish breakfast was served as we passed through the verdant countryside of south Armagh. We could see British army observation posts strategically placed on hilltops; their radio antenna silhouetted against the glow of the early morning sky. A troop-carrying helicopter droned towards its base in the village of Bessbrook. A shiver ran along my spine as I remembered the last time, I had been here in what we termed 'bandit country'. I had been serving in the S.A.S lying in muddy ditches, whereas now I was in a plush train travelling in excess of seventy miles per hour. Despite the rugged beauty of the place, I felt a sense of relief as we rolled down to Dundalk station where more passengers would board.

The enterprise slowed upon reaching Dublin's northern suburbs. The pretty coastal village of Malahide, which has a marina filled with expensive yachts, passed on our port side. Our train's wheels grated on the maze of points as we approached Dublin Connolly train station. The doors opened with a loud hiss of compressed air, and we stepped out into the sunshine of the Republic of Ireland's capital. Mingling with our fellow passengers we made our exit through the ticket barriers. We heard soft southern accents in striking contrast with the harsher tones of their fellow Irishmen and women from the northern six counties. And there he stood, head and shoulders above all others, Sergeant Major Michael Maguire of the Royal Irish Guards.

Although now in his early seventies Michael Maguire was still the most impressive man I had ever met. Ramrod straight and hair turned to silver he marched straight to me before snapping to attention and saluting. Liber fell into his arms, her eyes filled with tears of joy. Then it was my turn to be embraced in his giant bear hug. James McKinney appeared slightly embarrassed by the proceedings.

'Patrick Doyle, ye've grown into a fine figure of a man, ye were little more than a boy when I was best man at your wedding.'

The Sergeant Major, despite a lifetime soldiering in the British army, had retained his smooth Dublin brogue.

"Come, we have a lifetime of stories to catch up on, you will of course, be staying with me at Dalkey, but before then I'm taking you somewhere special for drinks and then lunch."

I took note that drinks came first in the order of priorities.

Michael, organized as ever, had a taxi waiting as we descended the escalator. The driver threaded our way through the chaotic Dublin traffic, enveloped in the cacophony of engine noise, agitated horn blowing and shouts, here it was every man for himself on the city roads. The wide bridge spanning the River Liffey at the end of O'Connell Street was thronged with tourists. Despite the troubles in the nearby north, Dublin seemed unaffected and was truly a cosmopolitan city. North Americans with their loud dress sense and voices to match seemed to be in the majority, coming to see the 'old homeland.' They all choose to include something green in their dress. They were joined by Australians, Canadians and camera-clicking Japanese. We passed the famous frontage of Trinity University, whose famous alumni included the playwright, Oscar Wilde. Entering Nassau Street, we turned south towards St. Stephen's Green. I wondered where the Sergeant Major was taking us. Our cab pulled to a stop at the steps of the Hibernian Club, a city centre gem and one of the most prestigious clubs in Dublin city.

The doorman greeted us warmly before escorting our party to the base of a sweeping curved staircase, complete with wooden balustrade.

"Sergeant Major, your table is ready Sir." The man preceded us onwards and upwards, and our feet sank in the deep pile carpet. Behind the long-curved bar was an array of spirits of well-known but also obscure brands from all corners of the world. Then we were invited to take our soft comfortable seats. The champagne was on ice and the barman, napkin over arm, came to pour. Glasses filled, we toasted the good health of all present. Pouring and toasts completed, the barman took his leave. "I will be back shortly with the luncheon menus."

I smiled, "Sergeant Major, you have done well for yourself." I looked around at the opulent settings. Michael returned my smile, "Ah sure we Maguires have had a lot of money in the family some of which has passed down to meself! I could never have afforded this on what Her Majesty paid me!"

And so, the stories began, and the years rolled away. An expert orator Michael had us in tears of laughter when we were summoned into the large dining room. The oculus circular roof window permitted natural light to beam down upon our table bedecked with the finest Irish linen.

Everyone decided to have traditional Irish dishes such as stew, Limerick ham, seafood chowder, ribeye steak served with champ. Each dish was accompanied by a wine of choice. I had the steak and champ and a creamy glass of Guinness. Appetite sated and with the stories still being told it was time for our cab to Dalkey.

Chapter 7. The hammer drops

Dalkey is an affluent suburb located to the southeast of Dublin. Very posh, it is complete with its very own castle. It has had its fair share of famous residents. Samuel Beckett was born in Dalkey, and Maeve Binchy lived nearby. When we exited the cab, we found the air to be tainted with the tang of the sea, but another surprise was in store.

Sergeant Major Michael Maguire was obviously a man of means. We found ourselves standing outside a two-storey red brick mansion, bedecked with ivy and late autumn flowers. The lawns were neat although mowing had stopped with the onset of autumnal rain and gales. The words, 'Millionaire Major' flashed through my mind causing a smile.

"Welcome to my humble abode." Michael escorted us along the path, gravel crunching beneath our feet. The house was vintage Dublin and must have been at least one hundred years old. Inside it was warm and airy and furnished in keeping with the home of a country gentleman. We went to the drawing room. "Michael, I had no idea that you are such a wealthy man, why on earth did you join the British army, you obviously had no need to work?"

Michael beamed his most charming smile. "Perhaps, no need in a monetary sense, but we must all find a way of getting satisfaction. My father was a successful banker, as you can see from this little lot, but bean counting was not the life for me. I wanted a life of adventure and to see the world and the 'Micks' gave that to me. So, I'm happy with my lot. I was an only child and the family home passed to me."

I was gob-smacked as were the others in our small entourage. The live-in cook served us a light supper before the stopper was removed from the brandy decanter. The cognac was smooth and warm and accompanied by a fine Cuban cigar. To my surprise Liber lit up and puffed away like the men. My wife, as ever, was full of surprises.

Liber asked, "And Michael, has there ever been a Mrs. Maguire?"

"No, unfortunately not, perhaps my only regret in life. I have been a travelling soldier all my adult life. Sure, there have been lots of ladies, lots of them, in fact I've had more than my share, but no woman in her right mind would have taken the likes of me on."

I noticed that Bruno, my bodyguard, seated on the far side of the room was busily engaged taking a call on his headset. Bruno was becoming more perplexed the longer the call continued. Something was radically wrong. He hung up and approached.

"Sir, I am most sorry to interrupt but I must speak to you in private now!"

My blood ran cold.

Bruno related the ill tidings, and I went back to my wife. My hands trembled with fear and my voice was breaking as I told her, "Liber, they have taken Miguel!" Who has taken our son?"

P.I.R.A. raided our cottage this evening and killed our two R.U.C. guards. The bastards have captured our son."

Liber stood up; her brown eyes were incandescent with rage. She strutted across the carpet, back straight, head up and her foot stamped as she pivoted like an enraged flamenco dancer who had reached the climax of the dance.

"Fucking bastards, I will kill them all with my bare hands," she shouted in Spanish. I fought back my tears and decided best not to translate her words. Bruno, a giant amongst men now seemed to stoop and be helpless as he told me, "Sir, a chopper will be here at first light to take us back to Thiepval."

There followed a sleepless night relieved only when I heard the thwack of the Sea King helicopter's rotors as it landed on the lawns at first light. A beautiful day had ended in disaster.

Chapter 8. The P.I.R.A. revenge plot

The team stood as I entered Thiepval's secure room and the only sound was that of chairs being pushed back across the flooring. "Gentlemen, please be seated." James Carter, my second in command took the floor. "Sir, the news is grim. Miguel has been abducted by P.I.R.A. operatives, some of whom we believe to be their most fanatical followers. We do have a mole in their midst, but as of yet he has been unable to obtain any intel as to where your son is being held. P.I.R.A. have sent us this statement, we know it to be genuine as the correct code words have been used.

"We the members of the Provisional Irish Republican Army notify Major Patrick Doyle that we have his son, the boy known as Miguel, in our custody. Our memories are long, and deeds done against us never go unpunished. It is fitting that you will be reunited with him before your execution. You will meet with us in Falls Park, on twenty-fifth of November, three nights hence; the place where you murdered our comrades Sean Gallagher and Noel Murphy. Miguel will be released unharmed providing you comply with the following instructions:

You will come unaccompanied to Falls Park.

You will come unarmed.

You will stand under the third street light at the entrance, where you will receive further instructions.

We are fully aware of the Brit's propensity for treachery; therefore, a cannula will be inserted into Miguel's artery, it will be loaded with a concoction of lethal drugs. It will be administered at the slightest sign of treachery. Also be aware that you and Miguel will constantly be in our sniper's crosshairs. It is your life in exchange for that of your son's safety. We expect you to confirm your acceptance through the normal channels. Should nothing be heard, you will receive instructions as to the location of Miguel's body."

Carter finished reading and there was an immediate hush and it felt as though the room temperature had fallen several degrees. Carter resumed, his voice trembling,

"Sir, there's more bad news. The body of Eamon Cousins has been found; he was shot in the back of his head execution style. A placard bearing the word traitor had been placed around his neck. Unfortunately for him, his former comrades had mistakenly deduced that he was in league with you."

The words hit me like a brick in the face. I recalled the shady characters who had watched me depart Nula Street. A wave of despair and remorse passed over me. It seemed that my every action caused a tragedy. Now Cousins, a reformed man, had paid the ultimate price for talking to me whilst my own son was at the mercy of killers. Why so much pain, why so much misery?

The man from MI6, Colonel Robert Conway, to whom I had given the moniker 'Basildon Bond' and an endless source of irritation to me powered up his plummy gob. It was unfortunate for him that he chose the wrong approach.

"So, the fucking crippled mick is dead! Good riddance, saves me one bullet!"

A red light flashed through my brain. My fist caught Basildon squarely on his jaw. He fell back arse over tit and crashed to the floor. Several pairs of hands, including Bruno rushed to restrain me. A befuddled Conway shook his head as he spat out blood and a broken tooth. Eventually, a dazed smile crossed his face, mixed with condescension as he continued to look down both nostrils at the rest of us humans not born to his imagined high station.

Basildon spoke after spitting more blood. "Patrick, my boy you pack a mean punch, that was quite a wallop that you just gave me. Absolutely not the way to treat a friend who has saved your life."

The plummy tones were distorted by his painful mouth, much to my satisfaction.

"First, you are not my friend. Secondly, the term mick is not to be used in a disrespectful way; you forget that I am a Major in the 'Micks' the Irish Guards regiment. And do not disrespect a man who risked and given his life to try and bring about peace.

"Quite correct Patrick, I do apologise for my inappropriate comments, however let it be on record that I want a proper boxing match with you when this little lot is resolved."

"Yes, you will get your boxing match, I will be pleased to give you a bloody nose and teach you some much-needed manners."

James Carter's patience had been stretched to the limit, he had more than enough of this behaviour, even though I was his boss.

"You two must focus on the problem in hand. We must save the life of this child."

My number two had just administered a stinging rebuke to two of his superior officers. He then continued, "By staging the meet three night's hence P.I.R.A. wish to make us sweat with trepidation. Ironically, we can use that time to prepare a nasty little surprise for them."

I interjected, "We cannot afford to try tricks. I am going to comply with their demands in order to save my son."

There followed a short silence. James chose his words with great care. "Sir, our mole has established that Miguel will not be spared. You are both to be shot. Their thirst for vengeance is such that they want your wife and family to suffer the most severe grief. If you sacrifice yourself, it will be to no avail. Please consider our plan, it is Miguel's only chance to survive."

Ironically, it was the man from MI6, the man holding a bloody handkerchief to his bleeding lip, who rose to his feet.

"Gentlemen this is my little proposal to deal with these bastards."

Chapter 9. Falls Park revisited

And so, midnight on 25th November found me entering the dark and foreboding place that Falls Park becomes in late autumn. The air was laced with moisture which mixed with the sweat upon my brow. Now I felt fear, but this was not fear as I knew it, this was fear for my beloved son, in the knowledge that the slightest mistake would bring about his demise. I fought to blink back tears as I walked forward alone, my army boots crackling the gravel path underfoot. In the distance came the sounds of dogs barking and close at hand an owl hooted its night-time call. I knew that eyes were upon me, but I could detect no sign of human life.

I was dressed in my khaki battle dress complete with peak cap of the Irish Guards, the regiment which I had served with distinction. If I had to die it would be as a soldier and an officer, though I certainly did not regard myself as a gentleman. Ram rod straight, shoulders back, chest out, I marched at a steady pace of seventy paces per minute to stand at attention at the appointed place.

The autumn storms had failed to divest the trees completely of foliage. Now the night's chill wind caught them causing the branches to bend with a soft soughing sound. It was eerie, no one appeared, nothing stirred except the wind. I stood, gazing straight ahead, the hairs on my neck standing erect. For some reason the biblical story of Daniel entering the lion's den came to me. Perhaps the Daniel of old had stood a better chance of survival than I currently did. I was also conscious that my standard-issue Webley revolver was conspicuously absent from my holster.

For a full five minutes I stood alone; if the bastards wanted me to sweat, they were certainly succeeding. Then I detected movement in the periphery of my vision. A figure, dressed in black fatigues and balaclava materialised from the dark. The arrogant bastard did not even bother to point a pistol at me. I also got no comfort in the knowledge that my head was now in the crosshairs of a sniper's scope.

"Well, would you look at the fine soldier boy!"

His harsh Belfast accent grated me as he continued with his mocking.

"Ah, the soldier boy from Belfast made good. An officer and a gentleman, and above all a traitor!"

"Where's Miguel," I snapped, "The deal was Miguel's life in exchange for my surrender."

"Now Patrick, you must show some patience, Miguel is close by and unharmed, although his arm is a little painful where we stuck the cannulae in."

Two more men emerged from the shadows, these guys carried AK47s.

"Now Patrick, we'll be going for a wee walk, and don't you be getting any foolish ideas. You still have a few more minutes to live, providing you behave."

A henchman pushed me in the back with his rifle. I hoped the bastard had placed the safety on. Then, reminiscent of what occurred twenty years ago, I was frogmarched to a small clearing. It was the very spot where I had killed Gallagher and Murphy. I had survived that attack although the odds had been against me.

"Patrick I'm sure that you well remember this wee place." The terrorist shone a torch illuminating two small marble monuments inscribed with the words, 'Sean Gallagher and Noel Murphy, comrades killed in action by forces of the British Crown.'

I managed a wry smile at that inaccuracy.

"Where's my son? I demanded, hoping my voice did not betray my terror. The provo gave orders, "Bring out the brat!"

A man led Miguel forward. Miguel had a long tube attached into his arm attached to a syringe held by the terrorist. The sight of which drove fear throughout my being.

"Papa!" the boy shouted.

"Release my son immediately!"

"Well, Patrick, it doesn't work that way anymore. It's us that give the orders not you Brits. We want you to enjoy Miguel's last moments as he convulses in agony due to death by toxins."

I spoke softly to my boy. "Miguel, quiero seas muy valiente. Cierra los ojos, con fuerza, cuando te diga que lo sabras estas malos se habran ido."

(I want you to be very brave. Close your eyes tight, when I tell you to open them the bad guys will be gone.) I snapped to attention and saluted my son. The signal had been given. Tongues of fire licked the darkness; it came from each of the four compass points. First to crumple was the guy holding the syringe, his head exploded like a watermelon struck with a hatchet. Then the three provos pirouetted as they parted company with their skulls. The stench of carbide and blood filled the air. I leaped upon Miguel and ripped the cannula from his arm, before sheltering him with my body.

The remaining provo had somehow been left alive; he came at me pistol extended. I had managed to conceal my officer's baton in my jacket lining. I flung it catching him a glancing blow across the face. Now he had a feral smile and I braced myself for the bullet's impact. The pistol barrel was thrust at my eyes, and I knew what was going to come from the dark aperture. Crack! Crack! I was still alive and found Basildon Bond standing beside me. The eye slits in the terrorist's balaclava provided an exit route for his brains.

"Really Patrick, I'm going to have to stop saving you! It's a little onerous and quite thankless."

I almost hugged the bugger with relief.

From the undergrowth stepped our four snipers. Even in the darkness there was something familiar about their leader. The man snapped to attention before me.

"Good evening, Sir. May I call you Paddy?"

"Good grief, Corporal Paul Shires!"

Then I spotted the pips upon his shoulders. He was now Captain Paul Shires.

"Of course, you may call me Paddy, congratulation upon your promotion."

Paul Shires was my mate from S.A.S. selection, he was the man who had helped me get through the seemingly impossible rigours of that process. Formality was dispensed with forthwith and we embraced warmly. My traumatised son, Miguel, joined in the group hug.

Paul nodded at the dead provos. "Another good result against P.I.R.A. This one is for Sergeant Willis."

He was referring to our dead comrade, killed during our raid to take out the infamous provo sniper at a raid at Corrybrackagh, eleven years ago. Many people owe their lives to the skills of Captain Paul Shires.

To my complete surprise, Libertad, escorted by a female Captain, appeared at my side. She quickly took our son into her warm embrace. But before she led Miguel from the field of carnage, she lashed out with her stiletto shoe dislodging the balaclava from the last gunman to die. She spat upon the eyeless corpse, "Puto Bastardo!"

Best not to be translated. Best never to mess with a lady's baby!

I removed the mask completely to look upon the dead distorted face of Nicko Mullen, who until now had been like Teflon man. All things come to an end. His body, together with the three other provos were loaded into a truck for the morgue. I remembered Yeshua's words, "Those who live by the sword will die by the sword." I shivered uncontrollably. Miguel made a complete recovery from his trauma, but we decided it was best that my family move to Malaga to live with Libertad's parents. I would join them in due course. In the interim I would reside in Thiepval barracks. With regret I gave up Moss Cottage.

But Spain would have to wait; our intelligence became aware that something big was coming down from P.I.R.A. We did not know what or when, but we gleaned that they would go for a 'spectacular' a major event that would force a British withdrawal from the province. My job was not yet done.

Chapter 10. Treachery at Trostan

The glens of Antrim in the northeast of the province are one of the most scenic locations in Ireland, indeed in all the world. The glens range from the magnificence of Gortin Glen's cliffs to the mountain of Trostan which stands at 550 metres above sea level. The nine glens have attracted visitors from all over the world to this part of the emerald isle.

A local historian described the glens as a place of culture, castles, churches and craic. Carved by glacial action they radiate from the Antrim plateau to the Irish sea. The original inhabitants were Celts who used the famous blue stone shale to construct wall, homes and tombs. Red squirrels play in the trees flanking the banks of cascading foaming waterfalls.

Yet the glens amidst the peace and tranquillity was a place also subject to human troubles. Ancient Irish Chieftains had fought for ownership of them and over many years much blood has been spilt here. Now in the year 1992 Celts are still the dominant people, with their own distinctive traditions and ways and accents: a people with no love for the British whom they regard as foreign invaders with no rights to be on the island of Ireland.

Early December and the people of Galboyle were preparing to celebrate a traditional Christmas. Decorations were beginning to appear in cottage windows and the village Christmas Fir tree had been erected in the square opposite the church. Situated at the foot of Mount Trostan Galboyle might even experience a white Christmas, not unknown at this high altitude. Fires roared in the hearths of the stone cottages as they had for many winters past. But problems lurked beneath the surface of serenity.

The stone cottage of Ruairi Savage and Kirsty Lee lies at the southern end of Galboyle. Dawn had broken in a cloudless sky allowing rays of golden light from the low winter sun to permeate the couple's bedroom window with a warm cheerful glow.

They both slept in the nude as they always had during their four-year relationship. Marriage had been discussed but never entered, their love was endless, and they felt no need to formalise it. Ruairi caressed Kirsty's back before gently easing her over. His tongue found her erect nipples in the centre of her pert breasts, and she willingly opened her thighs. Kirsty Lee's black shining hair tossed in contrast to Ruairi's red mane as they brought each other to a crescendo of pleasure.

When both were sated, they headed for their small shower. Kirsty's jet-black hair and almond eyes denoted her Chinese heritage whilst Ruairi's ginger red hair and pale Celtic skin stretched back in lineage to his Celtic forefathers. They had met while studying at Queen's University, Belfast, both had been active in student politics and found they had a shared hatred of all things relating to perfidious Albion. Sexual desire and shared political views cemented a somewhat unlikely relationship between two different cultures. Kirsty graduated with a degree in creative writing whilst Ruairi had majored in physics.

Now living together after their student days, their income was augmented by royalties from Kirsty's first novel, appropriately named 'Perfidious Albion in Ireland.' Ruairi's skills had been used in more nefarious ways. He killed those who opposed his political ideology. Ruairi was commander of the glens division of P.I.R.A. Between operations he had found work as a farm labourer. Today would be busy for both. Although now an active member of P.I.R.A. Kirsty had not been given access to the army council where strategic decisions were taken. Her failure to be admitted was a cause of some tension between her and her partner.

McGurgan's bar had a central place in Galboyle. It had whitewashed walls and windows in need of a good wash. Ruairi and Kirsty entered and as usual their noses were assaulted by the tang of disinfectant competing with the stench of urine coming from the gentlemen's toilets. The customers were mostly men, so on the odd occasion women frequented the bar they had to seek relief at a neighbour's cottage.

Six men sat at stools at the antique wooden bar, all wore flat caps woven from wool. Pints of freshly poured Guinness stood on the bar top waiting for the dark mixture to settle before they were deemed ready for drinking. Sam Greer, the barman, chatted convivially with his customers as he dried glasses. The six-foot-four giant of a man spoke in the brogue of the glens people. He was affable but had hands the size of shovels, which proved useful when dealing with ousting those too boisterous after too much imbibing. Sam's hair was greying at his temples, and he had taken to wearing spectacles as his septuagenarian years approached. He permitted no talk of politics at his bar, being all too aware of how inflamed passions and alcohol sparked violence. A sign above the bar mirror read, 'If you wish to talk politics then piss off to the back room!'

The back room boasted a long boardroom table and this morning thirty men were seated there. Each had a steaming mug of coffee placed before him and a coffee percolator bubbled merrily on a side table. The scene was reminiscent of any company board members meeting rather than a gathering of gangsters. Unfortunately, it was the latter. Ages of those present varied from those in their seventies to youngsters not long out of their teens. Some older men had been members of the original I.R.A. known by northern nationalists as the 'stickies' due to their habit of gluing easter lilies to their uniforms. Stickies had been a Markist-Lenist group whose ideology was to unite working people from both sides of the political divide against British imperialism. Their desire was a united communist Irish republic.

Ruairi and Kirsty made their entrance and filled their coffee mugs before taking their respective places. Ruairi rose to his feet. "Men, this morning's meeting is to enable me to brief you in the part you will play in 'operation chaos' which is going to happen on 17th December. That day will see the British and Ulster unionists brought to heel by the greatest attack against them in the history of republicanism. Such will be the effect of 'operation chaos' that the British people will clamour for their army to be withdrawn from the six occupied counties. Such will the scale of the deaths that there will be an emergency sitting of Parliament to table a motion for withdrawal. We expect that it will have the backing of the opposition and our nationalist MP's. The Tories will have no option but to go along with it."

There was a hush before one of the older men, Sean Loughlin stood. "Fuck Ruairi, this sounds like something mad, what makes you think the general public here will support that amount of killing? I am not sure that I can support this!"

"Sean, you can of course withdraw your support for the movement. But this movement is not a democracy, all members have sworn allegiance to the cause. Do you wish to leave? If so, I will arrange for you to be escorted to the top of Trostan."

The atmosphere in the room could have been cut with a knife, for all knew what that would mean. The two men held each other's gaze in a prolonged stare before Sean Loughlin looked at the floor. The matter had been resolved. Ruairi continued,

"Obviously, I cannot disclose to you full details of the operation, which is known only to army council. But I can tell you when this is going down there will be a simultaneous strike at selected R.U.C. stations. Your target is Coleraine R.U.C. station. Arms are to be moved to safe locations in that area. They are to be consigned in small quantities to avoid any suspicion. Your officers will brief you on the precise timing of the attack. Good luck when striking your blow for freedom."

The meeting was dismissed. All knew better than to ask unnecessary questions. That is except Kirsty and when alone in the hall she confronted Ruairi. "I'm very worried, not only am I concerned for you, but for all those whom you propose to kill!"

Ruari cupped her face with his large hands. "Please don't tell me you're losing your commitment to the cause. I have killed, you have killed, and you know that more killings will be required before we obtain our freedom."

Kirsty was guarded in her reply. "I cannot help but be terrified for what lies ahead."

Ruairi's touch was tender, but at her words his grip tightened perceptibly, was this man now threatening the love of his life? He lowered his hands to Kirsty's slim shoulders. "Darling, you will be informed of the details when the time is right. This is also for your own safety, should you be apprehended by special branch. We suspect that there is a mole within our ranks, and we are taking steps as appropriate to catch and deal with him. But as a sign of my faith in you here is a list of the R.U.C. stations which are being targeted. You must guard this with your life."

Kirsty hesitantly took the small slip of paper from his grasp; it contained the list of those who had been damned. She imagined her fingers smouldering at its touch. He once again cupped her face with his large hands.

"We must hurry, we are to meet the 4.30pm arrival from Paris. You are going to meet the key player in our plan.

Chapter 11. The French connection

People jostled in a friendly fashion awaiting their friends and colleagues at the arrivals area of Belfast International Airport. Family and friends hugged as they were reunited once again. Passengers from flight 6379 from Paris Charles de Gaulle wheeled their trolleys through the green customs lane before arriving out in the public concourse.

"There he is," said Ruairi, directing Kirsty's gaze to the little man now approaching the barrier. Didier Serusier appeared so small that she thought he may be a sufferer of dwarfism. However, he was immaculately dressed, he wore a double-breasted grey Armani suit, the trousers of which were pressed to razor-sharp edges. He sported a white shirt and jaunty tie and his highly polished Gucci black shoes had platform heels in a vain attempt to give him stature. Didier's head swivelled until he spotted Ruairi standing in the crowd.

He came forward, his hand extended. "Ah Ruairi, it ees good to zee you again. And who ees is this beautiful young lady?"

Ruairi completed the introductions.

"Mademoiselle, the pleasure is ees all mine."

The swarthy French Algerian took Kirsty's hand which he raised to his lips. Kirsty visibly recoiled at the limp wet touch and extracted her fingers from his grip. Didier remained smiling but the smile did not extend to his eyes. He wore small gold-rimmed glasses over dark eyes which appeared to be soulless. The Frenchman was a walking manikin doused in expensive aftershave which failed to disguise an unpleasant body odour.

The trio left the terminal and entered a waiting car whose driver had kept the engine running in case a fast departure was required. The Mercedes took route B38, avoiding the motorway to Belfast city centre. The destination was The Belfast Europa Hotel, which has the unfortunate reputation of being Europe's most bombed hotel. Two suites had been reserved and Ruairi was confident that no bombs would be detonated at the hotel during their stay. Check-in was completed and their visitor was invited to see a special place in Belfast's culture.

Just across Great Victoria Street, opposite the Europa is Belfast's pub gem, The Crown Bar. The exterior is decorated with polychromatic tiles which had defied bomb and bullet thus far. Once a Victorian Gin Palace the Crown has an atmospheric setting with period gas lighting and cosy snugs. They took an empty snug and ordered three pints of the best Guinness. The barman was instructed that they were not to be disturbed.

Didier said little but watched everything. Eventually he spoke, "Of course, in Paris, we have much better examples of architecture of this period. Your Crown does not impress me!" The Frenchman grimaced at his first sip of Guinness and the tone was set when he wiped the creamy froth from his thin lips and coiffed moustache.

"Please to get me a glass of champagne!"

Ruairi sauntered to the bar rather than use the antiquated bell push. He took a deep breath; he was glad to have a moment's respite from the insufferable little bastard. It was then that he coined the moniker, 'Didier Sore Ass'. It gave Ruairi no relief that he needed the small bastard rather than the other way round.

Glass of champagne in hand, he returned to the snug which had a distinctly frosty atmosphere. He had just regained his seat when his Nokia 1011 mobile phone rang. The Nokia had just come into mass production, and he was the proud owner of one of the first to arrive in Ireland.

"Yes Gerry, I can hear you, I'm listening. The harsh west Belfast accent grated over the airwaves. "Ruairi, we have a problem, we have a mole which could jeopardise our plans, I need to see you immediately. Where are you now?"

"The Crown."

"A car will be at the door in five minutes. Come alone."

Chapter 12. Fealty or infidelity

Kirsty waited with Ruairi at the kerbside, leaving the Frenchman alone inside. The car arrived and her partner departed, she knew something was wrong, things had taken an unexpected turn. She experienced a sharp sense of dread; what was Ruairi planning? What was the obnoxious Frenchman doing here? What part did he have to play in whatever P.I.R.A. were plotting? How many people must die? Would Ruairi and herself survive or were they to be sacrificed at the high altar of Irish Republicanism? There were more questions than answers and she shivered as she went back inside.

Didier stood politely as she joined him. Now that they were alone, she thought that she detected a subtle change in his demeanour. The haughty arrogance was still there in abundance, but Kirsty was good at sensing lust, and she knew that his soulless black eyes were mentally undressing her. They moved from her breasts to her thighs, and he did not try to disguise the looks.

"Mademoiselle, something troubles you, no? I Didier Serusier am always aware when a beautiful woman is troubled." She felt his cold hand resting upon her stocking-covered knee. The man's eyes seemed to bore into her brain.

"Perhaps you would care to share your trouble with me?"

Now Kirsty, on the verge of panic, took a deep breath to try to slow her rapid heartbeat. Why was Ruairi being such a bastard, when even this horrible man was aware of her anxiety? Ruairi had refused to share the P.I.R.A. plan giving a limp excuse that it was for her own safety. Was her partner some deluded fool who thought he was the monarch of the glens about to destroy the British imperialists? A modern Rob Roy on steroids? A useful fool for P.I.R.A. who would discard him after his task was completed? Her anger began to consume her.

"Mademoiselle!" Didier's hand had reached her bare thigh and when his fingers began to play with her stocking tops it jolted her back from her thoughts. Kirsty's immediate instinct had been to slap him, and hard. Something stilled her hand. Maybe, just maybe, she could get some information from this creep that would save both her and her beloved Ruairi.

"Ruairi treats me as though I am a child, he refuses to share plans with me, I don't know whether I can trust him anymore, I fear for him and I fear for us both."

The Frenchman snorted with derision, "But you are also part of his movement? You are part of his plan, yes?"

Kirsty nodded in affirmation and as she did so a look of lechery mixed with guile passed across Didier's face. "Mademoiselle, of course, I am appalled that your partner does not trust you" He continued, "Of course my help would have a price attached!"

Kirsty made a decision which caused her discomfiture and shame which would haunt her for the rest of her days. She made a quick call to Ruairi, and he confirmed that he would be unable to join them for several hours. He suggested that she should find a way to entertain their guest until his return. If he knew what she had in mind blood would flow. Her skirt had now ridden up to mid-thigh and Didier's fingers were exploring ways to enter her pants. "Come," she said, "Let's go to your suite."

The Frenchman could not believe his luck, this was much easier than he had ever expected. Kirsty's legs trembled as they climbed the marble steps to his suite. She thought that the concierge had given her a knowing look as they passed his desk, probably just her guilty conscience. Guilt and embarrassment were etched on her face.

Didier sat upon the bed as she stood before him. All pretence at politeness had now disappeared. "Strip," he ordered. She removed her dress and stood in her bra and pants, before undoing her suspenders and slowly rolling down her fishnet stockings. Didier's eyes followed her every move, he even licked his repugnant lips as though anticipating a meal.

"Now, take off the rest!"

Kirsty stood trembling, naked and very ashamed. Didier Serusier stood and undressed without haste. The little manikin fastidiously folded his shirt, placed his tie upon the tie rack and put his trousers into their sharp creases. But it was when he removed his boxer shorts that Kirsty got the shock of her life. Didier's erect and engorged penis was totally out of proportion to his diminutive body. The hideous appendage must have been ten inches in length and thick black veins encircled its thick girth. Kirsty's jaw dropped; how could she cope with this? She felt the urge to grab her garments and run. But the man had moved between her and the door, it was as though he had guessed her intention.

"You are pleased, I can see that," he smugly asserted. "We Frenchmen are very special, and I am the best!"

How could she have allowed this to happen? Was she so angry with Ruairi that she was about to betray him in the worst possible way? Or was she simply paying a price to find out what could be done to save them all? Should she scream for help or allow things to take their course?

It was resolved when Didier grabbed her and pushed her face down upon the bed. He was amazingly strong despite his small stature, and he roughly pulled her thighs apart and entered her from behind. Kirsty felt as though her lower body was on fire. Surprisingly it was over almost as soon as it had started. Serusier gave a convulsive jerk, groaned and she felt him go limp. He rolled away and his monstrous appendage now resembled a limp mouldy banana, going rotten and black.

"You like that yes! We French Algerians are the best lovers, I gave you much pleasure, yes!"

Kirsty was gripped with incredulity at his arrogance and stupidity but having gone thus far she decided to play for the end game. "My dearest Didier, it was amazing," she stroked his bare chest, "You must have given so much pleasure to so many women."

She was not to know that he had also completed this act with many men.

"Now, you must keep your part of our bargain and tell me what you know of P.I.R.A.'s plans and how my partner is involved."

Didier cleared his nose with a loud snort, crossed to the mini bar and poured himself a double gin. He offered nothing to Kirsty.

"Tomorrow, I will be the main guest at your so-called army council. They will then tell me what services they require and why they are going to make me a very rich man."

Kirsty placed his clammy hand upon her breast. "Will you share that with me?"

Once again, she got a smirk. "Perhaps, if the price is right. There are some more little tricks that you may wish to perform to make me happy."

"I am sure that we can come to an agreement. Is your speciality making high explosives?"

The bastard looked offended.

"I Didier Serusier do not make explosives. I am the renowned expert in the use of Sarin nerve gas. Tomorrow, when P.I.R.A. disclose their target I will instruct them in its use."

His words chilled Kirsty to the bone. "Deaths, perhaps thousands, would come out of this foolishness. Many of their supporters would no doubt be amongst the casualties. What has happened to Ruairi? Has his hatred caused him to take leave of his senses? And what of P.I.R.A. leadership, have they become so desperate as to even contemplate such a heinous act?

As soon as she could she made her way back to her room and immersed herself in a hot shower. Kirsty scrubbed her body until her flesh was red, but still she could not rid herself of the stink of Serusier.

Ruairi arrived back in time for a rushed dinner. He had tickets for tonight's performance of Handel's Messiah being performed by the Ulster Orchestra at its home venue, The Ulster

Hall in Bedford Street. He wanted to show the Frenchman that the Irish were not barbarians but were well-versed in music and culture.

It was a beautiful evening and they elected to walk the short distance to the venue. Christmas lights twinkled in the frosty air. A passing snow shower left flakes glistening and crunching beneath their feet. It may have been Christmas but tonight Ruairi and his companions would not be bearers of goodwill to all men.

The Ulster Hall, built in 1859, is a B1 listed building. Its pride and joy is the Great Mulholland Organ, the oldest working example of a classic English pipe organ. This great hall had witnessed many political rallies during its time, but tonight's audience of over one thousand people would enjoy Handel's Messiah, which was performed for the first time in Dublin in 1742.

Ruairi joined with great gusto in the Hallelujah chorus, Kirsty watched him sing enthusiastically. His behaviour was totally incongruous, tonight her lover was taking part in a Christian festival, tomorrow he would be culpable of instructing an act of genocide.

Chapter 13. Darius

My telephone rang incessantly, calls were coming through from section commanders in the security forces. Our agents were aware that something big was coming down upon us and that it would be soon. I instructed James Carter to assemble our key players at Thiepval. As I awaited the team's arrival, I mused over why people turned to subterfuge, spying and ultimately betrayal. Greed, ideology, power and sometimes a sense of entitlement. The dark side of Ulster was that many of its people were motivated by such base motives. These people were in both the loyalist and nationalist communities. They also worked for the security services; worse we needed and depended upon them to save lives. Some are double agents; some would slice your throat for a few pounds, and some would betray us to the highest bidder.

We had used them to successfully infiltrate P.I.R.A. But only at a low level, none of them were privy to decisions at P.I.R.A. army council level. That is until now, it appeared that at last we had struck paydirt. Colonel Robert Conway, the man from MI6, opened the meeting at Thiepval secure room. He paused his plummy tones for dramatic effect, "Other than G2," he looked at me, "None of you know that I am running a top-level informant whom I believe is about to gain information from a high source within P.I.R.A. We know the date of their 'spectacular' which is to happen on December 17th. We are also aware that selected R.U.C. stations will be attacked simultaneously to the main event."

Commander Thomas Herron of Special Branch interjected, "Bob, do we know your agent's track record? Is it possible that we are being fed false intelligence in order to divert us away from the real target?"

Conway sighed as though he was speaking to a paid-up member of the dimwit society. It was this tract of arrogance that had led to my initial dislike of him. I smiled as I resolved not to continue thinking of him as 'Basildon Bond.'

Bob continued, "My dear Thomas, I would stake my life on this agent's integrity. He has entered P.I.R.A.'s inner circle, with further access promised and already lives have been saved."

Did I catch a wry smile at Bob's use of the pronoun 'he'?

It was the turn of Commander Herron's turn to smile. "I have had the usual suspects rounded up and questioned at Castlereagh, and there has not been so much as a squeak from them."

All eyes then turned to the newest addition to our security cabinet. Bob did the introduction. "Gentlemen, this is Major Ronald Duff. Major Duff is a lecturer at D.C.B.R.N. "The blank stares showed he needed to explain the acronym. "The letters stand for the Defence, Chemical, Biological and Nuclear service, whose headquarters are in Wiltshire. The Major is a member of Falcon Squadron and has extensive knowledge of chemical warfare, especially in the use of Sarin nerve gas."

The words brought an audible gasp from the small audience. P.I.R.A. were ruthless, but surely not even they would commit murder on an industrial scale. It was James Carter who voiced what I was thinking. "P.I.R.A. would not contemplate such an action, not only would it bring the conflict to a totally different level, inevitably they would kill some of their supporters and in doing so lose the support of moderate nationalists in the six counties."

Colonel Bob Conway looked each of us in the eye. "Gentlemen, P.I.R.A. would be prepared to accept substantial collateral damage, providing the end justifies the means. If their action starts a clamour in Britain for a withdrawal of our troops, then they will have won. Nationalists will eventually forgive and forget for what they consider to be the greater good. I am about to show you who they recruited to their cause, this individual has the capability and the ruthlessness to do whatever they require, providing they can meet his price." He clicked a button, and an image of Didier Serusier was projected on a monitor.

"Meet Didier Serusier, aged 42, French Algerian, joined the Algerian FLN to fight for Algerian independence. Regards both Britain and France as imperialist powers. This man hasn't a chip on his shoulder, it's a complete log! He tried to become a successful industrial chemist but failed miserably. For this he blames both British and French government policies. This guy became an expert in the manufacture and use of chemical nerve gasses, especially the lethal gas Sarin. Motivated by resentment, hatred and greed he will sell his evil skills to the highest bidder, in this case to the provos."

It was Carter once again. "How in the name of everything holy, can you possibly know of his involvement?"

Basildon gave a smile which in all honesty was little better than a self-satisfied smirk. "I'm running an agent, code name Darius, named after the wise Persian leader of old. Agent Darius is in touch with me daily on what is a very dangerous and fluid situation. Allow me to pass the floor to Major Duff who will explain exactly what we are up against."

Duff spoke in the clipped middle-class tone of the professional army officer. "Sarin gas was originally developed by Nazi Germany in 1938. It is the most toxic of the nerve gasses and the fastest acting. Classified as an organophosphate, one small drop can kill. Sarin is easily vaporised and would spread rapidly throughout the environment, especially in low-lying areas. It's odourless, tasteless and extremely toxic to the human body. It attacks all internal organs, especially the lungs causing respiratory failure. It is twenty-six times more deadly than cyanide."

A hush descended around the table, and I imagined some faces to have turned pale with shock at the horrifying prospect of what this maniac could do. I asked, "Has it ever been used on humans?"

Duff responded, "The Nazis manufactured tonnes of Sarin, but for some unknown reason Hitler refused to use it. It's a puzzle, because he was a man without morals or conscience."

I took the floor, "If P.I.R.A. resort to something so horrible that even the Nazis declined to use it, then we have a major problem, thousands of lives may be lost."

It was Commander Herron who said what was becoming obvious. "P.I.R.A. will go for strategic targets, and in order to influence British opinion, it is most likely that target will be on the mainland."

Colonel Bob's phone gave its shrill ring. "Yes, I understand, I will inform the team."

"That was Darius, the target is Belfast Central Rail Station. The plan is to attack early morning commuters on 17th December."

To me this made no sense at all. We had already reached a consensus that the target would be mainland Britain. However, we had to act on the intelligence available; we had to plan now, and we had only two days in which to do so.

Chapter 14. Off the rails

Even though the rail station is located approximately two miles from the city centre, some silly person decided that it be named Belfast Central. Located in East Bridge Street, it does have an efficient bus service to the centre. The other main station in the city is in Great Victoria Street, which is indeed in the city centre. However, many rail services do route via the busy 'central' station, including the enterprise service to Dublin Connolly. It's estimated that six thousand passengers pass through Central daily.

On the morning of 17th December our people were in position from before 07.00 hrs. Commuter services didn't commence until 07.30 hrs but our people, both male and female, mingled with those queuing for tickets, having breakfast, pretending to read morning papers whilst scanning all around for any signs of suspicious activity. Despite the tension felt by us all we managed to fake an air of normality on this pre-Christmas commuter morning.

Ambulance crews were on standby at all Belfast hospitals and ED departments were told to expect a possible influx of critically injured patients. All my people had a supply of Hazmat suits which would be donned quickly in the event of a gas release.

As G2 in command, I was in constant radio contact with all units. Perhaps I should have occupied a central command point close to the scene, but I have always been 'hands-on' and I mingled with my operatives on the station platforms. My overcoat completely covered my MP5 compact submachine gun. The MP5 is favoured by the S.A.S. as it can fire 9x19mm parabellum rounds deemed to be of less risk to innocent passers-by.

All trains, both incoming and outbound had my people on board. Senior rail management were privy to the threat, but for reasons of security, drivers and conductors were not. All had to appear normal. Overnight had seen a substantial frost form and I stamped my feet and swung my arms in a fruitless attempt to keep the cold at bay. My boots left a frosted imprint on the platform, and I mused that I could see where I had been but had no idea of where I was about to go, or as to what may happen. I still had serious misgivings about the authenticity of the intelligence upon which we were acting. Was this a hoax in order to divert us from the real target?

The 08.00 hrs train arrived from Bangor with a squeal of brakes and one hundred plus commuters were disgorged and on their way to another tedious day at the office. I would cheerfully have changed places with any one of them. This morning tedium was much preferable to terror.

My sombre mood lightened considerably when I spotted Sergeant Les Cooper 'Cooperman' to his friends. He was amongst those disembarking from the Bangor train and was accompanied by his faithful dog, 'Jack' a tan and white Jack Russell terrier, who despite his diminutive size, was one of the best army sniffer dogs. I had not seen Cooperman for about three years, but the dog recognised me instantly, his pointed ears reached upwards and his tail beat a steady rhythm showing his enthusiasm.

Cooperman and I stepped aside from the throng. "Great to see you again Paddy." His soft County Armagh accent was pleasant to the ear in comparison to the harsh Belfast tones surrounding us. Les addressed me by my given name despite the differences in our rank. We had served together in the S.A.S. in various theatres of war. Although I had been a 'Rupert,' slang for officer, it made no difference to our friendship. Together we had risked life and limb. Cooperman was still serving in the S.A.S. and had been deployed on this mission. We clasped arms and Jack stood on his hind legs waiting for me to pet his small head. I asked, "See anything suspicious?"

"Absolutely nothing, nor did Jack sniff out a whiff of explosives. Sarin is odourless so all our dogs react to the smell of conventional explosives for which the terrorists may have a residual smell on their clothing. This, I'm afraid, is like looking for the proverbial needle in a haystack."

"I understand Les, we have three other dog handlers out on the platforms. Radio me instantly at the slightest whiff of suspicion."

Cooperman laughed at my unintended pun.

"Are you prepared if all goes pear shaped?"

This got another laugh as Cooperman patted the MP5 beneath his civvy overcoat. As a former Irish champion clay pigeon shot, taking out a terrorist would be small buns for him. He just adored his little dog companion. He once told me, "Dogs make great companions, they forever wag their tails, but unlike women they never wag their tongues!"

Man and dog made their way around the concourse. Midday came and went, still nothing, all seemed normal. I got 'Basildon' on the blower. In my frustration I had reverted to my former favourite name for him. "It looks as though we have been sold a pup."

For once Colonel Bob seemed less confident. "I simply don't understand this, until now intel from Darius has been extremely accurate."

"Perhaps P.I.R.A. are onto him or her?" There followed a short, stifled silence before he replied.

"I am due to liaise with Darius using a secure radio, this is to take place at 21.00 hrs, following the call I will immediately report back to you Sir."

At midday I gave the order to stand down. The order to stand down did not generate any sense of relief. In fact, it increased the sense of foreboding, the use of Sarin was going to happen, but yet we did not have a clue as to when or where. At 16.00 hrs I was patched through to the S.A.S. squad detailed to guard Coleraine R.U.C. station. As darkness descended P.I.R.A. had attacked the station. Vehicles had been spotted acting in a suspicious manner. As soon as they moved towards the station they were intercepted, and the occupants arrested without a shot having to be fired. The officer reporting told me: "A bit disappointing really, they are a gang of thugs from the glens led by a bad egg named Sean Loughlin. Had they fired a shot we would have saved the taxpayer a fortune in the costs of prison accommodation."

It transpired that several other attacks on police were thwarted that evening. Darius had been correct on that score, which caused me to shiver even more. What and where was the main event going to take place?

Chapter 15. For those in peril upon the sea

I asked the Colonel, "Can Darius be contacted before 21.00 hrs?"

"I could do so, but it may possibly blow his cover. If he was to be in the presence of the enemy, they would be instantly suspicious if he takes my call. And that would be the end of agent Darius."

The large grey Range Rover ploughed through the sleet and rain on the M2 motorway to Belfast docks. The slick surface reflected the vehicle's headlights in an unpleasant dazzle. Kirsty Lee sat in the front passenger seat beside Ruairi Savage. She reached across to adjust the airflow to the windscreen which was beginning to fog up. Seated immediately behind them were Didier Serusier, Anton Gracey, Paul Clegg and Dermot Casey. The latter three were P.I.R.A. foot soldiers, trustworthy, but also expendable.

"Ruairi, it's almost 6.30. The ferry check-in closes at 7.00pm." Ruairi could hear the frustration in Kirsty's voice. She continued, "We don't want to snatch defeat when we are so close to victory, by stupidly missing our check-in." Kirsty sighed; she had only been told of their destination within the last hour. She noted that Ruairi had not let her out of his sight since then. Was he suspicious, did he not trust her? The interior of the Range Rover was full of fishing bags, rods, reels and nets. Ostensibly, they were a group of fishing enthusiasts heading for lakes on the mainland. As they passed through security the rods drew some comments from the good-natured staff. There would have been no smiles had security spotted the vehicle's false bottom, leading to the compartment in which the real consignment was concealed.

All six passengers gave a sigh of relief when a crewman directed them to their parking bay and gave the signal for their ignition to be switched off. They found themselves to be parked amongst rows of freight trucks which suited their purpose admirably. Ruairi opened a canvas sack, "Everyone put your mobiles in here, army council has ordered that we be incommunicado until our mission is completed."

They complied as one and the bulky Nokia telephones clattered against each other as they dropped into the canvas. That is, all except one man, Didier Serusier objected, "You eeerish, you bring me here, then you offend me. My phone is mine and I refuse."

Everyone froze. Then there was a click as Ruairi cocked his tiny Tumbir pistol and placed the muzzle against the Frenchman's neck. The argument was resolved, and Didier's phone joined the others in the sack. Once Didier had served his purpose, Ruairi would take great pleasure in eliminating the bastard, he had no intention of paying him the extortionate fee which the fool thought he had negotiated with P.I.R.A. That money would be put to much better use.

The terrorists thanked the fates that no one had been frisked because each one of them, including Kirsty carried their personal weapons under their outer coats. They took the steps to the passenger lounge. When coffee had been bought Kirsty made her excuses, she had to visit the ladies, the tension was playing havoc with her bladder. Once in the cubicle with the door locked, she tore open the secret compartment in her leather satchel and extracted her small portable radio transmitter. As she pressed the transmit button, she became aware of the vessel having increased its speed. They had left the shelter of Belfast Lough and were now in the open sea heading south to Liverpool.

My top team were assembled at Thiepval, all our nerves jangled with expectation that something unknown and dreadful was about to happen and we were helpless. I was just about to order Conway to contact Darius when the Colonel's radio transmitter beeped together with an accompanying flashing small light. Was this our much-needed break? We sat with bated breath as he took the call. Finally, he broke the connection by saying, "Thank you Darius, good luck, I will pray for your survival."

Colonel Conway took centre stage. "Gentlemen, we have no time to lose, the terrorists are aboard The Silver Star ferry, Maid Of Erin, departed Belfast 20.00 hours, due Birkenhead 06.00 hrs. These ferries average 18 knots so that puts the Maid of Erin about here." He stabbed his finger on a map, indicating a point close to the southern tip of The Isle of Man. I asked, "Has Darius found out the details of the mission?"

The Colonel looked to be shocked, "Sir, that Frenchman has constructed a tiny device which will release Sarin into the atmosphere at preset times. The canisters containing Sarin will be attached to the undersides of lorry cabs using magnets like those used on limpet mines. They have chosen Birkenhead because of its proximity to the motorway systems. The M62 west-east trans-Pennine route stretches for one hundred and seven miles linking Manchester, Bradford and Hull. Seven miles is shared with the Manchester orbital route. Then, of course, some lorries will head south to London. These juggernauts will leave a trail of death in their wake before the driver eventually succumbs to the Sarin. That will also cause fatalities as the huge vehicles crash driverless and out of control.

I stepped in quickly with a series of rapid commands. "First contact the Captain of the Maid of Erin. Inform him that armed and dangerous terrorists are aboard his vessel. He must immediately secure the bridge and permit no access to anyone. Doors to the vehicle decks are to be locked and secured. No crewman is to approach anyone acting suspiciously, these terrorists will not hesitate to kill. He is to gradually change course to bring his vessel into wind and reduce to half speed to facilitate a boarding party from a helicopter. Major Duff have your bomb squad assemble immediately at the Helipad. As you will be handling the devices you will need to wear your hazmat suits. Captain Paul Shires (sniper) and Sergeant Les Cooper (dog handler) and Jack his dog will accompany me The pilot will plot his course and fire up the motor of the Sea King. Let's do this!"

James Carter my second in command interjected, "Sir, may I suggest that you oversee this operation from –"

I stopped him in his tracks, "James, first and foremost I am a soldier who has always led from the front. I will continue to do so and will brook no interference."

The ship's change of course was so subtle that it was undetectable to most of the passengers, but Ruairi did not fit into that group of people. He was also aware that the ship's engines had throttled back. A small pocket compass told him that the vessel was slowly veering from south to west.

"The bastards are onto us! Come we must get to the vehicle decks and fast!"

As one, the six terrorists made for the stairwell. As they descended the metal steps their noses were assailed by the smell of diesel and exhaust fumes which the large extractor fans never quite managed to completely extract. Dermot Casey, one of the henchmen, looked very much the worse for wear. "Sorry Ruairi, I can't help it, I've always been prone to sea sickness."

"Now you tell me, you dopey bugger!"

A large seaman wearing an oilskin coat and a woolly hat blocked their progress. "Hoy, you lot where do you think you're going?" He spoke with a broad scouse accent, but his tone was friendly. "The vehicle decks have just been declared closed, please go back and take your seats in the lounge. I'm sure this will be cleared up soon."

It was a pity that the man from Liverpool had disregarded his Captain's order not to intercept strangers. Ruairi shot him twice in the temple using his Tumblr pistol. The sound suppressor muffled the shots to putts as a trickle of smoke left the muzzle. The victim slumped then slipped on his own blood before toppling to the deck. It was all too much for Casey and he voided the contents of his stomach over his trousers and shoes with loud retching splutters.

"Ruairi grabbed him roughly by the shoulders, "Bloody well get a grip man, you smell worse than a blocked sewer in summer!"

The red-headed Irishman led his team to the Range Rover, the rubber soles of their boots squeaked on the metal decks as they ran. Quickly the fishing rods were discarded allowing them access to the vehicle's secret compartment. Ruairi carefully distributed the lethal canisters of sarin to his five accomplices. Serusier gave a quick review as to how to arm the weapons and attach them to the undersides of the lorry cabs. The devices' timers had been pre-set. The terrorists made their way along the rows of lorries, crouching beneath the cabs and snapping the limpet magnets into place. Each vehicle was secured by four lashing brackets on the four sides of their chassis. Their progress was unimpeded, for there was no sign of vehicle deck crewmen. Far from feeling relief, Ruairi now knew that the absence of crew meant they had been rumbled for sure. He chose not to inform the others, wanting them to get their tasks completed, but he anxiously watched the deck entrance points. When the soldiers arrived, he and his men would fight to the bitter end. He knew that he could not depend on the disgusting Frenchman, who would surrender to save his skin, that would not be allowed to happen. Ruairi watched as Serusier continually looked at Kirsty, lust imprinted on his face. Yes, it would be a pleasure to kill him, before his own death happened.

The Sea King helicopter, powered by its Rolls Royce engines, tore across the Belfast city sky and a myriad of Christmas lights twinkled magically from below its flight path. I momentarily spotted Belfast City Hall with its Christmas tree in the grounds and crowds enjoying the festive scene. Thankfully, they were unaware of the deadly cargo which had departed their port but a short time before. Aboard the shaking, vibrating helo beast communication would have been impossible but for our Dave Clarke headsets. Cooperman had his faithful sniffer dog, Jack, strapped to his chest in a home-made cocoon, it was only the little dog's upright ears which were visible in the dimly lit cabin. We donned night glasses to protect our eyesight efficiency when we landed upon the brightly lit deck of the ship. The sombre mood was lightened when Shires decided to poke some fun at his friend.

"Bloody hell, Cooperman can you go anywhere without that poodle?" To which he received the expected reply.

"Jack is no bloody poodle. If you annoy him, you will feel the effectiveness of his little white teeth! He sometimes wags his tail, but you are forever wagging your tongue!"

We all had a hearty laugh, even if it was a little forced. Cooperman then added, "Good luck to one and all. Paul make sure you shoot straight and nail the bastards!

Out of the murk our pilot spotted the red and green navigation lights of the Maid of Erin. The wake of the vessel appeared to glisten despite the darkness. Captain Mitchell had brought his vessel into wind and decreased speed. Correct judgement of both ship and helo was essential if we were not to crash into the sea and almost certain death. Our pilot, Ronnie Barr would position his machine just ten feet above the forecastle deck. At his signal we would abseil down to the deck. It's a manoeuvre I had made many times during my days in the S.A.S. Now, although a little rusty, I did not hesitate. The door opened and I was immediately hit by the downdraught from the rotors. The Sea King has a computerized flight control system, nevertheless the hover is a dangerous manoeuvre at the best of times due to the complexity of inputs required to maintain altitude and lateral velocity. However, Ronnie is a genius with pitch and cyclic levers. The yellow machine remained stable and all eight, including dog Jack, were on deck within seconds. A quick wave from me sent Ronnie on his way back to base. Now we were on our own and responsible for bringing an end to this madness.

Captain Mitchell led us to the vehicle deck door. He clasped each of us by the arm and wished us good luck. I led the way through the hatch and into the bright glare of the overhead lights. I could have had them extinguished but our opponents were professionals and would also be equipped with night vision googles, so no advantage in doing so. Row upon row of silent juggernauts stood awaiting their drivers. The only sound was the low throb of the ship's diesel engines. Where are the buggers, I asked myself? "Captain Shires, set up your sniping position on top of this lorry cab. You will be able to change position enabling you to have a field of fire down the lanes. Major Duff, you are to keep the bomb team here until we smoke out the baddies. Cooperman, take the starboard perimeter, I'll take the port side, maintain radio contact and move forward in unison. Bob, you take the centre lane, we will move forward like the three prongs of a trident."

Cooperman unleashed Jack and the little dog's tail wagged steadily as he preceded his master down the starboard side. Suddenly the air was filled with the screech of gunshots. Immediately in front of my position Anton Gracey and Paul Clegg opened up in an attempt to lay down covering fire whilst their cohorts in crime ducked towards an exit hatch. Bloody expendable fools, lambs to the slaughter laying down their lives for their devious masters. My MP5 was on full auto, and I sent a hail of 9mm bullets towards Gracey. Now it was time for me to play a very nasty trick. I allowed the hammer to fall upon an empty chamber with a resounding click. "Shit, out of ammo," I cursed. Too eager for the kill Anton Gracey moved forward from his cover. It was his last move. Paul Shire's shot took him centre forehead, slamming him dead to the deck.

On Cooperman's side of the ship Paul Clegg blazed away in a blind panic, his bullets ricocheting off surrounding lorries. However, that was the only damage that his wild firing inflicted. Cooperman shouted, "Lay down your arms, surrender and you will survive!"

Clegg replied in his south Armagh accent, "Go screw yourself you Brit-loving bastard."

Sounds travel well over steel decking, and I was able to pinpoint Clegg's position. Without further thought for the consequences I rushed him; the fool decided to fight rather than take flight and he took aim as I approached at the run. Still on full auto my MP5 almost took his head completely away from his neck.

There came cries of pain and curses mixed with growling and snarls. Jack, the intrepid Jack Russel terrier had Dermot Casey by the balls. A pistol came scattering out from beneath a lorry. "Get the bastard dog off me, please!" Casey pleaded in desperation. It was a sight to behold and one which I will never forget. The forlorn terrorist crawled out from under a cab, his trousers splattered in his own vomit. Jack was attached and continuing to sink his teeth into the poor man's groin. He would live, but he would never be a parent again!

"Jack leave!" The little dog reluctantly released his quarry. Cooperman laughed, "I guess it was his own stink that saved him, even Jack couldn't stand the smell."

During the fire fight, the three remaining terrorists, with Serusier in the lead, gained access to an exit hatch. It was the moment when I experienced that there was an understanding between the female terrorist and Basildon. He had the red-headed terrorist in the centre of his sights. Basildon was just about to squeeze his trigger when she flung her body in front of her man. Kirsty Lee was a woman in torment; despite everything she still loved Ruairi Savage and her action temporarily saved his life. After a brief nod to her Basildon raised his gun away from the target.

I led the pursuit up the stairwell and could hear the terrorist's footsteps running just ahead. With my MP5 extended in front and my finger on the trigger I emerged onto the stern deck. Serusier and Savage together with the girl stood trapped against the stern rail, they had nowhere to go. When a rat is cornered then it is at its most dangerous, so I dropped to one knee to take careful aim. Suddenly Savage encircled Kirsty Lee's neck with his arm and pulled her in front of him providing a shield against my fire. With his other hand he cocked his pistol and placed it against the girl's neck.

"You Brits must think I'm stupid. I know who has been forwarding intel to you. This bitch has betrayed me, her cause and the love which I gave to her. Put your weapons down and allow us safe passage or she dies now!"

Colonel Bob Conway and Cooperman appeared by my side. A look of understanding passed between Conway and his informant. Bob slowly nodded. The back kick from Lee was fast, vicious and immediate. Grasping Savage's gun hand, she swivelled and sank her knee into her erstwhile lover's groin. Savage gasped at the intensity of the pain, lost his balance and slumped back against the rail. His gun fell harmlessly into the Irish Sea. With a strength that belied her build the girl griped Savage by the shoulders, hoisted him up and over the rail. Arms windmilling the terror of the glens followed his gun down into the foam. The last sight of him was his shock of red hair, long locks spread out and floating briefly on the surface of the sea, akin to some weird creature arisen from the darkness of the depths. It reminded me of the story of Ethelred the Unready, the incompetent King of ancient England; this was the story of Ruairi the unready, failed terrorist. Kirsty Lee stood at the rail sobbing hard, her head in her hands. Conway put his arm around his agent. "Well done, Darius," was all he said.

Shouts came from the ship's bridge. Cooperman, Jack his dog, and I ran forwards. Didier Serusier stood on the open deck afront the wheelhouse door. In one hand he held a pistol which was levelled at Captain Mitchell's neck. In the other was a Sarin canister with his finger on the activate button.

"You bloody Engleesh, you think zee are so smart, but no, we the people will prevail against imperialism. Now listen carefully, I will say this only once! I wont zee small motorboat alongside and quickly! The good Captain will accompany me as I make good my escape. If you fail to comply, I will shoot the good Captain and this canister will be activated into the ship's air conditioning. The choice is –

His stream of threats was cut short as he let out a shriek of agony. Jack had come at him from behind and had buried his teeth to the bone at the back of his knee joint. The little dog's head rocked from side to side as though he was killing a rat, working his razor-sharp teeth further into flesh. Serusier was shocked and he tried to kick the dog away with his free leg. Thankfully, he had lost his grip on his pistol which rolled away across the deck. But he still had the sarin canister which he held aloft.

The French man spoke his last words, "Now ees the time we all die!"

Cooperman had his MP5 on single shot selection which gave greater accuracy. His first shot took Serusier just below the collar bone. I saw his mouth gape open in surprise and agony as the air was driven out of his lungs. He lost his balance and toppled over the sea rail, but in his dying moments attempted to lob the sarin canister at us. Cooperman's second shot entered Didier's right eye and erupted out of the top of his skull. His skull, coiffured hair and all went spinning into the spray. The diminutive body did not make much of a splash and his brain matter floated gently downwards seperately to join the body in Davey Jones' locker. Cooperman placed his safety catch to the 'on' position. No one else would die today.

"Bastard, he should not have tried to kick my dog! One Frenchy has gone to feed the fishes!"

The bomb squad, i.e. Lieutenant John Moakes, Lieutenant Alan McDowell and Lieutenant Paul Burkitt, led by Major Ronald Duff, successfully located and disarmed all the sarin canisters. Once safety checks had been completed the Maid of Erin was given permission to dock at Heysham. A major disaster had been averted but it had been a close call.

Our prisoner, Dermot Casey, restrained by zip ties, was led away, his guards had to hold their noses as they took him to his cell. After his trial he was detained at HM Maze prison, there he was forever known as 'septic' by his fellow inmates.

Chapter 16. Dunwoody from Dunmurry

An immediate press embargo was placed upon the sarin story. The government did not want the public to become aware at how close many had come to death. However, it was decided to have a special thank you dinner for all the teams who had brought the operation to a successful conclusion. I should say at the outset that this was not an exercise in self-congratulation, many had risked their lives to save others and it was felt they should receive some measure of recognition, no matter how small. Dinner would be served in the officer's mess at Thiepval and would include a very special Royal guest of honour.

Getting diaries aligned is no easy matter, especially when it involves the Royal household. Finally, it was agreed upon Thursday 8th April. HRH was in N. Ireland, ostensibly visiting a business group in Bangor, Co. Down. In line with protocol, I will not disclose the name of our Royal guest. For functions which involve Royalty, normal procedure is to involve all three of the armed services in providing the catering and hosting services. It is regarded as a high honour to be chosen and it appears on a person's C.V. for all time.

The winter of 1992 slowly passed and by mid-March 1993 planning for the Royal dinner was well underway. Able seaman Robert William Dunwoody from the village of Dunmurry was selected to be Maitre D. The honour was bestowed upon William for his long unstinting service in the Royal Navy, followed by service in the naval reserve. Unfortunately, our choice of William led to what may best be called a slight embarrassment.

The great and the good, including the N. Ireland secretary of state, the chief constable and senior officers were all assembled. The long dining table was resplendent with fresh flowers and rows of gleaming cutlery. We were all in full dress uniform and sat at our designated places. Cooperman, with faithful Jack sat on the floor at his side, was the subject of much conversation and raised eyebrows. Cooper was adamant, no Jack, no Cooper! After all, the little dog was a very special hero. Jack wagged his tail with excitement, he could smell the delicious aroma coming from the kitchen and he knew that food was in the offing.

All stood and bowed as HRH and his equerry entered and were seated. I knew that the best food was about to be served, but like the rest of my men, I was a little nervous, not being used to dining with Royalty. Once again, all standing, the Royal toast was taken. Picture the scene. Top brass bedecked in gold braid, more 'scrambled egg' than a best breakfast plate. Enter able seaman William Dunwoody from nearby Dunmurry, napkin over his shoulder and hat askew.

"Haans up for sloop!" The little man slurred and slightly swayed. There came a collective gasp. No one knew where to look, and a horrible silence momentarily fell. We all wished the floor would open and swallow us! That is, all except HRH who threw back his head in gales of laughter.

"Thank you, sailor, so much, I will be delighted to sample your best sloop!"

All followed the Royal lead and the room peeled with laughter, even though there were many red faces. Able seaman, William Robert Dunwoody was gently shepherded away to sleep off his enthusiasm for his Royal event. We found out later that William had been so delighted at his appointment that he had decided on an early celebration imbibing his favourite 'grogg.' However, he was told he would eventually get another chance, but only if he was 'groggless!'

Sergeant Timothy Heinz, known to his mates as '57' had prepared an exquisite meal of sea bass, celeriac puree, wild sorrel with smoked sauce shellfish. The dish was completed with wedge potatoes. HRH once again caused laughter, "Goodness it's fish and chips once again!"

Chapter 17. The Good Friday fight

Readers may remember that Colonel Robert Conway, (Basildon Bond) had once tested my patience too far when he made a disparaging remark about 'micks'. That had resulted in my fist sending him crashing to the floor. Robert apologised for his crass remark but insisted upon a rematch in the boxing ring. Now that the immediate danger was over and with HRH and other dignitaries returned home, he reminded me of his challenge. We agreed that the bout would take place on the day that became known as 'the day Dunwoody served dinner.' Officers and men who had vanquished the sarin threat assembled in Thiepval gym. Ironically, it was Friday 9th April, Good Friday.

I gave explicit instructions that absolutely no betting was to take place, for a reason which will become obvious to you the reader. My special guest of honour was Father John Feeny, who had been my boxing mentor at Holy Cross Boxing Club all those years before. My Opo took Basildon aside and warned him, "Did you know that the boss was once an Irish amateur boxing champion?" Basildon just smiled, shrugged his shoulders and said, "Of course, my dear James, remember I'm in the business of knowing things. No doubt he's good, but I'm sure that I am even better!"

It appeared that nothing changes with Colonel Robert Conway, the one and only Basildon Bond. It was decided that the bout would be named in honour of Able Seaman Robert William Dunwoody. Whereas gambling on the outcome was strictly forbidden, we decided to have a lottery for which the money generated would be paid to the Royal Lifeboat Association. First prize would be the newly laundered napkins from the top table at the Royal Dinner and who better to present them than the now infamous Dunwoody. Our bout would be refereed by Sgt. Major Michael McGuire, who is a qualified boxing referee amongst his many talents. We were very honoured that Michael travelled from Dublin for the event. And so, to the tune of Rocky belting out through the P.A. system Basildon and I made our entrance. The men stood, whistled, hooted, hollered and shouted. It was not every day they got to see two officers knock seven bells out of each other. The Sergeant Major gave us our prefight instructions then we each went to our respective corners.

The bell sounded for the first round and we both stepped forward. The arena was full of excitement and expectation. Bob and I were both conventional boxers, that is we led with our left fist with our right ready to deliver the power punch. In terms of height and weight we were evenly matched, but at forty-two years old, I was my opponent's senior by a few years and well past my boxing best. Our opening moves were tentative, throwing jabs and testing the other's moves and defences, with few power punches being thrown.

Bob was good, both in attack and defence. His left foot remaining flat on the canvas as he punched, and his right heel raised and ready for him to pivot. He maintained his fists high above his chin and after punching quickly returned them to the guard position. However, I did find some opportunities to deliver hooks which may have floored him, but something, or someone, stayed my hand. And so it continued thus for several rounds, each seeking an opening, our boots shuffling on the canvas floor. The men shouted encouragement to us both, baying for blood. Bob reacted enthusiastically, coming at me delivering hooks to both sides in quick succession. I did manage to block most of them successfully. Bob had a weakness, he tended to telegraph his intentions so I made my decision at the next telegraphed move. At the critical moment I dropped my guard, as though I had made a mistake. Bob's powerful right hook, with his elbow held high, allowed his fist to deliver a knock-out thump full to my chin. My vision dimmed, my legs buckled, and I crashed to the canvas. The men gasped; this was not the outcome they had expected nor hoped for.

I shook my head as Colonel Bob helped me to my feet. Then our gumshields were discarded and we both embraced in a bear hug. The officers and men gave us both rapturous applause. Michael McGuire gave me a knowing smile, "Young Sir, don't think that you fooled me, you saw that punch coming. The Colonel is very lucky to have you as a friend, otherwise he was a dead man walking!" Ours was indeed a lesson in reconciliation; we both had loathed each other at the start. Now we truly were comrades in arms. Sometimes, good things do happen on a Good Friday.

Chapter 18. Hypnosis at Harley Street

Although some good things had happened, all was not well with me. I had never professed to be religious in the traditional way, I believed that my thinking about violence and its use, had been influenced by experiences from my past and the very special person I had met in that past. Like all members of the armed forces, I was faced with the paradox of violence versus pacifism. My overriding ambition was to do good to others and for this I had often put my life at risk. In an ideal world there would be no need for violence, however we need to be pragmatic and recognise life for what it is, full of danger and threat. I accepted that my profession requires the use of violence and sometimes the need to take human life. Although I was no stranger to having killed, each death seemed to take away part of my soul.

It was when my mind was filled with visions of a lady in distress and about to die, not only in my dreams but in my daytime thoughts, that I realised that I needed professional help. Furthermore, the lady in question was someone who had been of very special to me in a past life. How could I possibly explain to Libertad that she had to share my love with a lady from my past. Despite all her love for me, that would not go down well. Then, one night, in a vivid dream, the young man with Chestnut coloured hair, the man called Yeshua beckoned to me. Known to Christians as Jesus, this man wanted me to come back to Jerusalem in a different time. He made it known that there was another mission for me in his service. Was I experiencing a calling, or worse, was I in the process of losing my mind?

I decided to list the help of my confident and friend, Reverend Jamie Douglas the Regimental Chaplain. We met in my office for coffee.

"Jamie, I'm greatly troubled, you are aware of my memories from the time I spent on life support and my belief that my spirit regressed to a different place and time. Now I have dreams in which Jesus is summoning me to return to ancient Israel. He has informed me that a lady named Batya is at high risk of losing her life. He has also told me that Batya was my wife in my previous existence. Moreover, Batya is not the only reason for his request; something much larger and involving many thousands of lives is afoot. Jesus would not disclose the nature of the threat at this point but said that all will be revealed should I choose to return. It's a very compelling request, but how do I return. What do I tell Libertad? Now, I not only fear for my sanity but also my ability to take whatever action is required to do my duty in keeping the peace in this province. Have you any suggestions?"

Rev. Jamie bowed his head deep in thought and perhaps offering a silent prayer for guidance.

"Paddy, I do not fear at all for your sanity; indeed, I believe that you have been chosen for something very special, something that may well change history!"

I was gobsmacked at his words. How could I, an ordinary person from a humble background be chosen to change something of immense importance? Jamie appeared to be reading my thoughts, "Don't forget that Jesus came into this world, not as a prince, but a boy born in a stable. I have no doubt that you met our Lord in a past life and now you are being summoned once again."

"You say that I am summoned, but I have no power to change the time into which I have been born."

There followed a long and silent pause before my Chaplain spoke once more. "There may be a way, have you heard of the use of hypnotherapy to help people who have had déjà vu experiences, such as past life experiences?"

"Not very much," I admitted, "But is that not a load of fanciful mumbo jumbo?"

Jamie stroked his chin, "It's true the practice has its sceptics and cynics who refuse to open their minds. But I know of one practitioner who has had some amazing results. His name is Doctor Richard Aldermatt, and his practice is in Harley Street. Would you be prepared to open your mind and give him a try?"

Harley Street, Marylebone central London, has been the home to large numbers of private specialists in medicine and surgery since the 18th century. Our chatty London cabby continued his monologue about the history of Harley Street, who was a good doctor and who was not, as we cruised past the beautiful Georgian buildings. The place reeked of money and privilege, and I feared what this experience was about to do to my wallet! For a working-class Belfast boy to come to Harley Street filled me with incredulity. But I needed help, and I pushed my socialist conscience to the back of my mind.

Richard Aldermatt was a silver-haired gentleman of average height, and I guessed him to be in his late sixties. His English was excellent and without accent of his Swiss heritage. The good doctor explained his procedure and the techniques which he would employ. A fully qualified nurse would continually monitor my vital signs, blood pressure, heart rate and my breathing and I would be free to end the session at any time of my choosing. After I had fully explained the background to my problems, we entered his surgery. Libertad and the Rev. Jamie would come with me but remained seated in the background. I was invited to lie and relax on a long couch whilst the nurse attached monitors in place. When the sound of low relaxing Chinese music wafted into the room, I struggled to suppress the urge to giggle. If I was being fleeced by a quack that would be no laughing matter. Dr. Aldermatt's tone was soft and subdued as he told me to clear my mind of everything in the present. After a suitable pause he asked me to think of ancient Israel and the people I had known there. At first my mind refused to respond, all I could hear was the doctor's voice and rhythmic tones of the background music. I began to drift into a pleasant reverie when I saw at the foot of the couch the angel with the piercing blue eyes. This was the man, or angel, whom I had encountered in the garden of Gethsemane, when I had threatened to stop Yeshua being arrested. The man had promptly despatched me from the scene.

"What are you doing here?" I demanded.

"Shalom, Ezekiel Ben David, the Master has need of you again. Will you return, with me, to old Jerusalem. It will be of your own free will, but it will require you to once again put your life at risk. Someone you love, a lady named Batya is in dire danger, we need your help to save her. But she is not the only reason; many things are wrong, and it is only a person such as you who can correct them."

My mind was decided, this person name Batya, had obviously been of great importance to me. "I will come immediately!"

The nurse spoke urgently. "Doctor, the patient's vital signs are slowing to a stop, he is about to flat line. You must call him back immediately!"

Libertad and Jamie came forward totally perplexed. She asked, "What's happening? Who is Patrick speaking with? There is no one there!"

In the far distance I could hear Dr. Aldermatt instructing me to wake up; but the die was cast. The man with the blue eyes beckoned me forward and together we walked into a grey enveloping mist. Libertad was comforted by Rev. Jamie as an ambulance, siren screaming and blue light flashing, took Patrick Doyle to a hospital nearby. Patrick's fight against time, had begun. Many dangers lay ahead; Patrick Doyle's Déjà vu might just be the end of him.

Part 2. Rome's Tentacles of Terror

Chapter 19. Ezekiel Ben David

Shalom, my name is Ezekiel Ben David. I am a killer. Yes, I know that this is a shocking opening statement, so please allow me to put it into context. As far as I can tell I am approximately thirty years of age. I was born in Battir, a small village near the holy city of Jerusalem. My mother, Miriam, was a beauty and my father, Jacob, was the envy of the village men. Jacob was an ironsmith, with a profitable business and we had prospered. But we were soon to suffer at the hand of Rome. An evil Centurion, Marcella Acilli, took a fancy to my mother, so much did he covet her that he had Jacob arrested on a false charge of terrorism against the state. Unfortunately, this was to be a reoccurring theme of my life – Roman's coveting those whom I loved. Miriam was forced to flee and live in hiding to avoid Acilli's clutches. Jacob was taken to the salt mines never to return to his family.

It was impossible for Miriam to support me, and it was decided that I be adopted by her uncle, a man known as Samson. Samson was kind and treated me as though I was his own son. I think I was about five years old at the time of my adoption. However, as good to me as he was, there was a problem about my adoptive father. Samson was the young leader of Zealots; they lived in the Judean desert and they existed to drive the Romans from the land given to us by our God. Between raiding missions Samson taught me many skills, some good, but mostly bad. I learned from an early age how to kill men using many methods.

And so, my formative years were spent in the desert camp of the Zealots. Another boy, Ismael was my friend and confidant. Together, we would hunt and play fight. I knew of the cruelty of the Zealots, but I thought it justified for I remembered Marcella Acilli and what he did to my mother and father. For me and for Ismael the Romans were the hated enemy and the only good Roman was a dead one feeding the desert vultures. It was when Ismael and I approached our late teenage years that Samson decided that the time was come when we were to be 'bloodied.' We were the next generation who would take the fight to Rome. Ismael and I were ordered into his tent.

"Boys, the time has arrived for you both to be indoctrinated into our band of brothers. Ezekiel, do you remember Centurion Acilli and what he did to your family?"

I replied tersely, "Yes, I how could I ever forget!" I felt the bile rise in my throat at the mention of the Roman's name. I was acutely aware of Samson's scrutinizing gaze. My adoptive father continued, "That man has now risen to the rank of Tribune, he has used his promotion to enable even more acts of wickedness. I have decided that it is time for him to die! And Ezekiel, I have chosen you to be the one to kill him. Ismael will aid you in your mission, for he too will kill a Roman of importance."

I felt a surge of pride in my being chosen, but also fear for I was all too aware of what Romans did to captured prisoners. Over the years I had developed skills as an archer, able to split a watermelon at one hundred paces, whereas Ismael was excellent at javelin throwing. We were told to practice nonstop for hours on end. We worked under Samson's watchful eye until he judged we were ready for the task in hand. Once again, we were summoned into the leader's tent.

"My agents tell me that Tribune Marcella Acilli is to lead a victory parade, showing vanquished prisoners, some of whom are my men, through the streets of Jerusalem. Doubtless he wants to relish in pomp and ceremony and then the eventual crucifixion of the prisoners. But you two boys will ensure that his pride and pomp will stick in his craw, literally."

The 'parade' of terror, the name we had given it, was to take place the week before our Jewish celebration of Passover, during which time Jerusalem will be flooded with thousands of worshippers arriving from all parts of Israel. Passover is the time when our people celebrate Moses leading our forefathers to freedom from captivity in Egypt. However, the Romans always fear that the annual spring event will lead to a mass uprising. It was not a coincidence that the parade of terror came immediately before Passover. We Jews had to be put in our place and told our fate if we should dare transgress against Rome.

Samson led our surveillance of the parade route, which would circumnavigate the walls of the old city. It would commence at the Fortress Antonia and in due course arrive at the way of sorrows. From there the prisoners, now roped to their crossbars, would go to Golgotha, the place of the skull, where they would be crucified. Overlooking this route, the rooftops came in all shapes and sizes, flat, conical, ridged, high and low. We expected that the enemy would place sentries at vantage points, ready to react to any threat. Samson, able to think like a Roman Centurion, knew where these guardians would be sited. Accordingly, our men were situated where they would emerge from hiding and take them out.

We knew where the prisoners' manacles would be removed and they would be roped to the crossbars, at the start of the way of sorrows. It would be there that the soldiers would be encouraged by their officers to lay into the unfortunates with kicks, fists and whips, anything which would add more distress in their last hours of life. We chose our location on a moderate size building which had a flat roof but importantly it also had a balcony. This place was admirably suited for our purposes. Samson had Ismael and me look down from our vantage point. He asked, "Can you nail the buggers from here?"

The range was no more than 50 paces and I nodded to affirm there would be no problem. The short range would also be aided by our elevated site.

Samson gave his next orders, "Ezekiel, you know your target. Ismael, I want you to kill the standard bearer, the soldier carrying the legion's eagle. Skewer him in the guts, that will rock the bastards."

We were then to escape using ropes secured to the rear of the building. Men with fast horses would be awaiting us, and we would ride at speed for the sands of the desert wastes. The day of our blooding dawned bright and clear, blue skies belied the dangerous deed with which we had been tasked. Although I was now fully grown and standing at over six feet, and strong as an ox, I quaked with fear at the thought of death on a Roman cross. We took our vantage positions early, long before there was any sight of the enemy. The rising sun crested the hills and the plains to the east of Jerusalem, casting all in a golden glow.

We did not have too long before the sentries, legionaries of Legio X Fretensis, arrived and took their allotted positions. They spread out in teams of 8 men, the Roman unit called a contubernium, each team under the charge of a Decanus. Clearly, they were not expecting any trouble, this should just be another routine parade and execution, soon they would be back in the relative comfort of the Antonia. They yawned and joshed, as soldiers do as they stacked their javelins, which they called pilums into piles upon the tiles. But in due course these bastards were in for the surprise of their lives, or to be more accurate, their deaths.

The sun had climbed a little higher injecting some welcome warmth into the frigid early morning air, when we heard the note of the cornu announcing the impending arrival of the parade. The sound was, at once powerful, exciting and intimidating. The players, known as cornicen hove into view at the head of the procession. They blasted their curved tubular instruments telling the roof top sentries to be alert and watchful. Those in front of our position rose and stood to attention. The players were followed by the Aqualifier, the soldier carrying the all-important standard. He was adorned with a lion head covering his helmet and he marched chest out and proud. To lose the standard in battle was deemed a terrible disgrace and would go down in infamy. Then the legionaries arrived, the sounds of their caligae marching hobnailed boots echoing on the cobbles. Centurions carrying vine canes marched to the sides of the ranks, distinguishable by their transverse horsehair helmets.

The chariot of Marcellus Acilli was pulled by a pair of white stallions. The pompous bastard waved enthusiastically to the waiting crowds. The chariot drew to a halt immediately below us. We were indeed well placed for our murderous task. Legionaries unloaded crossbeams from a cart as the prisoners were subjected to an intense bout of whipping. Then came the screech of a desert hawk; it was the signal for the sentries to die. Our assassins crept from their hiding places and took the unsuspecting men from behind, curved sicari daggers flashed as they cut throats from ear to ear. The dead bodies were dragged out of sight from view below.

Ismael and I crept forwards, each drawing deep breaths to still our beating hearts and stop our hands trembling. Below the legionaries stamped their boots, marking time. Baskets containing crucifixion nails were shown to the condemned, as a taunt as their crossbeams were roped to their shoulders. Marcellus stood proud in his chariot, red robe flowing in the light morning breeze. I saw that he held his head high, thereby helpfully exposing his throat. In an almost automated fashion, I nocked my arrow into my bowstring and drew my weapon to full tension. My arm muscles billowed with the exertion. Allowing for wind and elevation was by now second nature. There was an audible whoosh as I released, and my arrow flew straight and true. There was a squelching smack as it struck Marcellus in the neck, just below his Adam's apple. The arrowhead jutted out from the back of his neck accompanied by a huge gout of dark blood. Even at this distance I could see Marcellus Acilli roll his eyes upwards in utter disbelief. He grasped at the protruding shaft, coughed blood and phlegm and collapsed in a lifeless heap to the cobbles. Job done.

It was Ismael's time to shine, which was precisely what his javelin did as it inscribed an arc as it flew to the next victim. It punctured the Aqualifier's light armour gutting him. The unfortunate man wrenched at the shaft, pirouetted in a death dance, spilling his looping entrails into the dust and dirt. Orders were issued by blasts on the cornu. Centurions led their men up stairwells towards our vantage point; we had only minutes before they would be upon us. Ropes awaited our escape at the building's rear and Samson urged us to make haste. Ismael and I had just reached ground level when the first legionary appeared before us. A javelin split the turf between my feet. Despite Samson yelling to take to our horses, the Romans on the rooftop yelling insults was like a red rag to a bull. As though by magic my bow appeared in my hands. A Centurion stood at the parapet yelling obscenities about our Jewish heritage. My arrow took him full in the maw of his mouth and he 'couped' to the ground at my stallion's hooves. My good horse finished the bastard off in a flurry of hooves, smashing his skull inwards. It was time for obscenities to come from Samson. "You stupid bastard of a boy, you will get us all killed, get the fuck outa here!" Having vented his spleen, he slapped my horse's flanks, and we headed full tilt with the wind in our face for the wastes of the Judean desert.

Ironically, our success may have sowed the first infinitesimal hiatus in the relationship between Ismael and me. We were as close as brothers, but we were also highly competitive and me being chosen to kill the Tribune rankled with him. And so, the years rolled on, we continued in our war against the invaders, killing, maiming and causing mayhem. Then I heard the stories of Yeshua and his teachings. They would come to have a profound effect upon me and the way I thought of war and right and wrong.

Some form of turning point occurred when I saved some Roman captives from the gruesome death of crucifixion, which Samson had sentenced them to. To save them I had to defeat

Ismael in combat. This I did and was never forgiven by my erstwhile friend and lifelong comrade. My wife, Batya, and I were banished from the zealot camp. Those who have read my story "Combatant" will know that my actions that day opened a Pandora's box of problems. Now my story continues.

Chapter 20. The way of sorrows

The man with the piercing blue eyes, the man who called himself Gabriel, led me out from the grey mist. He addressed me,

"Come Ezekiel Ben David, you have, of your own free will, accompanied me back to Jerusalem in the year of our Lord AD33. It has therefore been decided to reveal to you that you will have a place in a future life. You will be born and live in a land known to the Romans as Hibernia. But, at the time of your future birth the Roman empire will have long gone. Personally, I think Hibernia to be a dark bog of a land and has always been inhabited by people of a savage nature unwilling to compromise or conform. But there are those superior to me who place importance upon the place and wish it to be successful and at peace. There, you will once again, play an important role in what the Lord desires. That is a story for the future, it is the here and now that is of the utmost importance. Your good wife, Batya, is in mortal danger, you must make your way immediately to the place known as the way of sorrows.

So, saying, Gabriel disappeared, leaving me alone in a Jerusalem Street. Although early spring, strangely the birds did not sing, even the cockerels failed to crow, everywhere seemed to be deserted in an atmosphere of gloom and despondency. As instructed, I made my way to the way of sorrows which commenced at the Antonia fortress. I was soon joined by a throng of others heading in the same direction, something was certainly afoot! We reached a point where the people stood three deep lining the route in an air of expectation.

Those who hoped to see blood would not be disappointed. A parade of those to be executed was heralded by the deep boom of a base drum which reverberated in the narrow space between the buildings, causing an added sense of dread. I heard the crack of a bull whip as it lashed a man's back. That man was Yeshua who bore a heavy crossbeam roped across his shoulders.

Some sadistic bastards had woven a crown of sharp thorns into a circular entanglement and pushed it down upon his forehead causing profuse bleeding. His robe was blood stained from the cruel whipping he had endured.

Pilate had decreed that the execution be carried out by Syrian auxiliary soldiers of Legio 111 Gallica. Pilate, already racked by guilt in condemning an innocent man, decided he would not inflict carrying out the execution upon Longinus, whom he knew to be a friend of the Nazarene. The procession ground to a halt. Yeshua, weakened by beating and stress had fallen to the cobbles. The heavy crossbar caused him to pitch forwards and he just managed to avoid dashing his head upon the cobbles. It was then that Batya dashed forwards with a drinking vessel, weaving her way nimbly through the onlookers and soldiers, wishing to slake Yeshua's thirst. She never made it to her friend. A load roar of anger came from the Centurion in charge. The soldier stood at least six foot-five inches tall and had a chest girth to match. He smashed his way through the ranks to reach her; if he did so Batya would die.

Without hesitation I man handled those in front out of my way, drawing level with the brute I slammed my shoulder as hard as I could into his side. The abomination grunted and staggered just permitting me sufficient space to grab Batya under my arm and dart for the cover of the crowd. But, big as the bastard was, he was also fast and recovered quickly and was drawing down upon us. I could feel the heat and smell of his foul breath when he was stopped in his tracks. A large, coloured man had placed himself in his way. Thus, doing so, he provided me with time to drag Batya to relative safety in a side alley. The crowd closed ranks behind us preventing pursuit by the auxiliaries; we were free for the moment, but only just!

I paused to draw breath and quickly looked back. The enraged Centurion had drawn his gladius, the Roman short sword, and was about to gut the black man who had dared confront him. An Optio appeared at his side and was just in time to stop the strike. "Sir, please wait, we have a use for this man. The prisoner, Yeshua, is totally exhausted, if we should force him to carry his cross beam to Golgotha he will die before we reach there. Now that would spoil your fun would it not!"

The brute turned to his subordinate, "What would you have me do?"

"Look at the size of this guy, the cross would be as a matchstick to a man of his size and strength. Have him bear Yeshua's cross to the place of execution, then do as you will with him."

I watched the brute try to think, despite his foul temper. Eventually, he saw reason and turned to the large black man. "What is your name?"

"They call me Simon of Cyrene."

"Then, Simon of Cyrene, carry the prisoner's cross or choose to die on this spot!"

Simon did as he was bid, lifting the rough wood and swinging it easily across his broad shoulders, no doubt wondering what he had just got himself into.

As this was transpiring, I had a chance to look at the sadistic Syrian. It was not just the creature's height and bulk which caused him to appear awesome. He wore his own form of uniform which most certainly did not conform to Roman regulations. A helmet, made of bronze, covered his head and jaws. A nose piece gave him protection to the front of his face and small eye slits allowed him sufficient forward and side vision. The helmet was topped with a sharp bronze blade honed to razor sharpness and no doubt he would use it in close-quarter battle. A protrusion protected the nape of his neck. Then a bronze breastplate was in place from neck to his upper legs. The ensemble was completed with a scarlet robe which billowed down his back. To be allowed to dress as a gladiator instead of a soldier meant that this man held considerable sway with someone in authority. No doubt his value was measured in the number of enemies he killed for his masters. This man, or creature was therefore extremely dangerous.

Once again, the procession started for Golgotha, Yeshua was just about able to drag his feet forward. I hoped his weak condition would provide him with an early release from the agony to come. Neither Batya nor I wanted to go and witness the horror at the place of the skull, but neither did we want to desert Yeshua in his time of need. His supposed loyal disciples had fled in order to protect their own skin. And so, with resignation, we walked onwards with heads bowed in sorrow. The path led us outside the city walls; Golgotha was indeed shaped liked a human skull. A small circular arena was placed in the centre of some large stones. To our dismay the former gladiators Akiva and Spirax were already hanging in agony from their crosses. These men, former comrades of Barabbas, had been led astray by the latter's outrageous antics with Pilate's wife and now they were paying the price, whilst their leader got off free. It was Barabbas who should have been the one to suffer. Ominously, a large upright between the two dying men awaited the arrival of Yeshua, the one who would pay for the sins of mankind.

A low murmur arose from the watching crowd as Yeshua was brought forward and forced upon his back arms outstretched. The man known to me as Ammar (Satin) yelled loudly, "Crucify him, crucify him!" He stood but ten paces away and I could smell the stink of his evil amora. I had to use all my will power to resist striking him dead. The nails and hammers were brought to the cross and I pushed Batya's head into my chest to spare her the horror. The soldiers took their positions, but it was the sadistic Syrian Centurion who slammed the spikes through Yeshua's wrists. Each hammer blow caused Yeshua's body to spasm in agony. Usually, it was the eight-man contibum who did this foul deed, but such was the Centurion's depravity that he took delight in his task. I felt a surge of hatred surge through me as never before experienced.

Whilst the condemned hung in agony, the soldiers sat upon the ground to drink and play dice. The main prize was Yeshua's homespun robe. Although it was but midday, it was almost dark; someone or some unknown power was indeed extremely angry. Cold downdraughts descended from towering thunder clouds chilling us to the bone. The man I hated, the sadist Syrian, decided to remove his helmet in order to imbibe more freely. Jet black hair knitted into dreadlocks tumbled down to his shoulders. His cheeks were covered in spiral tattoos adding to the hideousness of his visage. A well-dressed Jew beside me said, "That creature is called Zayin Krass, he's the spawn of the Devil himself! Did you see Ammar acknowledge him upon his arrival? Do not make an enemy of Krass, he will pursue you to the ends of the earth."

It was as though this stranger could read my mind and my intentions. "It may be already too late for that! How do you know of him?"

"My name is Joseph of Arimathea, I'm a member of the Sanhedrin, and I make it my business to know these things." Joseph hung his head in despair. "This was not supposed to happen, but I was powerless to prevent it!"

Despite Joseph's warning and that Yeshua would certainly not approve, I decided that I would make Zayin Krass have an ugly and painful death to pay for his crimes. By now total darkness had descended upon the land. The crowd were frightened, and some began to make their way back to Jerusalem. Jewish custom would not permit those executed to remain on their crosses on the sabbath which begins at nightfall on Friday. Pilate, fearing yet another riot agreed that the victim's legs be broken. Unable to prise upwards to exhale they would quickly suffocate to death. However, the process adds additional agony to their last remaining minutes. Thankfully, that fate was not in store for Yeshua. Longinus, the one Roman that I called my friend, arrived with men under his command. He carried a long spear and he was weeping openly. I knew his grim but merciful purpose. He stepped to the base of Yeshua's cross, not even Zayin Krass would dare challenge him. Longinus spotted me and signalled that Batya depart immediately. As I ushered her away, I saw the shape of a man dangling from a tree, a noose was around his neck. Judas Iscariot had also paid his price.

Chapter 21. The first Easter Sunday

Batya and I awoke together at dawn, her dark hair caressed my cheek and her arm rested upon my chest. Immediately we both sensed the atmospheric difference compared with the previous week. Gone was the heavy electrified air full of depression and sorrow, now replaced with warmth and early morning bird song. I left our bed and pulled back the drapes, a tiny, barbed warbler fluttered and tweeted in joyous greeting. I looked down into the street where, even at this early hour, the crowds were moving in their exodus from Jerusalem now that Passover had been celebrated and completed. Batya, naked, stood by my side. Once again, I marvelled at her beauty and thought I was the most fortunate of men. For the moment we were safe, and my thoughts were not predominated by fears for her safety. It felt as though the weight of the world had been removed from my shoulders. She instinctively knew what I wanted, and she pulled me back to bed and beneath the covers. Our love making was euphoric and joyous, then sated we lay bodies entwined.

As I gently stroked her cheek I said, "Batya you feel as I do, something has changed, though as yet I know not what, but despite the trauma of the past week I am now happy."

Batya fluttered her almond-shaped eyes. "Yes, but that's because you have just bedded a beautiful woman!" She giggled as though she was a girl.

"Yes, of course I love you and our love making was the best it has been for many days. But you tease me, you are aware that something wonderful has just happened, of that, I am sure. And we are going to find out!"

We decided that we would venture forth into the city, acutely aware that we were both fugitives from Roman justice. Those readers familiar with my previous story will be aware that I rescued Batya from the evil clutches of Carius Aquillas. He was a Roman of high breeding, destined to hold a seat in the Roman senate and a man used to getting everything that he desired. And for some time, he had wanted Batya, a woman who would never freely give herself to him. As is the nature of things, this only served to increase his longing and lust. We knew that Roman patrols were looking for us. Should we be arrested, Batya would be forced to his bed; I would be crucified.

We walked the side alleys of the old city, keeping our head garments wrapped tightly around our faces. Bird song echoed from the eaves of houses as pairs began their spring mating ritual, the awakening of new life after the darkness of winter. How I envied the little creatures with their uncomplicated lives. The spring sun shone from a cobalt blue sky with just a few fair-weather puffy cumulus clouds appearing over the tops of the hills of Judeah. Flocks of migrating wild fowl flew northeast in an inverted V, leaving Africa for their European summer nesting sites. The rites of spring were being observed in the time-honoured way.

The crowds were singing with great gusto; at first, I thought it was because they were returning home to loved ones. Then came the cry, "He is risen, the Messiah has come back from the grave!" Complete strangers clasped each other in exaltation. Batya and I exchanged looks. These were the people, who just days before had cried out for Yeshua to be crucified. They had been complicit in his appalling death and had chosen a rogue and scoundrel (Barabbas) to be set free. How fickle is human nature, had the scales of collective madness now fallen from their eyes. Too late had they realised the error of their ways. But Batya and I were intrigued; if Yeshua was indeed alive, that may well explain the change in atmosphere, could we dare for this to be possible? Neither of us could bear for our hopes to be dashed again by despair. Someone in the crowd said, "He was laid to rest in a tomb prepared for Joseph of Arimathea, but the stone is rolled away, and Yeshua has departed!"

Batya and I knew the garden's location and without further ado we walked hand in hand in that direction. We grew near to the city gate when a century of Roman soldiers approached. We covered our faces and stood aside. A sigh of relief escaped my lips; the Centurion in charge was my friend Longinus. We would come to no harm from these soldiers. Indeed, it had been Longinus who had been instrumental in Batya's escape. In doing so he had committed treason against Rome. Had his act been discovered by Pilate, Longinus would also have had an extremely painful death. Marching past, the soldiers' caligae boots echoed on the cobbles, as they followed the standard bearer. Longinus marched at their side; his vine cane tucked under his arm. My friend gave me a brief nod of recognition as he passed. In the midst of the century, eight men in chains shuffled forward.

Recognition dawned upon me, these men were the Syrian auxiliaries who had crucified Yeshua and had then been tasked with guarding his tomb. In the latter they had failed miserably and would bear the brunt of Pilate's anger and angst. Pilate the Procurator was incensed when he heard claims that Yeshua had risen from the dead. Now woe betide these soldiers who unwittingly had helped the rumour mill. Golgotha would have more occupants. But Zayin Krass was not amongst them. Some people in authority favoured the sadistic Syrian.

We followed the path outside Jerusalem's walls, which in part retraced the last steps of Yeshua. The garden was where rich Jews could have their tomb carved out from the cliff face. Legionaries from Legio X Fretensis surrounded the garden. Pilate wanted to ensure that no more rumours emanated from this place. Batya and I were about to turn for Jerusalem when a soldier with the rank of Optio beckoned us to come forward. His name was Titus Accius, and he was Longinus's second in command. My first instinct was we should make a run for it, but Titus smiled and signalled for us to halt.

"Ezekiel, you have nothing to fear from me, I understand why you are here, Batya and you may enter the garden."

Within the confines of the walled garden the warmth of the sun seemed to increase, and we experienced a feeling of profound serenity. However, when we decided to approach Yeshua's tomb, we both had a little trepidation as to what we would find. Indeed, the stone had been rolled aside from the entrance permitting us to peer into the gloomy interior. There was no body, only some discarded funeral linen. My pulse rate increased, and I turned away to face the sunlight. The man with the piercing blue eyes stood smiling. "Where is Yeshua? I asked.

He simply said, "The Lord has departed."

I found Batya looking at me strangely. "Who are you talking to, there is no one here?"

I decided not to tell her.

Such was the sense of peace and quiet joy, Batya and I decided to spend the remainder of the afternoon in the garden. Birds sang and flitted between budding almond trees. Red anemones flowered in wild profusion, a sure sign of the arrival of spring and life to be renewed. Hand in hand we sat on a bench until the sun had begun to near its destination in the low western heavens. In the crepuscular light of evening the sinking sun reflected from long lenticular clouds which were intersected with vertical components thereby forming a large cross towards the east. Perhaps this was the herald of a new beginning. We had not seen Yeshua, but our hearts were filled with joy as we departed the garden for Jerusalem. I wondered if all future days would be as joyous as today. We would soon find out.

Chapter 22. Barabbas and blackmail

How quickly things change! We entered our refuge to find Joseph Ben Gideon sitting head in hands, a picture of misery and angst. The euphoria and hope of today vanished as quickly as snow from a ditch. Now, I had little time for Ben Gideon, despite his providing us with a refuge from the Romans. During our short stay at his home we had witnessed the coming and going of some very unsavoury characters, including Aamar, the evil one himself. However, Batya and I had accepted his hospitality and for this we were indebted to him. His wife Niamoh was the essence of kindness; she and Batya had become firm friends.

"What's wrong Joseph?"

He slowly raised his head from his hands, his eyes were red from crying. "They have taken Niamoh!"

"Who are they?"

"That bastard Barabbas is behind this. Not satisfied and relieved at having escaped the cross, he has been openly boasting of how he bedded Pilate's wife at the Ludus (Gladiator school) before killing her. When Pilate heard of his drunken boasting in the taverns an arrest warrant was issued immediately. But Barabbas, brutal as he is, is not stupid. He anticipated Pilate's fury and took to the desert. Trouble is that he and his henchmen captured Niamoh and took her with them. I have received this ransom demand." Ben Gideon passed me a piece of papyrus. In Aramaic the message was brutal and blunt. It read,

"Joseph Ben Gideon, for many years I have regarded you as my friend. A friend in need is a friend indeed. Now I am your friend, and I am in very great need. I am pursued by our mutual enemy the Romans, even the zealot Samson has turned his back on me, and I am banned from his fireside. I am consigned to the desert wilderness with a few comrades and the desert animals. But not all is totally black as I have your beautiful wife to warm me during the cold desert night, and yes, she is really good at keeping a man warm. However, she is another mouth to be fed and we are fast approaching the time when my men and me have had their fill of her. Therefore, it is with great regret that I must inform you of my decision to slit her throat. As you know I'm an expert at doing this sort of thing and I will endeavour to make the process as painless as possible. Of course, there is the alternative, that being you pay me twenty casks of silver to ensure her wellbeing! That said amount to be deposited at the Wadi Ettu at midnight three nights hence. You may leave your reply by your garden gate tonight. I assume your answer to be yes, but you must know that should I detect any treachery or trickery Niamoh will have a very unpleasant death."

I was shocked at the brutality and ruthlessness, but also surprised that Barabbas could pass such a horrible message with eloquence. Batya turned pale as she read the scroll. "Ezekiel, we must do something to rescue Niamoh from that evil brute. Niamoh is my dearest friend and Joseph has provided us with a safe haven when no others would."

Ben Gideon looked at me pleadingly. "Ezekiel, you have a reputation for being able to save ladies in distress." He looked directly at Batya. "You saved Batya, and I know it is possible for you to save Niamoh. You have the contacts who can do such things under your direction."

Batya looked at me imploringly. I knew immediately that I had no choice; but how could I do this with both Romans and Jewish zealots after my blood? I needed a plan, and I needed it fast.

Pontius Pilate, Roman Prefect of Judea, sat in his office in near darkness. The small amount of illumination was provided by two wall torches, their flames guttering as their supply of oil dwindled. The darkness matched the Prefect's foul mood. Publius Galeria, Pilate's slave, cum advisor, an evil little man of influence, approached the entrance. Two Praetorian guardsmen, with crossed spears barred his progress. However, as he drew level, they withdrew their weapons. Both guards stared straight ahead but one whispered, "Publius, be careful, the boss is in foul humour. He has just thrown a rotten apple at me because I inadvertently coughed!" The large guard suppressed a laugh as small Publius passed him by.

"You wanted to see me master?"

Pontius Pilate looked up. "Of course, I bloody want to see you, that's precisely why you have been summoned!"

Publius adopted a grovelling stance, his hands clasped forward as though in supplication. "How may I be of service master?"

Pilate started one of his infamous tirades. "That bastard Barabbas has been openly boasting in the pubs and taverns of Jerusalem as to how he raped my wife Claudia before murdering her. And how I, the great Pontius Pilate, had been unable to hold him to account. Not only that, but how I had to crucify an innocent man in his place. Now Barabbas has fled to the wilderness to avoid justice. But still the mocking messages arrive from him in the desert."

As he spoke Pilate dipped his hands in a water bowl and roughly scrubbed them. Publius noted this habit had become persistent since Pilate had crucified Yeshua. A guilty conscience manifests itself in many ways. The Prefect resumed his tirade. "And all this on top of the debacle in my own praetorium when barbarians rescued that woman Batya and Ezekiel Ben David. Bad enough, but for that to happen in the presence of my boss, Lucius Pomponius Flaccus, Governor of Syria. That bastard always looked down his patrician nose at my lowly equestrian status. Now in Rome my name will be destroyed, I expect to be sent home in shame with no prospect of another post."

Publius Galeria's dark eyes flashed with intelligence and guile. After a suitable silence he ventured, "Sir, I have information that will redress the situation and will restore your prestige."

Pilate appeared to have calmed slightly. "Go on explain."

"I have been made aware that there is much dissatisfaction in the ranks of Legio 111 Gallica. These Syrian auxiliaries have long complained about their poor renumeration compared to Roman Legionaries. The last straw was when the eight men who failed in their duty to guard Yeshua's tomb were put to death on your orders. Rightly or wrongly, they feel deeply aggrieved and now that their Centurion Zayin Krass has backed their cause there is open talk of mutiny in the ranks. It's reported that Krass has formed an alliance with none other than Barabbas."

Pilate sighed deeply. Not only did he have problems with the Jews, but now auxiliaries sworn to serve Rome were about to revolt. The fact that they were Syrian troops, not Roman would not be seen as a mitigating factor. Pomponius Flaccus would have his head on a spike. Disgrace was certain. How he rued the day he agreed to take this post as Prefect in this stinking hell hole in the middle east.

Publius continued, "Perhaps we should view this situation as an opportunity, not a threat. We have a man who can find Barabbas in the wilderness. Find Barabbas and we find Krass. We will kill two birds with the one stone! The Syrians, having lost Krass will toe the line with no more trouble, especially when we crucify the remaining ring leaders of the dissent. Barabbas will die on a cross, which is long overdue. You will be seen as the saviour of the situation and Lucius Pomponius Flaccus will forever be in your debt."

Pilate's mood visibly lifted, how clever was Publius Galeria. Pilate ordered, "Send Centurion Longinus to me forthwith."

The soldier known as the desert fox had been summoned.

Chapter 23. Trouble at tavern

Longinus and I had a system of communication, but we used it only when absolutely necessary. If he was found to be fraternizing with the enemy, it would go very badly for him. Tonight, we met in a tavern in the western side of the old city. Longinus was dressed as a desert nomad, complete with a linen kaffiyeh upon his head and he wore long flowing robes and sandals. His skin was burnished brown by the Israel sun and the look was completed with several days beard stubble. To all appearances he was nomadic, not Roman; just as well as the invaders were hated in this hostel.

Beer is one of the most popular beverages in Israel and we supped the brew from large tankards. I knew that Romans preferred wine, but Longinus could adopt to meet every situation. Mind you, he was not complaining as he supped. My Roman friend told me of his meeting with Pilate and Publius Galeria. Longinus had been given orders to go undercover, find and kill both Barabbas and Zayin Krass. He sighed, Pilate was not an easy task master, and he knew he was only as good as his last success. Failure was not an option.

Joseph Ben Gideon and his wife Niamoh were known to Longinus, and he was genuinely upset at their predicament. "It looks like we have a shared objective my Jewish friend," Longinus laughed, "Once more into the jaws of death, how many more times can we survive these situations!"

I did not share his sense of humour! Especially when I became aware of several strangers from across the room watching us intently. We continued our conversation in hushed tones, but the four men left their bar stools and sauntered over. Their eyes were focused on me, not Longinus. Recognition dawned, the large bugger with the hooked nose and pock marked skin was called Abuya, a hench man of my former comrade Samson, the Zealot. He and I would certainly never be 'best buddies'.

"Well, look who we have here, its none other than Roman loving Ezekiel Ben David!" He stood hands on hips; he and his three backers wore contemptuous sneers on their weather worn faces.

I replied, "I'm afraid that you are mistaken. My friend and I are camel drivers, and we are currently seeking employment on a desert camel train."

He howled with mirth, "Camel drivers, my arse!"

Once again, I tried verbal de-escalation, "Please stand aside and allow my friend and I to depart in peace."

Longinus was watching me intently waiting for a signal. We both rose together leaving the table for the nearest exit. But Abuya was having none of it. He hocked up a wedge of green phlegm which he spat, hitting me between my eyes. I took a deep breath and calmly wiped the obnoxious spittle away with my sleeve. I opened my hands, palms outwards in a placating gesture, and moved towards the door. Yeshua would have been proud of me for my restraint, but then Abuya made a fatal error. A sicari dagger appeared in the oaf's right hand. Peaceful persuasion had failed.

Abuda mocked me, "You traitor! You are afraid even to admit your own name! The only peace you will experience is the pieces you are about to be sliced into." He brandished the wicked curved sicari blade in a threatening manner. Now it was fight, flight had been denied to Longinus and me. Sometimes the ways of a lifetime, or lifetimes in my case, die hard. Longinus and I looked each other in the eye, his pre-battle rage was reflected in my own eyes. Abuda made to slice my throat, he was fast, but not fast enough. I moved my head quickly to the side and the blade passed harmlessly by. Experience had taught me to stand slightly to one side thereby offering a slightly smaller target. I whipped off my outer cloak which served as a make-shift shield. Once again Abuda closed in, this time I detected a slight air of desperation in his movements.

My cloak deflected his knife, and I grabbed his knife hand with both of mine. A firm yank on my attacker's arm unbalanced him and his own momentum sent Abuya crashing to the tavern's floor tiles. I stamped my foot upon his wrist and the sicari flew from his grasp with a clatter. Leaning over my opponent I grabbed a handful of his filthy hair. This provided leverage to pull his head back before slamming his forehead into the tiles, in the process shattering several tiles. Abuya breathed his last in a dark pool of his own blood.

Goon number two came at me simultaneously swinging a weighted baton. If it had struck it would easily have shattered my skull. The fool raised it to strike thereby leaving himself completely open. My right hook crashed into his jugular rendering him unconscious and possibly dying. It was wrong but I found I was enjoying myself immensely. In the meantime, Longinus had despatched another idiot to join his ancestors and was in the process of toying with fool number four. The man made a break for the exit; mistakenly he thought he had made it when Longinus's pugio (dagger) lodged in his spinal cord after a short, swift and fatal flight.

The tavern's patrons, as one, broke into a round of spontaneous applause. These rough men had enjoyed the free entertainment. Such is human nature. The tavern keeper looked relieved that little damage had been done. He poured the two of us large beers as several big men took the bodies to be thrown into the lime pits. No one would mourn them.

Chapter 24. Suspense under starlight

The desert wilderness to the east of Jerusalem is called the Negev, and although small in comparison to African deserts it is an extremely unpleasant place for man to frequent. It stretches from northeast Israel to the salt-laden dead sea. Desert scrub and cacti, together with some brave animals compete for whatever little water is available. Some water is to be found in the small wadis where the soft sandstone has allowed it to accumulate in underground springs. It's at these springs which the nomads call wadis, that the animals come every evening to drink. Hydraxes, reddish brown, cat-like animals, take their turn along with gazelles and desert foxes to approach the water. Most wadis are found in north facing canyons which are sheltered from the burning rays of the sun.

And now Longinus and I found ourselves in this unfriendly location, as we sought help from the rogue of the desert, David Ben Efron. We sat and warmed our outstretched hands at a small fire which we had lit between a circle of stones. Skeins of scudding clouds crossed the face of the moon, their progress across the heavens helped by a freshening wind. Tiny ice crystals hung suspended in the air as the humidity increased. A weather front was approaching from the west. Most moisture is divested on the western side of the Judean hills, but this one had managed to rise above them without losing all its precipitation. In short this meant that the Negev was about to receive some precious life-giving rain. However, for the moment the stars still shone brightly in the heavenly firmament. It was then that we heard them, the low-pitched moans of the desert dunes, known to the nomads as the singing sands. Longinus looked at me, "They say it's the moans of those who have perished here in the wilderness."

I just nodded and said nothing. How could I explain to this Roman that I had received an education in the 20th century where I learned that the "moans" were caused by low seismic waves as wind passed through the dunes. Better by far for my friend to believe he was listening to the sounds of tormented souls.

The adrenaline of the previous evening from the tight spot in the tavern had now dissipated to be replaced by guilt. Did I really have to dash Abuya's brains into the tiles? Truth was that I had enjoyed the action and the killing, once started it was difficult to stop. It's the dark side of human nature which lies dormant within us all. Subject to some stressors the latent violence quickly surfaces to the fore. I remembered the words of my Greek comrade, Alketas, with whom I had fought side by side in the arena. "If you want to live never poke a sleeping bear with a stick." As though on cue a scorpion rushed out from underneath a stone. The little creature is harmless unless provoked, but if so it has a deadly sting in the tail. Such is the way of life with men like me and Longinus, we too have a deadly sting in the tail when provoked.

Suddenly the peace of the desert night was shattered as a spear embedded itself with a crash into the centre of our campfire. Flames spluttered, hot ashes and embers flew in all directions, some hitting Longinus and me in our faces. Instinctively I reached for my gladius, but Longinus placed a restraining hand on my arm. "This play-acting is quite normal for David Ben Efron; he loves to make a dramatic entrance! This he had certainly achieved. A large man, built like a man-mountain emerged from the darkness. Four men followed him as Longinus and I slowly came to our feet. A smile crossed Ben Efron's knife scarred visage. "Greetings Longinus and Ezekiel, its very good to see you both once again. But this must mean that you once again require my services, what is it that you desire?"

Longinus explained our joint mission to save Niamoh and to kill Barabbas and Zayin Krass. Ben Efron listened intently before asking, "And why should I risk my life and that of my men for that bastard Joseph Ben Gideon? That man has made more money from nefarious deals than Pontius Pilate." He laughed and added, "I may be a rogue, but at least I'm an honest rogue!"

Longinus knew it was pointless to appeal to his better nature, David Ben Efron simply did not have one. The man was motivated by money. Such was his avarice he would sell his soul to the Devil, and probably had already done so. Longinus simply stated, "There will be a reward."

David Efron pretended to be deep in thought and then proceeded to surprise us. "Of course, I will demand a reward. I am fully aware of what Barabbas has been up to. I have spies, even in his camp. Joseph Ben Gideon is a fool if he thinks leaving 20 casks of silver at Wadi Ettu will save his wife. I have already planned to have the silver collected tomorrow night. The silver becomes my property, Niamoh is saved; do we have a deal?" Longinus did not really expect any better, "Do I have any choice?"

Once again Ben Efron laughed, at least the rogue had a sense of humour. "Of course not, if you had you would not have come to me!" The man had a point. I asked, "And what do you know of Zayin Krass?"

The smile disappeared from David Ben Efron. "That monster is pure evil. He tried to form an alliance with Barabbas and Krass's rebel Syrian legion. But even Barabbas had the wit to chase him. It's reported that Krass and his men are going to cross the border into Parthia. Now that's another interesting problem that's about to come the way of Pontius Pilate!"

I was amazed at the scope of intelligence available to this nomadic will of the wisp. My immediate concern was to save Niamoh, "Do you know where Niamoh is being held?"

Once again, the smile reappeared on the big man's face, "Of course, I know where Barabbas's camp is, its but a four-hour march from here. Get your stuff together for we leave immediately."

Chapter 25. Barabbas in a bag

The heavens decided to erupt sending a deluge into the desert sand turning it from powder into a sticky quagmire, making our progress difficult. Rain driven by the freshening wind ran in rivulets down our faces stinging our eyes. Our hair was plastered to our faces and our sodden robes clung to our bodies. We shivered and strode grimly on into the mouth of the storm. Motivated by the need to save Niamoh lent energy to our legs.

Ben Efron took the lead setting a fast pace despite the difficult conditions. Longinus and I found ourselves positioned in the middle of his marching men. "How do you know we can trust him?" I asked my Roman friend. "What's to stop him from slitting our throats, pocketing the silver and disappearing into the night? Longinus replied, "If that is his intention, he would have done it by now. Despite his greed somewhere deep down there's a streak of goodness lurking in David Ben Efron; we have nothing to fear from him."

We arrived atop a cliff which overlooked a desert valley. The rain had played itself out and dawn was breaking in the eastern sky. Situated at the base of the cliff ten tents stood, but yet, there was no movement, no sign of life. "Don't be fooled, the buggers are there, but we will not act until tonight. Today we will survey and assess their strength." David Ben Efron continued, "I must find out which tent Niamoh is being held in." I nodded agreement.

The sun climbed high in the sky and the desert heat reasserted itself. Seeking shelter, we pulled our robes over our heads. Soaked and frozen by night, roasted by day, such was the life of the desert nomad. Eventually the camp came to life. Men lit cooking fire and gathered water from an underground spring. Others worked on their weapons. Swords, spears and hatchets were being edged and burnished to a bright shine. The scene resembled any army on the march, even if this was a small army of thieves and ne'er-do-wells.

"There he is," Longinus nudged me as we lay at our observation post at the cliff edge. The large man, former gladiator, murderer and rapist, emerged from the tallest tent. I knew him well and watched as he stretched his stiff limbs. He spoke with a booming voice. "Bring water to the woman, lets make her last day a little pleasant. Tonight, after I have had my way with her once again, I will slit her throat!"

I squirmed with anger and was almost overcome with an urge to rush down the slope and slice him to pierces. Once again Longinus showed why he had been selected to become an army officer. "Patience Ezekiel Ben David. The brute will never get the chance to make good that threat. I promise you on my sacred oath."

And so, we bade our time awaiting nightfall. The sun sank and the shadows lengthened, and a mule-drawn cart entered the camp. Six thieves had been selected to go to Wadi Ettu to collect the silver. David Ben Effron grinned and punched me lightly in the side. "We have a little surprise in place for those guys. The only metal which they will collect tonight is arrow heads in their guts!"

The six men and the mule left on their futile mission. Despite everything I felt a little bit sorry for the fools. The light of the campfires glowed in the crepuscular as sentries took up positions at the camp's four compass points. Then, taking us all by surprise, music arose from flutes, lutes and drums and drifted up to our position. The thieves sat in circles around their fires and seemed to be sniffing something from pottery vases. The music increased in tempo, and some got up and stamped their feet before swaying and twirling in a frenetic dance. However, we noted that Barabbas did not indulge in either the dancing or snorting. Was he saving himself for something altogether more pleasurable? Ben Efron enlightened me. "The idiots are imbibing the white powder of the poppy plant; they will not trouble us tonight. Within two hours they will sleep like babies and then we will cut their thieving throats!"

Barabbas ambled to the edge of the circle. To my horror he led Niamoh on a long leash which was secured by a collar around her neck. Then in a loud voice that carried above the music he ordered her, "Dance and strip!" At first, she refused to obey until he lashed her with a whip held in his other hand. The rabble applauded and laughed with glee in their drugged state. Niamoh had no choice, it was dance or die. Slowly she began to sway and discard her clothing. When she was naked her head hung in shame, and she made a futile attempt to cover her breasts with her arms. The rabble was now aroused and began to chant a litany of lust and profanities. Once again Longinus placed a restraining arm on me. "Not long now Ezekiel, she will be safe. Barabbas will suffer and will be sorry for his actions.

A man, obviously sober, left the camp and began climbing towards our vantage point. Ben Efron said, "Do not worry, its Nathan, he's my eyes and ears in Barabbas's camp. Nathan will guide us into the camp. Down below the poppy powder was working its magic, the thieves slept where they fell; but Barabbas had taken the naked Niamoh to his tent. The perimeter sentries had no chance, Efron's men quickly sliced their throats with sicari daggers. They gurgled and choked on their own blood as they fell to the dirt. Efron signalled that the same should be done to the sleeping thieves: I stopped him. "Killing them serves no purpose, alive they will continue to be a thorn in Pilate's side. Let them be!"

David Ben Efron was not used to being spoken to thus and I momentarily wondered if he would defy me. He looked at Longinus before making a sign indicating that he thought I had taken leave of my senses. It was with a degree of trepidation that Longinus and I entered the tent. We feared not for ourselves but for what we would find had happened to Niamoh. Barabbas the brute had her naked and strapped to his bed, legs wide apart. Also naked he loomed above her like the angel of death about to descend. His face was coated in a sheen of sweat and lust; so intent was he on his pleasure to come he failed to notice us until it was too late. No doubt his missing ear, lost in a fight, did not help. Sex was simply a means of imposing pain and control for this animal. He was about to commit rape when I called softly, "Barabbas!"

He froze in his tracks as though he had been struck by a sledgehammer, then slowly he turned to face me; I laughed at his manhood shrivelling into a useless flaccid flap of skin. It would have been so easy for me to just plunge my sword into his neck but that was not to be. Longinus simply said, "Ezekiel, this is not your fight, but I have my orders and now I am going to carry them out!"

The shock and surprise on Barabbas's face was replaced by guile and cunning. "So Roman what are you going to do, kill a naked and unarmed man like the coward which you are. Or would you dare face me in a fair fight?"

Longinus said, "You will have your fight, get dressed now!"

I was horrified. Longinus, as good a soldier as he is, had never fought in the arena. I had fought Barabbas as a gladiator, and I knew his moves and tricks. This was extremely foolish and dangerous for my friend. Once again Barabbas sneered, "If I am going to be sent to meet Yahweh, then I prefer to be presented to him as a Thracian gladiator, so I will fight you in the outfit of the Thraex, a man who fears no one." He proceeded to don a loincloth and a protective belt, and his arms were protected by leather greaves. His head was protected by a wide brimmed helmet called a galea which was adorned by a scarlet crest. Barabbas's weapon of choice was a Thracian curved sword which had a bronze blade honed to razor sharpness. With this formidable weapon he could slit a man down the middle from head to groin. To my amazement I recognised the sword, it had once held pride of place in the weapons display cabinet of Caseo Collina, for whom Barabbas had fought as a gladiator. The weapon was rumoured to be the sword of Rhesus who had fought at the siege of Troy. This may be just folk lore, nevertheless the sword had precious stones inlaid in its handle and was worth a considerable fortune. Barabbas, master thief as he was, had spirited it away from his master's ludus. Barabbas held nothing or no one to be sacred. The arena was formed by a circle of Ben Efron's men. Others stood guard over their drugged adversaries and had orders to slit their throats should they stir. The firelight reflected off Barabbas's parmula, a small rectangular light shield which would not hinder his dexterity. I had to admit he appeared a frightening opponent. Once known in the arena as the 'wolf man' Barabbas had killed hundreds of men and I shivered with fear for my friend.

Once again, I pleaded with Longinus to allow me to take his place, but my words fell upon deaf ears. Longinus would fight with a spear and a gladius, the Roman short stabbing sword and chose not to be encumbered by a shield. I briefed him, "Speed is your survival. Barabbas is also fast, but his vision is impaired as his visor has only two small eye holes. Try to tempt him to take off his helmet, that will give you a much larger target for a killing blow. Also watch for him drawing his arm back to launch a killing slash, when that happens move quickly to the side, remember his peripheral vision is impaired. He has limited hearing due to his missing ear, try to discombobulate the bugger!"

David Ben Efron took it upon himself to act as referee. At the drop of his spear the contest began. Barabbas immediately gave a fine display of his gladiatorial footwork, reminding me of my boxing in a different time and place. He stepped, slashed and twirled and changed direction, but Longinus led him a merry dance, this way and that and around the circle of men. Barabbas was aging and getting fat and I could hear him panting from within the visor. His great bronze blade slashed and flashed but found only fresh air. Even though it was night, I knew that inside his visor it would be hot as hell. Dare I begin to hope that this may yet end well? I had already resolved to step in should Longinus suffer a bad wound; I knew it would be cheating but I had a spear at the ready. I had my friend's back.

The watching men were placing bets and the odds began to swing in favour of Longinus. Suddenly, Barabbas found a reserve of energy from deep within his being, his blade flashed at speed in the firelight; this was it the bastard was going for the kill. "Longinus move now!" I yelled at the top of my parched throat. He heard me just in time moving to the side and losing just a slice of his sleeve instead of his arm. I tightly gripped my spear, ready to dart forward and impale the brigand. But Longinus's evading swerve allowed him inside the arc of Barabbas's swing; he gripped that wide brimmed helmet and sent it spinning into the night. However, Barabbas's speed saved him; he backstepped out of immediate danger. The men howled as they had been cheated out of seeing Barabbas shed his blood.

Barabbas was coated in sweat which ran down his face and stung his eyes. Now it was Longinus on the offensive, his gladius stabbed and found his opponent's shoulder. The bronze blade of Rhesus fell to the compacted sand and blood flowed down Barabbas's arm. "Well Roman, you have me now. Will you grant me mercy?"

Longinus lifted the sword of Rhesus, gently swinging it to feel its perfect balance. Longinus looked to the heavens as though seeking guidance from the night sky. Barabbas followed his gaze and in doing so tilted his head back exposing his throat. Once again, the bronze blade flashed, and Barabbas's head bounced torn from his neck in a clean sweep. My relief was palpable. Longinus ordered "David Ben Efron bring me a bag for this bugger's head!"

Fast forward to four hours later in Wadi Ettu, the six men on the mule drawn wagon were in good spirits. Barabbas would be certain to give them a share of the spoils of silver which they were about to collect. And there they were, the casks reflected in the light of a campfire. A hunched figure sat beside the flames.

The cart driver shouted, "Joseph Ben Gideon!" Joseph slowly rose to his feet and sauntered over to the edge of the firelight. The mule driver drew his dagger, this was going to be fun, tonight he would have silver and sport! He ran towards his target; he was filled with blood lust. A spear came from the confines of the shadows and rent his head asunder. His five comrades were startled and tried to form a defensive circle; this was not supposed to happen! A second thief fell with a dagger protruding from his throat. Panic struck the remaining four who turned tail and tried to flee. Arrows took them in their unprotected backs.

The silver was duly loaded into the cart destined to be banked by David Ben Efron. A good night's work!

Chapter 26. In from the cold

The next part of my tale is told in the words of Longinus. Approximately one week after our return from the Negev desert, we met in our usual tavern. Few others were present, and no one interrupted us. This is the tale told by my friend.

Ezekiel, you know of my friendship of Yeshua and how I was sceptical about the tales of his resurrection after his cruel death on the cross. But two nights ago, he was with me. I had dismissed my squad and being tired retired early to my small, cramped but private quarters. I had just begun to drift off into a dream when I heard his familiar voice.

"Longinus, Longinus, awaken, I have a task for you which is of the utmost importance." And there stood Yeshua, looking young and renewed, not as I had last seen him in excruciating agony. I rose to embrace him, but for whatever reason he stopped me. A strange radiance came from his person, some power which was not of this world. I was overcome with guilt that it had been my spear which had ended his earthly life, even though it also ended his pain. He sensed my discomfort and said, "Longinus you did what was destined for you. But now I need your help once again."

I began to wonder if I was indeed dreaming, but this was really happening. Yeshua continued, "Ezekiel Ben David is here for a very special reason. Tomorrow Pilate will summon you and others to tell of a threat from the east. The Parthians, under King Nambed have amassed an army of 60,000 men on the banks of the river Euphrates, thereby forming a direct threat to Rome's control of Syria. Nambed's demands include excessive tributes to allow Roman trading caravans to pass through his territory which is necessary to gain access to the silk road in the east. If Governor Lucius Pomponius Flaccus does not agree to Nambed's terms the Parthians will invade Syria. Flaccus does not have sufficient troops to repel an invasion, especially after Legio 111 Gallica mutinied. It is my task for Ezekiel to prevent the needless deaths of thousands on both sides, but first we must bring him in from the cold. You can bring this about during your meeting with Pilate tomorrow; and this is how it can be achieved. Remember that knowledge gives power, and you must use this knowledge to good avail.

Chapter 27. Pilate's pragmatism

We all stood as Pontius Pilate, accompanied by his assistant Publius Galeria, entered his spacious office. Assembled were Tribune Carius Aquillas, the spoilt patrician snob of noble Roman lineage. Dido Valerii, Roman Camp Prefect and commander of the 10th Legion, Legio X Fretensis. I, Longinus, a humble Centurion, was in exalted company, far above my station in life.

Pilate was pale and appeared to have the worries of the world upon his shoulders. Although the senior person present, he was not of aristocratic lineage; the others excluding myself and Galeria, were Patricians whose families had connections with the Roman Emperor. We were all aware that Aquillas looked down his upturned nose at Pilate and that it galled him to have to address him as sir.

Publius Galleria gave me a sly wink as he took his seat beside his master. The little weasel of a man had undue influence upon Pilate, who depended upon his information gathering and high intelligence. What the others did not know was that I had met with Galleria in the early hours of this morning. The weasel and I had what may be called a symbiotic relationship i.e., we occasionally exchanged information to our mutual benefit. This was one such time and the little man and I had a plan. Pilate gestured for us to be seated before he called the meeting to order.

Pilate addressed his assistant, "Publius, what is the first order of business?"

"The first item on our agenda is Barabbas, may I call forward Centurion Longinus?"

I snapped to attention and stepped forward, linen bag in hand. Pilate waved his hand, "Relax Longinus, you are not on the parade ground!" He pointed at my bag, "And what have you here for us?"

I deftly put my hand in and extracted Barabbas's waxen-like head. Congealed blood had dried where the head had been severed and the smell was rank. Hands rushed to cover mouths and noses and a guard was instructed to take it away for disposal. I thought that Pilate, already pale, was about to vomit. Galeria was quick to hand him a bowl of water and a napkin. Pilate squeaked, "Centurion, you have carried out my orders, you have my gratitude in bringing this villain to justice."

I was about to be dismissed for the remainder of the agenda was well above my pay grade. However, Publius Galeria intervened, "Consul, I met briefly with Centurion Longinus early this morning. I beg that you all listen now to the Centurion's tale. We are aware of the Parthian threat, but bear in mind that Longinus had not been privy to that information. Despite this Longinus is going to tell us things which are hard to explain.

A hush descended and the eyes of the privileged and powerful fastened upon me. I cleared my throat and began. "Last night I had a dream. The Great God Jupiter, who shapes all our destinies appeared to me. He informed me that the Parthian King Nambed has amassed an army on the banks of the Euphrates and Syria faces imminent invasion. Following Syria, Israel will be next to fall. But Jupiter does not want this to happen. Nor does he wish thousands of Romans to die needlessly. Instead, he has instructed me that I make good his wishes. Procurator, I beg your indulgence to hear my request."

Pilate looked at Galeria, who nodded. "Proceed Centurion!"

"The Great God Jupiter has told me that disaster is imminent. Governor Lucius Pomponius, Governor of Syria will command Legio X Fretensis to make haste for Damascus. Then together with Legio XV1 Flavia Firma, both Legions will march to the river Euphrates. But I have been warned that both Legions, consisting of only 12,000 men will be annihilated by the Parthians who number 60,000. Rome cannot find additional

Legions in time to stop Nambed. We will be overrun and put to the sword, including you Procurator. Rome will lose its trading routes to the east and all of us will die in shame. Our families' dignitas will be destroyed and never allowed to hold high office."

I paused at this point for effect. Pontius Pilate, known to be highly superstitious, squirmed in his seat. Carius Aquillas looked at me with defiance. How could a lowly Centurion foretell such momentous events. Dido Valerii Gratus, remained impassive, but I knew that below that stoic persona, I had struck a nerve. For Patricians family honour was all important.

"But Jupiter has revealed to me that there is one man who has the powers of persuasion, one who has the diplomatic skills to prevent this rout. Procurator Pilate you have the power to appoint this man as your special envoy to King Nambed. This man will save the day for Rome."

Aquillas asked the obvious question, "Who is this special person to whom we should put our faith in.?"

"I told them my champion was none other than Ezekiel Ben David. I thought that Carius Aquillas was about to be seized with apoplexy. His face burned crimson and when he tried to speak his words were accompanied by a shower of spittle. Aquillas rounded upon me as though I was the devil incarnate."

"That is the bastard who humiliated me in the arena. This man is a criminal, a fugitive from Rome, a man who has stolen my woman. An envoy? I will have him crucified as soon as I catch him."

Pilate allowed the tirade to continue for some minutes more before telling the Tribune to shut up. He reminded Aquillas that his humiliation had been of his own doing and that the woman in question was not his in the first instance. Publius Galleria whispered in his master's ear. "It appears, despite the good Tribune's misgivings that we have no choice but to appoint Ezekiel Ben David as special envoy. I would advise you Sir, that to fail to do so, will be against Jupiter Great and Good."

That was sufficient to seal the deal. Pilate had enough problems without offending the gods. It was decided that Ezekiel Ben David be given a full pardon for previous misdemeanours. In addition, he be appointed to the honorary rank of Tribune, for what use is an envoy without status when he must negotiate with a king.

Longinus concluded his tale in the tavern, and I listened with incredulity. We sat in silence before Longinus asked, "Will you accept Pilate's pardon and take on this task?"

"How do I know that when I arrive at his office, he will not have me crucified?"

"Pontius Pilate is rattled. He believes that Jupiter has informed me of impending disaster. Put simply, he has nothing to lose by your appointment. Carius Aquillas has been warned to put up and shut up. I just hope that Yeshua will forgive me for changing his name to Jupiter; it was a case of needs must!"

Chapter 28. Ezekiel Ben David soldier of Rome

It was with a feeling of great trepidation that I entered Pilate's Praetorium. Longinus accompanied me and I noticed that the Praetorian guards nodded recognition to him as they parted their spears to allow us entry. We were joined by Publius Galeria who escorted us into the presence of his master. Pilate was seated behind his large desk and looked up as Longinus snapped to attention. Pilate gave a wry smile before speaking. "So, Ezekiel Ben David, zealot, gladiator and hater of all things Roman, you have now decided to work for the hated enemy, may I dare ask you why?" His tone was heavily laden with sarcasm.

"Sir, you are correct, I have hated Rome and all that it stands for. Nor will I ever accept that Rome has any right to rule Israel. It is my fervent wish to witness your armies board their triremes and depart these shores. But that said I have met a man who teaches that violence is not the way to bring about change, and that we should not overly concern ourselves with the evil ways of this world, but better to prepare ourselves for the better life that awaits us in the next. My friend, Longinus, has informed me that a great disaster is impending which will not only affect Rome, but also all those who live in the land of Israel. Both Jews and Romans will be put to the sword by the dark power which is coming from the east. Longinus says that your God, the deity whom you call Jupiter, has chosen me to be a mediator and to prevent war."

Pilate scratched his chin, "Quite a speech Ezekiel, but what makes you think that you, a mere Jew and a fugitive to boot, could possibly influence a Parthian King?"

I panicked momentarily until the answer formed in my mind. "If God has faith in my abilities, then that's good enough for me. Therefore, I am prepared to try and possibly die in the attempt."

Pilate's grin widened, "Well, you probably will die, but your altruism for your Jewish people does impress me." Once again, the words formed in my mind, "Sir, it is not only altruism which motivates me. I no longer wish to be a fugitive; I want to provide a home for my wife and to enjoy a normal life."

A man in the uniform of a Roman General stepped from behind a large curtain dividing the office. Pilate introduced him, "This is General Valerii Gratus, Commander of Legio X Fretensis. General, what have you to say about our new soldier of Rome?"

The General's face was totally impassive. When he spoke, his voice resonated with authority and power. "Ben David, are you prepared to swear the Roman soldier's oath, known as the Sacramentum?"

This was a total no brainer; it was do so or die a painful death on a cross. So, with reluctance I swore to be loyal to the Emperor, the Senate, the people of Rome and to my Commander General Valerii Gratus. I swore to fulfil my conditions of service on pain of punishment including death should I fail or commit an act of treachery.

When the oath had been taken, I thought of my parents, of how they would have felt shame and disgust for their son. Of my mentor, now my enemy Samson, and his band of zealots. I had betrayed all of them and all the people of Israel. In my mind I could hear their cries of denunciation, traitor, scum, lover of Rome, I could feel their visceral hatred for me, and I felt intense shame and despair. I had sacrificed my principles on the high altar of expediency, or put simply, betrayed my beliefs for the greater good. Ironically, my actions were being taken to save those who would point the finger of blame at me. It did not make me feel any better when General Gratus said, "Hail, Ezekiel Ben David, Tribune and soldier of Rome."

The Sacramentum had just been completed when a loud knock reverberated from the entrance door. Two Praetorian guards escorted two captives into the office. The senior guard apologized, "Sir, our apologies, these two have just been arrested upon entering the Praetorium grounds." He pointed to the two muscular men, whose arms had been bound securely to their sides. "They claim to be comrades of Ezekiel Ben David!"

I was astounded, "Hacerlo and Alketas! What in the name of all that's good are you doing here? You are both escaped gladiators with a price on your heads. Why have you both chosen to walk into the Lion's den?"

It was Hacerlo, always the more talkative of the two who replied, "Alketas and I had the same dream in which a man with piercing blue eyes commanded us to return to Jerusalem. He informed us as to where you could be found and that you faced an extremely important and dangerous mission. Also, that if you are to succeed you will need our help: here we are at your service.

Once again, Carius Aquillas went red with rage. "Procurator, these two were complicit in the fire arrow attack on this very building. They escaped into the night with that scoundrel." He pointed an accusing finger at me. "The law says that these three scum be crucified. I request that you now pronounce the death sentence."

Pilate fixed the two ex-gladiators with an unblinking stare. "Where were you when you allegedly had such dreams?"

This time it was Alketas who spoke. "I was at home in Corinth, I have a successful business there and most certainly had no desire to return to this hell hole. Hacerlo was in Spain running his vineyard; he sells fine wines to Romans."

Pilate, clearly rattled, asked, "And when did these dreams occur?"

The answer came spontaneously from both men, "Three months ago, we have been travelling since then. We did not meet until yesterday when we arrived in Jerusalem."

Aquillas spluttered, "Sir, this is a set-up. For some unknown reason these thugs have pre-arranged this situation!

Now it was Pontius Pilate's turn to throw his toys out of the pram. "First, Aquillas you will not address an officer of equal rank as scum and scoundrel. I don't give a damn about your aristocratic stuck-up ass; if you do so again, I will have you flogged. On weighing the evidence, it would appear to me that Jupiter has tasked these men to help us. They are willing to do so though they have no motive and indeed are placing themselves in danger by so doing. Therefore, my decision is that they be appointed to serve Tribune Ben David in whatever role he so desires. Furthermore, you will apologize to your fellow officer and in future treat him with the respect due to him. If you do not, I will have your balls pickled and returned to Rome in a jar!"

Aquillas's face changed from red to white and again I thought he might suffer a seizure. Once again Hacerlo the likeable but dangerous Spaniard and the sullen Alketas were reunited with me. Before we had fought as a team in the arena. Known as the three threshers we had taken on and beaten the best of the gladiators. Now we faced another dangerous adventure together.

Pontius Pilate had placed himself in jeopardy by taking on the obnoxious Aquillas. I had no love for Pilate, but nor did I hold ill will for him.

Chapter 29. The Tenth Legion leaves for war

On the eve of departure General Gratus assembled his senior commanders, of which I was one. The news was grave indeed, a communication had been received from Lucius Pomponius Flaccus, Governor of Syria, saying that General Elbaz, former commander of the rebel Legio 111 Gallica, had been executed by his own soldiers. We were instructed that soldiers of this legion must now be treated as the enemy. In due course they would be punished in the way fitting for traitors. Rome's first imperative is to safeguard the isolated city of Palmyra, the major staging post on Rome's silk road, the trading route to the far east. It had been decided by the Governor that Legio XV1 Flavia Firma depart immediately from Damascus to strengthen the Palmyra garrison. We, the soldiers of Legio X Fretensis would leave Jerusalem at first light en route for Damascus. The journey was 150 miles heading northwest from Jerusalem and we would do a forced march of one hundred steps per minute. Even so it will take us two weeks to reach our destination. Governor Flaccus would then accompany us on the second leg to Palmyra. This stage is 130 miles northeast of Damascus and involves a crossing of the river Euphrates. Emperor Tiberius, in Rome sent explicit orders. "Stop the Parthians by any means and at any cost! Failure is not an option."

I was ordered to dress according to my rank; that is a Battle Tribune of Legio X Fretensis. I donned the uniform, and never had I felt so uncomfortable, and not just because of the garments. The breastplate, known as the Lorica Musculata, felt very foreign to a man used to fighting in free-flowing robes. The Paludamentum cloak complete with its neat folds, would serve little or no useful purpose in a free-for-all fight. However, my helmet with nose guard may be good for banging an enemy's brow. An ornate belt encircled my tunic, below which I wore a form of short trousers. My shins were protected by long metal greaves and on my feet, I wore the standard issue caligae, the

Roman soldier's hob nailed marching boots. I could feel the other officer's contempt for me; never had I felt so incongruous.

However, General Gratus was fully aware of my past and now he summoned me forward. "Tribune Ben David, I have been told you are something of an expert at desert warfare." The General raised an eyebrow awaiting my reaction; I gave him none and he continued. "This map shows our intended route to Damascus. If you were planning an attack upon the tenth Legion, where would you strike?" He placed emphasis upon the word 'you'. Without hesitation I tapped my finger upon the Pass of Elijah. I answered, "I know the enemy awaits us here."

General Gratus said, "Yes, it's a natural ambush point. Now from your experience what can you tell us about this pass and how can we turn the tables upon our enemies?

Chapter 30. The Pass of Elija

On a large chalk board, I sketched out the pass. As my chalk etched out the diagram, I gave the following narrative.

"About one thousand years before this time when King Ahab was on the throne of Israel there was a prophet named Elija. Elija was fiercely loyal to our unseen God Yahweh. Elija detested those Israelites who worshipped the Canaanite deity, Baal. Such was his anger with those who worshipped this false god that he brought fire down from heaven as punishment. After this he needed time to rest and reflect and he travelled to Mount Horeb to meditate and seek solace. Mount Horeb is sacred to Jews as we believe it is the mountain where Moses received the Ten Commandments from Yahweh. It is said that Elija travelled through this pass on his way to Horeb. Hence the pass is associated with Elija and Elija is associated with fire. I believe it is fire that our enemies will use against us but two can play at that game!"

My sketch showed that the pass lay on a north-south axis and stretches out for approximately two miles, which is about the same length as our marching legion. I continued, "Sir you will note that this line represents a ridge on the western side of the pass, it's at an elevation of one hundred and fifty feet above the valley floor. This is the ideal location from which the enemy can pour boiling oil down upon us." My chalk now moved to the sketch of the eastern side of the pass. "A similar ridge exists here, but higher and has a clear view of the pass below. It is from this point the enemy will deploy their slingers and archers. Our Legion will be caught in a deadly crossfire of burning oil and missiles."

The General thought before asking, "Is it possible to circumvent the pass?"

"It is," I replied, "But it would add at least one week to our march."

General Gratus muttered, "Time which we do not have, we must go through the pass."

Once again, I sketched a dotted line on the western side, running north-south. "This is a very narrow path along the top, much too narrow for a full legion to use, but big enough for fifty of our best men to cause mayhem. I have a plan which I will present to you and your officers when we make this evening's marching camp. Gratus gave a short harrumph! It was evident that he felt ill at ease at having to entrust the lives of his men to a Jew, and a former enemy to boot!

We left Jerusalem at first light. The vanguard of Legio X Fretensis was formed by the calvary, about three hundred mounted soldiers which the Romans called equites. They were closely followed by light infantry and archers. Then came the standard bearers, with the Legion's eagle in pride of place. The colour party marched immediately before the mounted command group which comprised the general and his tribunes including me. Carius Aquillas rode alongside me, he stared into the middle distance and nary a word passed between us. We were tightly encircled by bodyguards and trumpeters. The latter would use their instruments to pass on commands. Last, but not least came the covered wagons pulled by teams of mules and oxen. The wagons brought all our essential equipment. Batya had elected to travel with the Legion rather than stay in the relative safety of Jerusalem, and she rode in a wagon. I assigned Alketas as her bodyguard, my friend Hacerlo marched along at the side of my horse. Nothing daunted the sprightly Spaniard. Longinus was appointed as Senior Centurion, the Primus Pilea. It was his task to maintain the marching pace and he did so by marching to the outside of the columns of men, vine stick in hand and ready to use if any man tried to slack. Legionaries are fit men, they must be as their load includes a pickaxe, its sharp edge encased in a bronze sheath. The rest of the soldier's kit was carried on a forked stick, the pila muralia which each soldier bore across his shoulders. The heavy leather sleeping tents, each designed to sleep eight men were hauled by the mules.

Usually, a Legion will march six men abreast, however our departure to the east of Jerusalem was steep and perilous and it was only possible for three men to march abreast in the narrowest confines. The elongated line restricted progress but was necessary for safety. Jerusalem sits at an elevation of two thousand feet above sea level. We were now descending into the Jordan rift valley towards the city of Jericho which is eight hundred feet above sea level. The difference in respective altitudes causes a climatic microcosm moving from warm pleasant spring conditions to a burning desert. Dusk was falling as the pass of Elija came into view. The General gave the order, and the trumpeters blew the command to stop and make camp for the night. I had discussed my attack plan with General Gratus during the first day's march. He had listened carefully before approving the strategy. He gave one of his rare smiles, "Tribune, I know that you are speaking from experience gained when working for the other side. Now it's time to use that experience to give these bastards a nasty surprise."

Centurion Longinus approached and requested permission to speak. "Sir, you will know that I have my spies out there in the sand. I have just received this message. Gratus scanned the parchment. It read as follows, "Beware of the fire of Elija. In the pass lurks four thousand enemies. They are under the command of Zayin Krass. Note: the sadistic Syrian has promoted himself to the rank of General of Legio 111 Galicia. Samson and his band of zealots have been sufficiently stupid to join them, adding a further five hundred men to oppose you."

In place of a signature were the letters D.B.E. General Gratus gave Longinus a long look before saying, "Centurion, you have just confirmed the Tribune's extremely good situational awareness. The letters D.B.E.? "There was an awkward silence before Gratus simply said, "I suppose it's better that I do not know who this man is!"

Longinus did not respond!

Chapter 31. Elija's fire

The Legion vanguard drew to a halt approximately half a mile from the pass's entrance. Soldiers set to work constructing the night fort. A perimeter ditch was dug, and sharpened spikes erected. The purpose was twofold. First, it was essential that the enemy believed that everything was normal and that we would bivouac here for the night before resuming the march come the morning. Secondly, we needed a strong fall-back position should my plan go awry.

Darkness descended and my teams assembled. I use 'my teams' because General Gratus had given me overall command of the attack. I knew it to be a poisoned chalice; success and I would be a momentarily hero, failure and my name would be the laughingstock of the legion. Should I fail I knew that death would probably come during the attack. Marcellus Sextus, a hardened veteran, would act as my Centurion, however, it was Hacerlo who would act as my right-hand man. It was he who would pass my commands down the line. Fifty of our strongest legionaries would man-handle kegs of oil, normally used to create fire with missiles from siege engines to the top of the pass. Sextus would command a company of archers following in their wake. Centurion Longinus, an accomplished horse man would lead a charge of calvary into the pass at the appropriate signal.

Dusk had now given way to the black darkness of the desert. I led our small expeditionary force, and although I knew well the cliff top pass, it was steep and narrow and fraught with danger from falling. One slip and a man would face a precipitous fall to the valley floor and alert the enemy below. Hacerlo, as sure footed as a Spanish mountain goat ran from danger spot to danger spot, shepherding the legionaries through the narrow points. It was tough going and I was worried that small rocks dislodged by our progress would alert those below. The soldiers bearing the burden of the oil flagons grunted under their burdens and I prayed they would not be heard.

Eventually, with the help of Hacerlo we safely ascended to the top path along the pass of Elija. Despite the darkness, I knew well the position of the assassins below us. I chose the positions for the oil flagons which were now being fitted with fuses. They were evenly spaced, and I knew they would roll at speed down the steep incline. Hopefully, they would reach the enemy before shattering amongst them. The burning fuses should ignite the highly flammable oil spreading and sticking to the enemy and quickly devour them in the fires of wrath.

Hacerlo arrived with me and said each soldier had his barrel ready to roll. I held aloft a burning brand and as one the fuses were lit, and the barrels pushed out into the abyss. With bated breath we watched the flickering fuses bump and burn. On and on they rolled, forever gaining speed. Some did not make it, crashing and burning as they hit large rocks. If this failed, the enemy would be upon us. Then came the sounds of crashes and explosions.

The howls from below were at first from rage and surprise, followed immediately by cries of agonising pain. Flaming figures of men threw themselves to their deaths to the valley floor. It was as though all the fires of hell had unleashed themselves on the traitors of Legio 111 Galica and Samson and his zealots. Then came the pungent smell of roasting human flesh, not unlike roast pork. Now I thought I knew why pork is not permitted in the Jewish diet! The fires illuminated the whole of the pass and the discombobulated slingers positioned on the eastern side rose to their feet. Now it was the turn of Marcellus Sextus and his archers to unleash their volleys of arrows upon their exposed targets. Slingers and soldiers died together in the onslaught of arrows which were barbed not permitting victims to pull them free from arms or legs. The enemy fell like the rain into the void. Hacerlo, at my command sent a flaming arrow high into the southern sky. Longinus and his equites, hooves thundering, charged along the valley floor of the pass. Their orders were to kill all. No prisoners were to be taken.

I led my men, crawling and rolling down in the path of the barrels. Battle rage was upon me, and the sword of Rhesus sliced heads from necks and limbs from bodies. Pleas for mercy were ignored, a killing frenzy was upon me and my men. Yet through out the frenzy of battle I was looking for one man, Zayin Krass. Despite the teachings of Yeshua, I would kill him, and slowly, he would not get the mercy of a fast death. At last, the carnage came to a stop. The battle was won. Surprisingly, despite the no-prisoner edict, survivors of Galicia 111 were still alive and being chained together into groups. They hung their heads dreading the fate which was surely coming to them. I searched amongst the fallen and the survivors, of Zarin Krass there was no sign. Had the bastard escaped?

Chapter 32. Promotion and provocation

As is normal after a battle General Gratus assembled his officers, including Centurions and Optios, for a post-battle analysis. The discussion ranged from what had gone well to where improvements could be made in future operations. Overall Gratus was well pleased, the pass had been secured, Legio 111 Galicia defeated and the 'butcher's bill' only two of our soldiers dead. He had almost completed his speech when I was summoned forward to join him on the podium.

General Gratus beamed like the cat who had got the cream. "Gentlemen we owe an immense debt of gratitude to this officer who masterminded our victory at the pass." He placed his hand on my shoulder as though he was my new uncle. "Therefore, I have decided that for the duration of our mission in Syria Tribune Ezekiel Ben David be promoted to Senior Tribune Primus and he reports forthwith directly and only to me. He is the officer in command and therefore all officers present must address him as 'Sir.' General Gratus gave Aquillas a pointed stare, "Is that understood by you all?"

"As one the officers of the Legion, including Carius Aquillas replied, "Yes General!" All saluted the General, none would dare argue with this commander. I knew that the words must have burned the throat of Tribune Carius Aquillas as he said them. The meeting was dismissed, and we left the General's tent, each officer returning to his command to issue orders for the day's march. Centurion Longinus stepped alongside me after giving me a smart salute. "Permission to join you Sir?" He tried his best to refrain from smiling.

I replied, "Of course Centurion, and stop taking the piss my Roman friend!"

We both convulsed with laughter at what the fates had bestowed upon us. Here was I, a former Jewish zealot, guilty of having roasted Roman soldiers alive, now second in command, albeit on a temporary basis, of a famous Roman legion. Perhaps the Pax Romana, Roman law, was not so bad after all! I dismissed the treacherous thought from my mind.

However, there was one person who was not in the mood for making jests. Carius Aquillas was fuming with anger and was spitting nails. I was on my own as I reached the tent allocated to the Tribunes. He had been awaiting my arrival and now he stepped outside to accost me. To make matters worse he had been sipping rough red wine. Aquillas's face was filled with such evil maleficence the equal of which I had seldom seen either on the battlefield, or indeed the arena.

His voice was slightly slurred. "Come here, you fucking jumped-up Jew!"

He shoved his face close to mine simultaneously gripping my tunic and pulling me towards him. His hot spittle hit my face. I completely forgot Yeshua's teachings. I would not, this time, turn the other cheek. I growled, "I have taken enough shit emanating from your fat asshole! I care not a fig for you dog of a patrician parasite. Your family and you made it to the top of the Roman dung heap by exploiting the weak and defenceless. I no longer fit into that category."

So, saying, I smashed my forehead into his nose. There was a satisfactory snap as Cartlidge snapped. Blood and snot flew in all directions. My 'Belfast banger' had broken and twisted his large hooked Roman nose. Aquillas now had another facial flaw to match his battle-scarred cheek. I pushed the bastard back, rocking him onto his heels. A quick left jab, my arm fully extended gave power to my punch, sending him on his arse into the dust of the desert. Skills I had learned in a place called Belfast, had stood the test of time.

I was now in full flow and my pent-up rage erupted. "You spineless bastard, you forced my wife into your bed. She fixed you with her sharp teeth, and now you're almost cockless after she severed your miniscule manhood! I believe your halfway to becoming a eunuch; best blow job you ever got! Tears of rage and anger welled in the Tribune's eyes. I could not believe it;

the cretin was about to cry. I stood over him and ordered, "Soldier, get to your feet, stand to attention!" I was enjoying my moment in the sun. With reluctance Aquillas obeyed. I continued, "Now address me as Sir. Or should you wish, you may challenge me to a duel. I should have finished you in the arena, when you cheated and tried to kill me. Next time you cross me you will die."

Tribune Carius Aquillas collected himself. He stood to attention, ramrod straight, a disciplined soldier of Rome. The tears had disappeared, but he stood alone and friendless. I was aware that I had made an implacable enemy for life. In future I would need to watch my back.

Chapter 33. Decimation but with a difference

Despite the 'no prisoners order' incredibly five hundred legionaries from Legio 111 Galica remained alive. Somehow, they had survived the fire and carnage caused by Legio X Fretensis, who had fought with the ferocity of men who detested traitors. Although alive, some of the Syrians were grievously wounded. Some had lost limbs and would shortly bleed out unless they received medical attention, which would not be forthcoming from the Romans. When my soldiers were about to cut the throat of the defeated, I had given the order to desist. Again, my order had caused Carius Aquillas's ire to rise. I cared nothing about Aquillas, but my decision had caused problems for General Gratus, and it was with some trepidation that I joined my fellow officers when summoned to the General's tent.

It was immediately apparent that Gratus's mood had deteriorated and gone was the warm congratulatory tone when he had promoted me over the head of his seasoned veterans. Now, I knew that I was going to be judged on my actions. Aquillas looked smug and confident, was he about to get revenge for his previous humiliations? Gratus paced his limited floor space. His face was as inscrutable as ever, but he shot a quizzical look at me. Finally, he spoke directly to me.

"Tribune, I gave the order that no prisoners be taken. Why did you deliberately disobey me? Are you going to give me cause to regret your promotion? The Roman army runs on discipline; hence we are the finest fighting force in the known world. You now have an opportunity to explain yourself!" Aquillas was having to restrain himself from laughing. Now, it was my turn to be angry, I would wipe the smirk off that smug bastard's face! The words which I needed flooded through my mind as though someone was prompting me.

"Sir, I know that my action contravened your orders, however when in the heat of battle, when it's impossible to approach one's superiors, I believe that an officer must be allowed to use his initiative!"

In this instance the battle was won, and Legio 111 Galica would pose no more threat. General Gratus gave a loud "Harumph! Then may I ask what is to be done with these men? We are on a forced march to face an enemy of superior numbers and we have no provision for the care of prisoners. You have solved one problem by clearing the pass, but now you have caused another. You have forced me to order a mass execution of five hundred men."

Aquillas could not hide his delight.

I cleared my throat and attempted to muster as much confidence and courage as possible. "Sir, please hear me out. It was not just an act of mercy to spare the lives of these men, I believed that I was also being pragmatic. Our two combined legions total only twelve thousand men. In all probability we will lose men during the forced march in the desert heat. King Nambed has a force of between sixty and one hundred thousand warriors. The Parthians are expert horsemen, and they possess sophisticated weaponry. We will need every man we can muster so I ask why kill those prisoners who will be only too willing to fight for us in return for their lives?"

Aquillas could contain himself no longer. "Sir, please do not listen to this man. He is proposing that we arm and take traitors into our trust. Furthermore, a large number cannot even stand, never mind fight!"

The General was not pleased with Aquillas's unwanted interruption. "Aquillas, you will be quiet! I will ask you should I want your opinion!" Gratus signalled that I should continue. Aquillas had been put down yet again and I began to have hope.

"General, I am well versed in the procedures of the Roman army. There is a precedent that after punishment, which you call decimation, the surviving prisoners be allocated to various other legions. These prisoners have nothing to lose and everything to gain by fighting for us. Furthermore, their former commander Zayin Krass, deserted them in their hour of need. It's known that Krass is on his way to enlist with the Parthian army. These men would love to catch and tear him limb from limb. Now, that is what I call incentive!"

The next part of my plea gave me no pleasure, but it had to be said. "I would request that you mercy kill those prisoners who are in pain and facing a slow torturous death. We will still have some four hundred men who will not make the same mistake again."

The tent went quiet, I had concluded my summation for the defence. General Gratus bowed his head in thought before asking, "Who and where is the surviving officer of Legio 111 Galica?"

Centurion Longinus answered, "The man is Tribune Faisal."

"Have him brought before me now!"

Tribune Faisal was a bedraggled and bloody figure. He was escorted in by two burly legionaries and the man had difficulty shuffling forward in his tight leg irons. Faisal's forehead was encased in dried blood, but he stood to attention, shoulders back and chest out. This was a proud man who would never beg for mercy. Gratus let him stand for a full five minutes before firing a broadside.

"So, Faisal, you are a traitor, a man who bit the hand of those who fed him. You and your men are a disgrace to the people of Syria who benefit greatly from the largess of Rome. Do you know that I am considering having you crucified? Why did you betray me? I would think carefully before you answer!"

Tribune Faisal did not waver. "General, I am not going to stand here and make excuses for my men and me. What we did was very wrong and unforgivable. So, crucify me if you will, but please spare the others who were coerced and misled by Zayin Krass, who deserted us when he knew the game was up. Some of my men are now dying from their wounds. Please grant them a speedy end with a sword thrust."

It was an impressive speech by a wounded man who faced death by crucifixion. General Gratus was impressed by the man's bravery, although his face was wearing its usual inscrutable mask. Again, there was silence as the General weighed the options available to him. Finally, he lifted his head. "Before passing sentence, I am going to consult five of my senior officers for their opinion." So, saying he selected the five who would have the choice of life or death for Faisal and his five hundred.

"Gentlemen, the choices are as follows. Leniency for those who survive the process of decimation, if they swear an oath of allegiance to fight alongside us against the Parthian horde. Or immediate execution of the five hundred. I will call each officer in turn.

"Tribune Aquillas?"

"Death to each one of them. Faisal to be crucified."

"Centurion Longinus?"

"Mercy."

"Centurion Sextus?"

"Death, but no torture."

"Tribune Brutus?"

"Mercy, but 50 men to be decimated."

"Tribune Ben David?"

Therefore, I had the casting vote. The General was a wily old fox and had clearly passed the buck down the line to me. I cleared my throat, "Mercy, and I ask that Tribune Faisal be spared. Clearly, he is a brave man and I believe he will fight to the death alongside me."

There was a sharp intake of breath from all present. The defence had won the day. Although previously warned, Aquillas could not and would not accept defeat lightly. "General, I wish to make an official complaint re your decision. You have decided to take into your hire traitors who may turn their swords against us in the heat of battle. I will inform my father Senator Aquillas and request that you be removed from your command due to incompetence."

You could have heard a pin drop and I expected General Gratus to let fly. But our General was an old soldier and remained in full control of his emotions despite the provocation. He rose to his full frame and approached Aquillas until he stood inches from the upstart's nose.

"Please give the good Senator my best regards. However, soldier, if you wish to play either at politics or personalities, I suggest that you learn how to do so properly. I think that my friendship with Emperor Tiberius trumps even the House of Aquillas. Furthermore, you have shown disrespect to your commanding officer in front of other officers. I am very tempted to demote you to the ranks and place you in the vanguard of forthcoming attacks. Last night you assaulted Tribune Ben David, neither of you saw me but I witnessed everything that was said and done as I stood outside the tent of the Tribunes!"

Gratus paused for effect. "This is my decision. Ten men from Legio 111 Galica will be executed. They will fall to their deaths from the ledge where they lay in ambush for us with flaming oil. Tribune Faisal will be the last of the ten to fall after witnessing what happens to traitors, he will then join them. Tribune Ben David, you are not without guilt in this sorry mess. Your unorthodox management style does not meet with my approval. Therefore, you are ordered to be the executioner who will sever the men's lifeline, sending them into the abyss. As for you, Aquillas, you are on latrine digging duties until the Legion reaches Damascus. You should thank Ben David for breaking your nose, at least you will not be able to smell the stink! Have the executions take place immediately, the Legion must march without undue delay."

The nine unfortunates who were to join Faisal in his fall were selected by whoever drew the shortest straw in groups. Apart from Faisal, they were clamped in leg irons, and they shuffled slowly forward. Tribune Faisal marched at the head of his doomed soldiers, his shoulders back and his head unbowed. He was a proud man leading his soldiers on their last march. He would never have deserted them in their hour of need, even if he had the choice.

The ledge, known to the locals as the fall of Judah, was a narrow path atop a perpendicular drop of two hundred feet to the floor of the pass of Elijah. Ten poles, spaced apart at small intervals were placed like gang planks over the pass. Those about to die were bound by rope around their ankles. The rope was secured around the plank and the victim swung upside down over the drop. It would be my job to slash the rope. I stood with the sword of Rhesus awaiting my instructions. General Gratus would select the order of the drops. Aquillas never learns, I heard his laugh, "At least they will have an eagle's eye view of their descent."

Had there been an opportunity my shoulder would have sent Aquillas over the edge on his first and last flying lesson. General Gratus called out the numbers and I moved from execution pole to execution pole. At the General's command it took but one downward slash from my bronze blade to send the victims into free fall. Their arms were not bound, and some sought to emulate a swallow with their arms outstretched as though they were wings. Others rolled into a foetal position; no doubt they had their eyes tightly closed. None cried out as they fell. Such was the high velocity of the falling bodies that we heard the smack of breaking bones as they hit the rocks on the valley floor.

Nine had fallen and I moved to Tribune Faisal's pole and awaited the command. General Gratus moved to my side. He ordered, "Pull this brave man up, he will fight at your side Ben David, but you must accept responsibility for his actions."

That evening, following the day's march, it was my task to smirk as Aquillas joined the soldiers, shovel on shoulder on latrine duty. I told him, "Do not worry Tribune, this is just a case of the affluent joining the effluent."

He growled, "Jew, when I get the chance, and mark my word, it will come, you will die a long and painful death."

Chapter 34. Jericho

The Legion resumed its forced march pace under the watchful supervision of Centurion Longinus. And soon we entered the town of Jericho, a place of great importance to Jewish people. For according to the Torah, it was here that God had assisted Joshua in capturing the town from its Canaanite occupiers. Following the blowing of trumpets and encircling the perimeter, the walls had collapsed, allowing the Israelites to prevail. Regardless of the truth of that tale, Jericho is the oldest inhabited town known to man. People have lived here for at least seven thousand years before our present time. It is located at the southern end of the Jordan valley at the top of the Dead Sea.

Jericho is located below the level of the sea, but it has abundant freshwater springs and a very pleasant climate. This is a green oasis amid a harsh desert landscape. Favoured by Herod the Great, he built a magnificent winter palace in Jericho in order to escape the winter cold of Jerusalem. Herod, in outlook and education was more Roman than Jewish and he sought to emulate Rome's grandeur by building big in Israel. Herod was a personal friend of Mark Anthony and had gained Roman citizenship for himself and his family. This was a much sought after privilege as it conferred many rights and safeguards in a very turbulent time. However, during his later years Herod became mentally unstable before his death at his winter palace. Rome appointed Archelaus as Tetrarch, but his rule was that of a cruel tyrant, before he was eventually exiled. Jericho was of great importance as a gateway town and its walls were built with fortified towers. The Herodians also fortified the surrounding cliffs to protect themselves from eastern enemies.

Now the sound of Legio X Fretensis's marching hob-nailed boots, caligae, echoed on the town's cobbles. My last passage through Jericho had been in very different circumstances. Then, I had accompanied Yeshua and his twelve chosen. Yeshua had decided that the time had come for his return to Jerusalem. We had pleaded with him not to do so as it would be fraught with danger. Crowds filled Jericho to see him and once again there was a dangerous crush from the multitude.

It seemed to me that this had happened only yesterday, not months past. Yeshua had stopped mid-stride as though he had found someone for whom he had been searching. Finally, he spotted a small man who had climbed a sycamore tree in search of a vantage point. Yeshua had beckoned the man to come down and join him. The little man was called Zacchaeus; however, Zacchaeus had thrown in his lot with the Romans. This small man was a tax collector. Tax collectors were regarded by the Jews as the lowest life form on two legs. Were it not for the protection of Roman soldiers, people such as him would be torn limb from limb. Tax collectors would tax imports, exports, town dues, cattle and much more. It was known that they would skim money off the top for themselves. The Romans tolerated this, providing Rome received the taxes due to them. In effect, Zacchaeus was a social outcast, a man disdained by his fellow race.

To our surprise, Yeshua instructed the tax collector to prepare the evening meal for Yeshua and his twelve, plus me. Whereas, at the time, I had reservations about doing so, Simon Peter was livid with anger. Yeshua had to remind him that it was people such as Zacchaeus that needed his help most, not the self-proclaimed do-gooders, such as priests and pharisees.

After the meal we judged the mood of the crowd to have deteriorated. They were not yet hostile, but they certainly were not in favour of our dining with the scoundrel who robbed them on a regular basis. So, we began the ascent from Jericho for Yeshua's date with destiny in Jerusalem.

Now months after his crucifixion, I marched through Jericho as a senior officer in the Roman army. Simon Peter would have sneered, expecting no better of me, but Yeshua would understand I had been given a mission to fulfil. I marched under the sycamore tree, the former vantage point of Zacchaeus. He stood, now at ground level beside the gnarled tree trunk. Surprisingly, he knew me as he watched us pass with his friends. He fell in alongside me keeping in step. "You may be glad to know that I no longer collect taxes for Rome. But something tells me that you are dressed in Roman robes for a very special reason." Zacchaeus then disappeared into the mob with his newfound friends. I thought the little man to have amazing prescience.

Chapter 35. Saul of Tarsus

And so on we tramped due north towards Scythopolis crossing the River Jordan at one of the shallow fording points. Lake Kinneret, better known as the Sea of Galilee, appeared like a blue gemstone surrounded by lush pastures. I remembered this was one of Yeshua's favourite places and was where he recruited some of his most important disciples. Our track continued northwards along a mountainous ridge, known today as the Golan Heights. Lake Kinneret shimmered in the sunlight, its waters glittering on our left-hand side.

The lake is beautiful but is noted for the squalls which can blow up alarmingly fast and with little or no warning. The fishermen treated these waters with great respect. The skies darkened and our progress was impeded by a torrential downpour. Jagged forks of lightning plunged into the lake waters accompanied by cannons of thunder. Centurion Longinus marched beside my horse. "Sir, I must reduce the march pace, otherwise we are going to incur injuries amongst the men. The Governor will not thank us if we arrive at Damascus like the walking wounded."

I gave a grim smile of acknowledgement as I wiped the rain from my eyes. It was then that we spotted the small group huddling down to find some shelter from the elements.

As we got closer, I saw that they were trying to protect one individual from the torrents of rain. He appeared to be lying on his side and was trembling violently. So bad was his shaking that his fellow travellers were having to restrain him. We approached warily but received a warm welcome. Their spokesman ran to greet me.

"Thank goodness, we are much relieved to see Roman soldiers. Our comrade here is having seizures after being struck by a lightning bolt."

"Who is your comrade, and why are you journeying to Damascus?" I asked. The fellow adopted a haughty air as though he was of great importance.

"We travel on business of the Sanhedrin. Unfortunately, Damascus has become a haven for those who call themselves 'friends of Yeshua.' This new movement is spreading falsehoods that their leader has returned from the dead. The Sanhedrin, and Caiaphas in particular, view this movement as a threat to their authority and to peace and stability. A number of these people are currently detained in Damascus and our duty is to escort them back to Jerusalem where they will stand trial before the Sanhedrin before being executed."

Longinus and I exchanged glances, these travellers were certainly not our friends. General Gratus drew his steed to a stop overlooking the haughty one. Gratus growled, "You have not yet identified your ill friend."

Haughty appeared not to be intimidated by being addressed by a general. "This man is Saul of Tarsus. He works on behalf of Rome, and of course our Sanhedrin. He personally supervised the stoning of a blasphemer named Steven!"

My ire rose and I watched Longinus, for a moment I thought the Centurion might strike the man. General Gratus ordered, "Have this man Saul see the Legion doctor. We will escort you into Damascus."

I gave Longinus a warning look to remain silent. The Legion joined the great Roman road the Via Maris and the Road of Kings. Our marching pace increased and soon the city of Damascus lay before us. Damascus, capital city of Syria then and today, is a natural oasis. The Rivers Abana and Pharpae irrigate over four hundred square miles in which crops, orchards and gardens thrive. Governor Flaccus awaited our arrival at his fortress. Although soldiers of his Praetorian Guard patrolled atop the walls, the Damascus military garrison was severely depleted with the departure of Legio XV1 Flavia Firma for Palmyra.

Prior to our entry into the city, I wanted to speak to this Saul of Tarsus, although due to my 'special situation' I knew more about him and his future than he could ever have guessed. For it had been agreed with the angel Gabriel that details of my 'other life' would not be withheld from me any longer. Having had the benefit of a good education in the 20th century, I was cognizant that Saul of Tarsus would become St. Paul, the man who did most to spread the gospel of Yeshua. From being appalling he would eventually become appealing to those who would call themselves Christians. This was a man of destiny and I simply had to talk with him. The doctor had ordered that Saul travel in one of the supply wagons for he had not yet recovered his sight. Some instinct told me to take Alketas to meet Saul. Alketas had a successful business in Corinth, the place that Saul/Paul would send his epistle to.

I found Saul in the care of Batya. The doctor had administered an opiate and Saul's shaking convulsions had ceased. However, he was still as blind as a bat, and he continually rubbed his eyes as though they were on fire. Batya introduced me as her husband and used my full title of Tribune Ezekiel Ben David. Saul moved his hand from his eyes to his stubbled chin. "But you are a Jew, how did you become a Roman commander?"

I countered, "And you are a persecutor of the newly named Christians. Why do you think Yeshua spoke to you on the road to Damascus?" There was a long silence before Saul replied. "So, you believe it was the voice of Yeshua who spoke to me before the lightning strike?"

"I know it to be so."

Saul mused. "My companions said that it was simply the lightning that caused my confusion. They do not accept my story. Only you believe me, may I ask you why?"

Obviously, I could not, and would not, tell him my story of another life, to do so would invite ridicule and he would think that we had both lost our minds. But I could tell him. "You are

Saul, born in Cilicia, slightly older than the man you persecute. You too are Jewish but both you and your parents benefit from being Roman citizens. Jerusalem was your boyhood home and you studied under Pharisee Rabbi Gamaliel. You were led astray in your thinking and as a result you have committed some grievous crimes. Despite this you have been chosen to spread the gospels and it is for this work that you will be remembered and honoured by mankind. I cannot tell you how I came to know these things, but it is the truth."

Saul was dismayed, how could I know that he who hated Yeshua with a passion would become a devout follower of the man he despised. He spoke in slow measured tones. "Ezekiel Ben David, the voice told me to go to the house of Ananias at the place named Straight Street. But how can I do this? I came here to arrest him and bring him to trial."

This much I could tell him. "I will assist you to find Ananias. You will be treated with compassion and your three days of blindness will end. Saul much more than your eyes will be opened. And so, it was. Saul had found his purpose. The rest, as they say, is history.

Chapter 36. Damascus - the good, the bad, and the ugly

Our Legion arrived at the outskirts of the walled city of Damascus. This is another city of antiquity and of huge importance to those civilisations who inhabited it, past and present. Damascus has many facets, the good included skilled craftsmen who produce many things of beauty. Home for centuries of skilled artisans who produced high-quality steel. They had learned the correct mixture of iron and carbon to forge steel of strength and beauty. Swords made from Damascus steel are reputed for their ability to pierce and slice better than any others. However, it is only those of means who can afford its pleasing aesthetics whether for decoration or for weapon of war. Weavers of Damascus wove fine patterned fabrics, in later times known as Damask. Damask was originally produced from silk only, but commercial pressures demanded the introduction of less expensive materials.

Damascus is a further gateway to the far east for travellers engaging in much needed commerce. People lived happy and peaceful lives in this green and pleasant oasis city and supplied essential items to those about to brave the harshness of the eastern desert.

We marched, ramrod straight, proud soldiers behind the Legion standard bearers through the wide gates into the castle of Governor Flaccus. Trumpets and buccinas sounded our orders to manoeuvre and we formed into units in the parade square. I remembered the tall men in bearskin helmets of the Royal Irish Guards under the command of Sergeant Major Maguire doing similar things in another time and place. Some things in the army never change.

Governor Flaccus appeared and gave a rousing speech as to how we would defend Palmyra, Syria and Israel at all costs; the Parthians will not be allowed to prevail. The Governor would accompany us at first light tomorrow on our mission to defend the silk trading road. Legio XV1 Flavia Flama should now have arrived at Palmyra. The men of Legio Fretensis would shower and rest at the Damascus barracks for what remained of the night. Under normal circumstances the men would be permitted to sample whatever pleasures the city had to offer, but not tonight! Men and officers were confined to barracks. I and the other senior officers would dine with Governor Flaccus before retiring early to our bunks. Several things played on my mind. First, no communication had been received from Legion Flavia. It is operating procedure for a despatch rider to return with a situation report. Our men were aware of this, and I had a concern for their morale. Second, had the expedition Legion succumbed to the Parthians, and were we leading Fretensis into a death trap, thereby exposing all Syria and Israel to the enemy? I had no way of knowing.

Dinner with the Governor had been fast and informal. A limited amount of watered wine had been served. Sobriety was essential come the morning march. My sense of unease prevailed as Centurion Longinus and Tribune Faisal accompanied me to the tent of the Tribunes. Somehow, I knew something was amiss; this was confirmed when I saw Aquillas was not in his bunk. No other officer would speak as to where he was, they claimed they did not know. I called for Longinus and Centurion Felix. Within minutes both stood before me.

"Have you checked that all your men are accounted for?"

Felix replied, "No, surely no man would be so foolish as to go absent without leave tonight. They would be flogged within an inch of their life."

I thought Felix was trying, in vain, to convince himself.

"Both of you go and do a role call inspection. Report back to me immediately. Aquillas has disappeared, this augers ill for all of us."

Twenty minutes elapsed before both officers returned. The look on their faces said it all. "How many are missing?" My unease had turned to dread. Felix hesitated, not his usual confident self. "Come on man!" I impatiently snapped.

"Six soldiers in total Sir. Legionaries Sicio, Manlianus, Justus, Sirius, Cato and Thaddeus."

I thought for a moment, "The name Manlianus sounds most familiar to me. Now, I remember him."

Felix appeared to be somewhat embarrassed. "You should Sir, you shared a cell with him the night prior to his flogging for cowardice in the face of the enemy." When he is caught it will be the end for him!"

For those readers familiar with my first tale entitled 'Combatant' will recall that I had shared a cell with the terrified man. Felix had been an Optio and my jailer! How times and circumstances had strangely changed.

"Gentlemen, we must save all six of the silly buggers. Executions prior to our departure to Palmyra will result in rock bottom morale. If that means also saving that bastard Aquillas, so be it!"

While we officers had dined in the Governor's palace, Aquillas had sent a note of apologies feigning a stomach upset. The duplicitous sower of discord had conspired with those whom he had suffered the ignominy of latrine duty. The pompous patrician had found his true level with the worst men of the rank and file. He approached Sicio, a Decanus, a soldier in charge of a contubernium of eight men. The latter was a bully and known to have used his hobnailed boots on men who failed to do his bidding. The Decanus wondered what the bloody patrician wanted with the likes of him.

Sicio, stood rigidly to attention. "Sir!" There was a strong inference of sarcasm in the man's tone. Aquillas noticed but ignored it.

"You are a Decanus, a man of some influence, are you not?"

Alarm bells sounded in his head, but Sicio decided to play along, who knows what may come out of this for him. "Of course, Sir, what is it that you require of me?"

Aquillas lowered his voice. "Do you know the men of the night watch?"

"Yes, old mates of mine. They owe me a favour. When I say jump, they ask how high."

"Could you, or would you entice them with a small bribe to look the other way whilst we left to take in a little of the Damascus night air?"

Sicio feigned puzzlement. "Night air? Hot or cold air?" He fully knew what Aquillas wanted. The scoundrel guffawed.

All centres of human habitation since time immemorial have had their 'red light' districts. In this respect, Damascus was no different. The guards were bribed with money which Sicio coerced from his eight-man contubernium. Two decided not to take the risk but had to pay their share of the bribe regardless.

Tonight's destination for the 'seven sinners' was known to the locals as the place of Eden, the red-light district of Damascus, where beautiful girls engaged in the world's oldest profession. I knew that Carius Aquillas had a voracious sexual appetite, my wife Batya had suffered because of it. Aquillas had convinced himself that tomorrow the legion would be marching to its doom. If that were to be so, he would not be denied one last moment of pleasure from a woman. He was prepared to enlist the help of scum like Scipio to achieve his needs. The seven passed the magnificent temple of Jupiter before turning into back streets full of bars and danger.

Legio X Fretensis would leave at first light come the morning on their 130-mile trek through the desert to Palmyra. All the absconders knew that should they be caught time would not permit a proper court martial. They would be summarily found guilty of desertion and justice would be swift and brutal. However, crafty Aquillas knew that the Governor would be reluctant to execute him because of his family position. The others would be crucified, but Carius Aquillas cared nothing for their fate. Again, how I regretted having met this pompous prick. I know the importance of discipline, but it made no sense to execute men prior to marching to war; moral would hit rock bottom at a time when we needed every Legionary to be keen to kill the enemy, not pondering the cruelty of their commanders. I had a plan, but it was not without its own risks.

"Centurion Felix, you have been stationed in Damascus, we know what entertainment these men seek, may I ask where you would go to?"

Felix gave a wry smile before answering. "Before I changed my ways, I sometimes would visit the house of Madam Kayla. In my own free time of course, never on duty!"

I asked, "And do you think you could find the house of this Madam Kayla?"

The Centurion began to blush. "Of course, how could I ever forget! The Madam is in an area of ill repute known as the place of Eden. I am sure that is the place that rogue Scipio will lead them to."

I thought, the place of Eden, further disrespect to our religion. Those who ran these establishments needed to be taught a salient lesson.

"Centurion Felix, choose six of your strongest and most trusted legionaries. Bring no man if his mouth tends to run away with him. Equip them with arm manacles and sturdy batons. Felix, Fasil, Longinus and I plus the six strong men made our way to the guard house gate. We were all dressed in Arab robes with our weapons concealed beneath them. The guards recognised me immediately and smartly snapped to attention. I was short and abrupt to this lot of morons. "Who's in charge here?"

An Optio stepped forward, head low and crestfallen, the man knew he had been rumbled and was in deep trouble.

"Why did you lot of cretins permit Tribune Aquillas and his party to leave camp tonight?"

For a moment the junior officer was tempted to deny it, but the point of my gladius against the nape of his neck, made him change tack. "I am sorry Sir; it was foolish in the extreme."

I let the man sweat with a long silence falling. Then I looked at him in the eye. "You will tell no man of what is transpiring here tonight. You will donate the bribe money to the Legion welfare fund, and I may have mercy on you and your men. Now open the gate and watch carefully for our return."

I estimated that approximately three hours of darkness was remaining. We would need to be fast if our rescue and retrieve mission was to be successful. I was fully cognizant that if Flaccus caught us it would be me and my men hanging from crucifixion crosses.

Felix led us into a much different Damascus. The streets were lined with bars and hookers. All sorts of drinks and drugs were on sale by street peddlers. Girls gyrated in time to lutes, flutes and cymbals, their oiled bodies glistened in the torch light. Heavily muscled men with bored expressions stood on guard at the entrances of the prostitution dens. Some fools, their pockets now empty, were roughly ejected into the street. They lay face down as the heavies laid into them for sport. We stepped over and around them following Feliz who obviously knew where Madam Kayla plied her trade. I hoped, for all our sakes, that this was where the wayward seven had headed. We did not have time for a prolonged search.

In contrast to the seedy backstreets, the house of Madam Kayla was surrounded by lush gardens and decorative fences of wrought steel. Obviously, prostitution paid! Six heavies, men with bulging biceps stood guard at the gate. They were questioning 'would-be' customers. You would not gain entry if you did not have sufficient funds to pay for the services. Felix decided that it may be best if he were to make the initial approach. It appeared that he was a man of experience in these matters. He duly marched up to the gate. Even out of uniform he exuded authority and confidence. "Good evening, gentlemen, does Madam Kayla still reside here?"

Bulging biceps waddled forward. "Who's asking?" Biceps voice was full of menace. "My name is Felix, for many years I traded in Damascus. I am a very good friend of Madam Kayla. Would these coins help you to allow entrance to my friends and myself?"

Felix dug deep in his pockets and his hand emerged with a handful of silver coins which he duly poured into the large man's outstretched hand. Biceps grunted and uttered, "More!"

Felix duly obliged and we were waved through the gate.

The interior of the house was dimly lit, the subdued lighting attempted to add an air of mystery to proceedings and no doubt helped to hide some of the ladies' flaws. Girls floated from the darkness offering glasses of wine of dubious quality which we politely declined. A lady, a little past her prime appeared. Her hair was dyed jet black and she had managed to retain her svelte figure. She looked at Felix, and instantly recognised her customer from the past. Her voice was sultry and seductive, "Why goodness me, it's my Roman friend Felix, what good times we enjoyed in the past."

The two entered a warm embrace and Felix had the good grace to blush. The Centurion came straight to the point. "Kayla, I need your help. Some foolish soldiers have absconded on the eve of march, they face execution if we do not rescue them from their stupidity. They total seven in number, please tell me if they are here."

The Madam paused as she decided what to do. Then she said, "Felix please follow me." She swayed as she walked up a staircase, we followed with bated breath, not quite knowing what to expect. Madam Kayla turned the knob on a bedroom door handle. The six enlisted soldiers had satisfied their base needs and no doubt, under the influence of the cheap wine, lay snoring beside their young courtesans. Several pitchers of cold water were placed on nearby bedroom tables. I snatched them, and poured them over the sleeping imbeciles who coughed, cursed and spluttered their way back to consciousness.

"What in the name of Jupiter's balls is going on here?"

A naked and drunk Carius Aquillas had been in a private boudoir, and now he swayed in the doorway. I faced him, nose to nose and was instantly revolted by the stench of stale wine.

"Tribune Aquillas, once again you are a disgrace to your uniform!" Get these rags on so that you and this scum may leave here intact."

I tossed him rags which would pass as Arab clothing. The smile had disappeared from Madam Kayle's face. Now she was spitting nails. "Felix, these soldiers have not yet paid me for services provided."

Felix ignored her and instructed the six strong legionaries to restrain 'the seven sinners' with the arm manacles. They were then unceremoniously pushed and bundled down the staircase. Kayla shrieked for her men with the bulging biceps to come to her aid.

I gave the order for no sword play; I did not want an enquiry into the killing of civilians. But that did not prevent us from banging a few heads. The six strong Legionaries were ordered not to interfere but to remain guarding the deserters. Longinus, Felix, Fasil and I pulled batons from beneath our robes. These cudgels were blunt but made from hard whalebone and would help even the odds against the cavemen coming at us! The six brutes were fast for men of their height and bulk. Fast, but not fast enough to get the better of six seasoned soldiers of Rome. The smack of bone upon bone resounded around the room. The heavies crashed, one after the other, to the floorboards, shaking the room to its foundations. The girls squealed and ran. We whistled while we worked. I was thoroughly enjoying the moment, sometimes old ways die hard, even when we know to the better!

The fight was short lived, no others stood before us. Felix wiped the sweat from his brow and stinging eyes and apologised to Kayla.

"Upon our return I will ensure that you receive due compensation for this little debacle. But may I suggest that you employ a higher quality of guard. He indicated the six unconscious brutes strewn around the floor.

We frog marched the seven back through the streets from whence we came. This, most certainly, was the ugly side of Damascus. The first streaks of light were beginning to appear in the eastern sky. As the light strengthened the whores began to disappear, work for the night was done. The guards at the gate were awaiting our arrival. I gave them their final order for the day.

"Ensure that these fools are put in the equipment wagons. They are to remain in chains until I say otherwise. The wagons will roll with the Legion. I will list them as ill. Do this and no more will be said of your stupidity."

The guards fell over themselves to carry out the instructions. Within the hour the trumpets sounded, and we were on the march. I was glad to see the back of Damascus; this had been a close call. I steered my steed into the officer's section and wiped tiredness from my eyes. Now we faced the demons of the eastern desert.

Chapter 37. The serpent in the sand

We shook the dust of Damascus from our boots as the Legion marched east into the interminable Syrian desert. The trek was arduous, mile after mile of sand, scrub and monotonous red dunes. The wind blew and grains of sand stung our faces in a torrent of pain. Sand clogged our noses, entered our ears and caked on our drying lips. We shared this sea of sand with the snakes and scorpions who scuttled and slithered out of our path. We were aware of the watchful eyes of wolves and hyenas; they would attack if they found signs of weakness in man or horse.

General Gratus pulled his horse over beside mine. He warned me, in no uncertain terms, to be wary of Governor Flaccus. "He is of the old school and believes that to be in command you must be of Roman blood. Should trouble arise between you and Aquillas, it is likely he will side with your enemy. Speaking of Aquillas, is he still in the sick wagon?"

I answered, "Yes Sir, together with six other soldiers. When our march stops for the night, I will check upon them."

"Yes, do and get them back to their units if they can crawl. No one is going to get a free ride in this Legion."

I thought about what the General had said about the Governor. Perhaps if the Governor had treated the men of Legio 111 Galica better by giving them respect and good pay, the uprising may not have happened. We stopped and the routine for setting up evening camp commenced. Legionaries dug the defensive ditch and sharpened perimeter stakes were erected. The sun set, permitting the first evening stars to shine. I made my way to the sick wagon. As I approached, I heard a mixture of shouts, groans and curses. Immediately I drew the sword of Rhesus from its scabbard, the sharp blade gleamed in the star light.

I opened the wagon's canvas flap. Inside a scene of chaos and pandemonium. Scipio lay moaning and rolling. The man was in abject agony. Legionaries were knocking each other over in a panic to get away from the vile serpent confronting them. Their task was not made easy as they were restricted by their arm chains. The source of their fear was a huge Levantine viper which was highly venomous, one bite was sufficient to induce a painful death. The snake had a khaki colour, covered in bluish blotches and stripes and was now slithering with deadly intent towards Carius Aquillas. To his credit, Aquillas stayed still and calm. The brute raised its flat triangular head and opened its jaws ready to strike. Its forked tongue flickered, and deadly venom drooled from its reddish lips. I was filled with fear and revulsion.

Tribune Aquillas spread his arms as wide apart as his arm manacles permitted. Bravely, he tried to ensnare the snake in his chains which if successful would have allowed him to throttle it. He missed. The viper was now inches from his unprotected face, and I could hear it hiss as again it prepared to strike. Whoosh! The sword of Rhesus came to life in my hand. My downward strike was straight, steady and true. The snake's head bounced from its coiled body and landed with a thump several feet away.

Aquillas was bathed in sweat. He held his arms out and I unlocked his shackles.

"Ah, my Jewish saviour arrives again in the nick of time!"

Gratefulness and humility were not in the man's lexicon. I replied, "Tribune, I most certainly am not your Jewish saviour. You Romans crucified him, but despite your deeds one day you may be fortunate enough to meet him."

I moved to the stricken Scipio. He was still rolling with severe abdominal pain where the viper had struck. The area around the bite was blistering badly. Blood and drool dripped from Scipio's open mouth as he struggled to breathe. Batya arrived and attempted to help, but it was clear that the man was done for. His chains were removed, and he died within the hour. Men of his contubernium buried him and placed rocks over the grave top to keep the desert scavengers away.

I instructed, "You men, including Tribune Aquillas, report back to your units immediately".

How ironic that a snake like Scipio had met his end by another serpent.

I lay down for what remained of the night. In the distance I heard the bark of a Hyena, it sounded like the animal was laughing. mocking the folly of men.

Chapter 38. The River Euphrates and the Silk Road

As we approached the mighty River Euphrates the topography changed from barren desert to green fertile flood plains. Meadows of rushes, wildflowers, and scrub grass were a welcome replacement to the hated harshness of the sand. Birds flew high and flitted from bush to bush and small mammals watched the marching men with curiosity. High in the sky Red Kites soared in the thermals, entering and leaving the white fair weather cumulus clouds. Fishermen laboured unloading their catches from small fishing vessels. The banks of the river were lined with fishing nets put out to dry and awaiting repairs. The Euphrates flowed and brought life as it had done for many aeons. Originating from snow melt and rainwater in the Armenian highlands it meanders through Syria and Persia before joining the River Tigris at Shat El Aval. After a journey of one thousand seven hundred and forty miles it reaches its destination when it spills into the sea in the Persian Gulf. Its long trek takes it past the ancient site of Babylon and the homes of other ancient civilizations. The Hebrew bible teaches us that the Euphrates is one of four rivers which flowed directly from the Garden of Eden at the dawn of time. Now I was being given the chance to cross these waters of great historical importance.

Our path led to the crossing point of Napta al Abour. At this point the river is sufficiently shallow which allowed for a fording point to be constructed. In times long before the Romans, men had laboured moving boulders into the water which afforded safe passage to men and horses. Floating platforms carried merchant's wagons. These ferries were manoeuvred by men on the banks using ropes and pulleys. Therefore, the ford at Napta al Abour facilitated the ancient Silk Road whereby goods, services, ideologies and even religions moved from west to east and vice versa. Silk and jade arrived from China in return for horses and cotton. Roman glass was much prized in China and traded for bales of silk. Providing the river was not in spate business was brisk for the ferrymen.

The men of the Legion waded into the calm waters enjoying its cool, cleaning freshness after enduring the dirt, heat and sand of the desert. My horse lowered its head to drink, and I allowed it sufficient time to do so. A loud shout of alarm turned all our heads in unison. I did not understand the language, but it was not necessary, the trouble was apparent. The supply wagon in which Batya was travelling was on board a ferry which had broken free. Now it was drifting downstream and as it hit the shallows its speed increased at a frightening pace. The draw horses attached to the wagon shafts were stomping and I was afraid that they would panic, and all would be smashed on the jagged rocks protruding from the foaming waters. But most importantly Batya was in imminent danger. And I knew that she had never learned to swim. After all that we had come through I was not going to allow this river to take her from me.

I urged my horse into a gallop downstream and passed the adrift ferry. A pulley rope had snapped and now drifted behind the platform. Longinus, Felix and Fasil were mounted and followed closely behind. To my surprise we were joined by Aquillas who also was riding like a madman. We plunged into the waters trying to avoid injury to our horses from the rocks. Then, as one we grabbed the trailing rope and heaved with all our strength. The ferry had gained a frightening momentum and our horses had to dig their hooves into the riverbed to avoid being pulled after it. My brave stallion, Sarum, stumbled badly and almost dismounted me. While I struggled to regain control, Aquillas was fast to react. Holding fast to the rope he used his heels to urge his steed out of the river and encircled the rope around a tree. Sarim had recovered his balance and we followed, hauling and drawing the rope around the wood. Now we hoped the tree would withstand the strain. Thankfully it did and Legionaries arrived to haul and steer the vessel to the bank.

Batya stepped from the wagon, she smiled nonchalantly, she ignored Aquillas, fully knowing that it was he who had saved her.

"Ben Ezekiel, my husband and Senior Tribune, I never doubted that you would save me."

She moved to stroke my sweating stallion. I turned to face Aquillas. "Thank you, I guess that makes us about even!"

His reply was curt, "Don't thank me Jew, we need the supplies in the wagon. I care nothing for the other cargo on board!"

I stifled the reply which was forming on my lips. Instead, I smiled and looked into the waters of Babylon.

When we arrived back at camp, to my horror, I found that the ferryman in charge had been stripped naked and bound to a tripod frame. A Legionary with a large whip which had sheep bones imbedded in its leather, stood ready to deliver a flogging. My relief at saving Batya now turned to raw anger.

"On whose orders is this man to be flogged?" I demanded.

"Tribune Brutus Sir."

"I am the Senior Tribune here; no man can be subjected to corporal punishment without my express authority. Untie this man immediately!"

The Legionary hesitated until I dismounted and faced him. He knew I was in no mood for nonsense, and he carried out my order. Governor Flaccus and General Gratus sat upon their steeds watching the proceedings. Flaccus gave me a look of contempt and said, "Why did you release that man? Clearly, he is guilty of dereliction of duty, our supply wagon may have been lost."

The fact that Batya may also have been lost was of no importance to this Patrician snob. How could such a stupid man rise to the rank of a provincial governor?

I tried to keep the anger from my voice. "Sir, with the respect due to your rank, the ferryman is not a soldier, he is a civilian not subject to military rules. We have been sent here on a delicate mission which is try and prevent a major war. Our cause will not be helped by alienating the civilian population!"

Flaccus's face was filled with anger. I knew the bastard would love nothing more than to have me flogged for insolence. Without further ado I steered Sarim away without permission to leave. I knew that for the present the stupid bugger needed me more than I did him. As we trotted back to my command I muttered under my breath, "To hell with him and his bloody Romans!"

Chapter 39. The dream of Ezekiel

After having crossed the Euphrates, we made camp for the night. As I lay awaiting sleep, I reflected on what a complex character Carius Aquillas was proving to be. Born into privilege and obviously spoilt by doting parents, he was deceitful, lecherous, snobbish and vain. The list of negative adjectives could stretch all the way back to Rome! But today I saw another side of this man. When required, he could be brave and be prepared to put his life on the line. Without his timely help Batya may have died. I wondered if I was now beginning to think like Yeshua; endeavouring to see good in the most unlikely of men.

The day's exertions, both physical and mental, had taken their toll and a deep sleep soon overtook me. I dreamt that Yeshua was sitting beside me. As always, he addressed me as a dear friend.

"Ezekiel, your bravery will soon be put to the test, not because I doubt you and not because it is my wish to do so. The Romans think that you are 'their' emissary, but, you are mine. I have tasked you with finding a peaceful solution to an evil situation which is about to spiral out of control. If it should do so thousands will die throughout the countries of the Levant.

But we have one big problem. King Nambed is a narcissistic tyrant; worse he currently holds all the aces. Nambed will not engage in any serious comprise unless he feels the need to do so. So, despite his superior army we must create doubt in his mind that he is not invincible. Doubt will create fear. Fear will allow reason. To this end you must steel yourself to face death on at least two occasions. What I am about to reveal to you will show that you will not die in this desert. You have been chosen to do good things for your fellow man, not just now but also at a time in the distant future. Please watch your own story in a different time and different land. In your darkest hour remember that this is not the end."

Images began to form in my mind. I saw a place called Belfast, it was bombed and torn apart by sectarian strife. My alter ego appeared; a young man called Patrick Doyle. Athletic and an expert in the art of boxing, Patrick was not interested in religion nor politics. Through no fault of his own he becomes entangled between the warring factions and must leave his native Ireland. A life of service follows, both in the British army and in a civilian role. Patrick has a beautiful woman at his side and my lips formed the word, 'Libertad.'

The images ceased and I asked, "What nature of test will I face that is so frightening. For in this life, I have faced many challenges. How will these affect the attitude of Nambed?"

Yeshua smiled, "All will be revealed to you in good time. Nambed will know that despite his superior numbers there is one who is stronger, one who he must fear and respect." Yeshua's smile broadened, "That one is me!"

I awoke in a cold sweat. What sort of sorrows did the next days hold for me?"

Chapter 40. Vasillis the good Greek

Legio X Fretensis topped the crest of a small desert rise to see the beautiful walled city of Palmyra before us, dazzling white in the sun. However, it was not the beauty of this oasis city that caused a rapid increase in my heart rate. The Parthian host stretched for miles upon miles and in doing so had completely encircled the city. Thousands of soldiers stood in serried ranks, pennants fluttered gaily in the light desert breeze. But most awesome was the sight of the twenty mighty war elephants with their mahouts in place in their howdahs high upon the backs of the massive grey beasts. Even at this distance we could clearly hear the trumpeting of the Pachyderms as their trunks were raised in roars. Sepoys, wearing turbans confirmed the Indian influence upon the Parthians gained from their control of the Silk Road to the sub-continent. A short distance from the city's walls lay an enormous, tented village which had been laid out in a grid system worthy of any Roman planner. At the centre stood a massive tent with pennants flying and armed guards at attention. No doubt, this was home to his Majesty King Nambed.

It was obvious that this huge army was no mere expeditionary force, this was a full-blown army on a campaign of invasion. When Palmyra was taken, the road would be open to Damascus, then all of Syria. Next Jerusalem and all of Israel. If these places were to fall easily, as I knew they would, Nambed would set his greedy eyes on the riches of Egypt. Although the Parthians had Palmyra at their mercy there was no sign that battle had been engaged. The city gates were barred firmly closed and the Legionaries of XV1 Flavia Flama could be seen patrolling the ramparts and the Legion pennants were on display. In the open space between both armies no bodies lay.

As I surveyed all this a scene from my life to come flashed before me. My alter ego, Major Patrick Doyle seemed to appear in my mind. What would Doyle do in these circumstances;

negotiate, the only viable option. Even the combined might of two Roman Legions could not stop this force. How I wished that I now had possession of the surveillance equipment which Doyle would have at his disposal. But there was no point in stupid wishful thinking. I would have to play with the cards dealt to me.

General Gratus convened a council of his senior commanders. When we were assembled, he paced before us, vine cane held under his right arm.

"Gentlemen, we have an enigma. Clearly Nambed has the numbers to take Palmyra, so what is holding him back? He is aware of us marching to the city, I thought he would have struck before reinforcements arrived. Perhaps his strategy is to draw both of our Legions to join him in battle on the open plain, thereby leaving us exposed to his army's might. Without any defensive positions we would be annihilated. This would leave both Syria and Israel without adequate protection and enabling the Parthians to make an easy conquest. Or perhaps he has doubts about his army's ability to take the city?"

Even as General Gratus spoke a horseman detached himself from a group of Parthians who had been watching our progress. The man was a skilled and confident rider, sitting upright and holding his reins loosely, guiding his Arabian steed with gentle pressure from his knees and heels. The movement of man and horse appeared to meld as they approached at speed in a cloud of desert dust. A white flag of truce fluttered from his saddle horn. The guards observed the flag and allowed him safe passage to rein in before our command party.

The stranger wore a white turban for protection from the sun. A linen face mask protected his face, this he removed exposing a tanned face, but he did not have the darker hue of a Parthian or Persian. His eyes were unusually blue and were filled with a flashing intelligence, and his mouth creased into a warm and friendly smile.

When he spoke, his tones were sonorous. "Greetings men of Rome, King Nambed sends you his warm salutations. My King has no wish to engage you in a costly battle but would rather attempt a negotiated settlement to end this impasse. I come, not only to offer you a safe passage into Palmyra but to invite Governor Flaccus and his senior officers to dine with King Nambed this evening. Your safety is guaranteed by my personal code of honour.

Governor Flaccus tried his best to sound imperious. "What is your name and your title man?"

The smile reappeared on the face of the horseman. "My name is Vasilis. I am honoured to be special advisor to his highness King Nambed of Parthia. I have been in the King's employ for ten years and my master trusts me implicitly. As you may have guessed, I am not Parthian by birth, I come from Athens, Greece. We Greeks are a nation of culture, philosophers and mathematicians. Dare I be so bold as to say much of our learning has been copied by Rome. Now may I have the honour to escort your Legion into the city of Palmyra?"

General Gratus looked at me questioningly. I nodded and said, "It would appear that at this moment we have no other card to play. Let's do this."

Legio X Fretensis marched towards the gates of the city. Vasilis drew his horse alongside mine. "If I'm not mistaken you are a Jew. A Jew who is also a soldier of Rome, something I thought I would never see! As for me, a Greek who is an advisor to a Parthian King! What an enigma we two are! If we do survive this little debacle perhaps, we can discuss how we both arrived in such positions?"

I replied, "Our survival depends on how we can influence our masters during the next few hours, we need to stop the impending slaughter."

The massed ranks of Parthians parted to allow our Legion safe passage. The enemies' faces were impassive, and they avoided any eye contact as we filed through their ranks. These troops were highly disciplined hardened veterans. They would fight to the death rather than suffer dishonour. A fissure of fear tingled my spine as I passed their gleaming lances.

Cries of welcome came from the Legionaries manning the wall ramparts. The gates of Palmyra slowly rumbled open, and our two Legions were united in a common cause. I held back with Vasilis until the last Legionary passed through the gate. Vasilis said, "I and senior Parthian officers will arrive back before dusk to bring you to our King. May our respective Gods look down upon us tonight!"

Chapter 41. Palmyra – the jewel in the sand

As the city's gates rumbled closed General Titus, commander of Legion Flavia Firma came forward to greet us.

"Greetings Governor Flaccus and General Gratus, I and my men are much relieved to have you join us. May I suggest that we convene in my quarters with all senior officers so that I may present a situation report."

"Yes, immediately!" Flaccus snapped, "We have little time before the Parthians come to escort us to meet with their treacherous King."

There was a low hum of conversation in the control room until General Titus rose to his feet and coughed politely to gain his officers' attention.

"Governor Flaccus, my men and I arrived at Palmyra several days before you, only to find that the Parthians in situ encamped outside the city walls. The Roman garrison here is small and the Parthians could have easily taken Palmyra before our arrival. To my great surprise the enemy despatched a lone envoy, a Greek named Vasilis, who offered safe protection to the city. Vasilis knew that Legio X Fretensis was on the march to meet us. However, the Greek informed me that King Nambed wished to have a conference with all senior Romans to reach a settlement amicable to both parties in order to prevent massive casualties to both Parthians and Romans. We accepted his offer and we have watched and waited for your arrival. Each morning Nambed parades his army's might by marching men and animals around the city walls. Other than this intimidation no offensive action has taken place. Your arrival was a repeat of our own, being greeted by a Greek."

A smart-ass seated at the back quipped, "Beware of Greeks bearing gifts!"

A low ripple of laughter spread around the room until Governor Flaccus rose, his face locked in a scowl of disapproval.

"All very funny, but we find ourselves trapped and facing a force numerically much stronger. Bear in mind that if we fail here, either by diplomacy or by force, all the countries of the Levant will fall to tyranny. If I fail here my family will face disgrace. No doubt Emperor Tiberius will send Legions to take back that which is rightly ours but at tremendous cost in money and men. As is my place, I will lead this evening's delegation to ascertain if it is possible to negotiate with Nambed. I will be accompanied by General Gratus, and officers Aquillas, Longinus, Ben Ezekiel and Fasil. If for any reason, we fail to return General Titus will take command. In such circumstances Titus it will be your responsibility to inflict as many casualties as possible upon the Parthians. I expect you and your men to fight to the very last man. Good luck to one and all."

Palmyra was known as the jewel in the sand. Springs from Wadi Al Qubur provided the garden city with fertile soil in which crops, olives, and date palms grew in abundance. Fresh drinking water was plentiful and was provided by a Roman-built aqueduct. In theory the city should have been able to withstand a prolonged siege. But the Parthians had siege engines capable of hurling large boulders at high velocity smashing the walled defences to smithereens. Machines together with the might of the elephants would quickly provide a breech into which the Parthians would pour through in thousands.

When at school I had learned the history of Palmyra located on the eastern outskirts of the Roman empire, at a crossroads between eastern and western cultures, home to a nexus of ideas. The city's architecture and sculptures reflected a diverse blend of Greco Roman and Persian influence. The central way, known as the great colonnade, stretched for three-quarters of a mile from the temple of Bal. Palmyra was the last place of refuge for the many caravans of traders who were about to risk their lives on the eastern deserts of the Silk Road. Whoever controlled Palmyra would be in control of the riches provided by the Silk Road. Now, I was a soldier, a Roman soldier about to take part in the defence of this refuge of trade and prosperity. It brought no comfort to know that Roman General Mark Anthony had failed dismally to conquer the Parthians and after incurring huge losses had left licking his wounds.

At dusk the Parthian escort arrived as Vasilis had promised. Bright pennants flew from their saddles together with a white flag of truce. Vasilis was accompanied by four horsemen and to my horror I recognised one of them to be Zarin Krass, the abomination who had taken such pleasure in crucifying my Lord. It came as no surprise that he had joined the Parthians. He was a man without morals, a cretin who had deserted his men at the pass of Ezekiel. This creature of the night would and probably had sold his soul to the devil. And now the bastard's eyes were fixed upon mine, I wondered if he remembered my intervention on the way of sorrows. I hoped so because I wanted him to feel fear before I gave him a painful death, something I had promised to do.

As we left the relative safety of the city Vasilis drew his horse close beside mine. "I could not help but notice the looks of mutual hatred between you and General Krass. May I ask, have you two met before?"

"Yes, we most certainly have, he committed a crime of great evil and now he will pay for it at my hand!"

Vasilis sighed, "My friend please remember our mission this evening is to seek peace. Unfortunately, Krass has great influence with our King. Nambed was so impressed with his ability as a ruthless warrior that he has promoted him to the rank of General in command of a Germanic tribe that has aligned itself to Parthia. Be warned that Krass and his Germans are absolute bastards, my advice is to give Krass a wide berth."

Chapter 42. A divided dynasty

(Family quarrels are bitter things. They do not go to any rules.)

King Nambed was ambitious, greedy and tyrannical, but he was also a man with severe family problems. His three children were jealous of each other and were as devious and scheming as their father.

Prince Haman, the eldest was handsome, muscular, and strong. Haman craved power, wealth and glory above all else. He would readily kill anyone who dared stand in his way. That threat most certainly included his two siblings.

Prince Ramn did not possess the physical strength of his older brother, but he possessed a superior intellect and could set clear and achievable objectives. That said, Ramn was also quite capable of skullduggery to achieve his ends.

In short, King Nambed was a man with many problems. He was fully aware of his children's flaws and that a house divided against itself could not hope to stand. Nambed depended on two strong allies. The Greek, Vasilis, whom he had befriended many years ago, was a man of wisdom and culture whom he trusted implicitly and General Arsaces, a man who had been his boyhood friend.

That evening, Prince Haman and Princess Nazanin met in secret. Much political intrigue was afoot.

"Greetings sister, do come and sit beside your loving brother."

Nazanin gave Haman a look which clearly told him that she was not fooled by his false fondness.

Undeterred, Haman pressed on, "The Roman delegation will shortly arrive in our camp. We will have Governor Flaccus and General Gratus at our mercy, but I fear our father will not press home on our advantage. The old fool has lost his ruthless streak which once allowed him to rule without challenge to his authority. It is time for change; time for a new King!"

Nazanin flashed her warmest smile, "You mean it's time for you to become King, do you not?"

Haman returned her smile, "Only if the Gods will it to be so, for I would take no action to harm either our father or our brother."

They both knew that to be a lie.

Haman took his sister's chin in his large hand. Princess, I need your help tonight to bring about a circumstance making it impossible for father to allow the Romans to leave our grasp. Now, dear sister, please listen to my plan. Do as I say, and you will be rewarded greatly.

Chapter 43. Entrapment

The headquarters tent of King Nambed proved to be nothing less than a mobile palace. We were subjected to a perfunctory search for weapons before being escorted into the King's inner sanctum. Before us was a long table which was laden with flowers, foods and fine wines. The air was filled with sweet incense and as we walked our feet sank into deep pile Persian rugs. The walls were decorated with artefacts from different lands. A beautiful Leopard skin, complete with the animal's head was positioned by the King's seat. Walls were festooned with assegai tribal spears from southern Africa. There were an elephant's tusks and a water buffalo's head with magnificent horns emanating from a central boss.

Vasilis escorted us to our seats at the long table. Introductions were made to Princes Haman and Raman and General Arcases. Other Parthian nobles were ushered to their seats. The wall torches had been adjusted to provide adequate but subdued lighting and a small group of musicians provided background music from lutes, lyres and cymbals. The atmosphere was created to fill all present with awe and expectation as we awaited the arrival of His Majesty King Nambed, Monarch of all of Parthia and Persia. There was little conversation between us Romans and we were amazed at the grandeur of the Parthian's mobile headquarters, especially as this was an army on a war footing. How different these people were to the Romans. The highest-ranked Roman General led a spartan existence when on campaign. They would not understand the need for such rich trappings in the field of conflict.

King Nambed entered, and conversation stopped. We all stood; the King was accompanied by one of the most beautiful women I had ever laid eyes on. The Parthian nobles, including the two princes, bowed in reverence to their King. In contrast to his surroundings Nambed wore simple robes with no adornment upon his head. This man did not need to try and impress anyone. He was of medium stature, had a tanned face which was creased with laughter lines. His beard and hair had been curled with tongs, adding to his Royal appearance. His dark eyes reflected intelligence but something about his demeanour told me this was a man not to be trusted. The King was in his early sixties but moved with the ease of a younger man. His eyes moved from noble to noble to satisfy himself that all was in order. Only then did he pay attention to his Roman 'guests.'

"Salutations Governor Flaccus and General Gratus and members of your entourage. Thank you all for accepting my invitation to join me this evening. Of course, we have serious business to discuss, but business can wait until morning. Tonight, you are my honoured guests and as such I hope you enjoy my hospitality. Now I would like to introduce you to my pride and joy, my beautiful daughter, the Royal Princess Nazanin."

Princess Nazanin gave us a warm smile and a small inclination of her head. Her blue-black hair was long and lustrous and fell from a bob to her slim shoulders. Her decollate allowed her firm breasts to be partially exposed. She had an oval face with almond shaped eyes which had a greenish hue which seemed to glow in the low lighting. It was her eyes that warned me. This beautiful creature in her early twenties, was like a large predatory feline. She was a cat waiting to pounce on her prey. Those eyes focused on Tribune Carius Aquillas, seated next to me. Aquillas emitted a sharp intake of breath, and I knew this may be trouble as Aquillas's brain was positioned in the region of his groin. Female slaves, also beautiful, fanned us with Ostrich feathers as other slaves poured rich red Falerian wine from Italy. Nambed upset me intensely by saying, "I do not serve any of that cheap Israeli rubbish which they pass as wine!" I decided there and then that I would not imbibe, tonight I would need to have my wits about me. We were in a house of vipers.

Waiters brought forth platters of roast chicken, tender lamb, beans and a garum fish sauce, a Roman favourite. Desert was almonds, figs and sherbets. Falerian wine flowed copiously with every course. Aquillas was thoroughly enjoying all the food and wine placed before him. The fool should have had more wit! The Parthian officers were joined by their wives and dancing commenced. The atmosphere, helped by the alcohol was becoming very relaxed and I thought it was now at its most dangerous. Governor Flaccus, General Gratus, Longinus and Fasil were also being careful not to consume too much drink. They also sensed impending doom.

Prince Haman noticed my sobriety and came over to engage me in conversation. "Is all not well with you Roman? Is the filarian wine not to your liking?" His Latin was flawless, but I replied in Aramaic, the native tongue for both our races. "Prince Haman, please note that I am not Roman, I am a Jew."

Haman continued to press me as to how I had become a senior officer in the army of Rome. I knew that I must be diplomatic, so whilst trying to be evasive I did my best not to be rude or offensive. It dawned on me that Haman was trying to divert my attention and with trepidation I realised why.

While Haman had been engaging me with polite blether, Princess Nazanin had approached Aquillas, now well intoxicated by both wine and the vixen's beauty. They danced and she swayed provocatively. Turning she pressed her rounded buttocks into Aquillas's bulging groin. By the time I realised what was afoot she had led him from the dance floor.

Nazanin took Aquillas by the hand and brought him like a lamb to the slaughter into her boudoir. With a wave of her hand, she dismissed her female attendants. When they were alone, she plied her drunken victim with kisses and placed his hands upon her breasts. Carius Aquillas was well versed in undressing girls. His grasping fingers found her robe's clasps and with a small click it slipped from her shoulders to lie at her feet. Deftly she removed the Roman's uniform and took his engorged manhood in her hand. Carius Aquillas, fool of fools, thought he had passed through the gates of his own heaven.

It was when his hands moved to her undergarments that the cat's purr changed to a scream. Nazanin screamed so loud that she was heard throughout the encampment. "Help, help, I am being raped by this Roman!" She ripped her own pants and scratched herself on the cheek.

"Guards, guards, come quickly. This Roman, a man without honour has defiled me." When her playacting was completed, she collapsed sobbing onto the thick pile carpet. Two bodyguards, swords in hand, appeared in an instant and pinned a stupefied Aquillas against a wall. Prince Haman appeared on the scene and struck Aquillas knocking teeth from his bleeding mouth. King Nambed entered, he gasped at the scene. He ordered, "Take this man, Aquillas to the cells. Tomorrow, he will pay for his treachery by taking a different ride! Tomorrow, he will ride the mare of steel and will feel her sting!"

The Roman delegation was bunched together into a corner by scowling guards with spears. Nambed, his face contorted with rage, turned to face us. "So, this is how you Romans negotiate!" Tonight, you will be placed under armed guard and come morning you will witness Parthian justice being implemented. Aquillas knew that it was pointless to protest. The foolish deceiver had finally been deceived himself. He was placed in chains and led away.

Chapter 44. King Nambed's nasty predicament

The wall torches were guttering in a gentle breeze that wafted through the tent as Vasilis made his way to the King's bed chamber. The guards uncrossed their spears allowing him access. Although it was not yet dawn, Vasilis found the King propped up on a cushion and fully awake.

"Ah Vasilis, what troubles you at this early hour my Greek friend?"

"Many things, my King, and I feel that these troubles are mutual to both of us."

King Nambed shifted position on his pillow, "I never sleep well on the eve of an execution, and it feels particularly uncomfortable to have to do this one. Why did the Roman have to be so stupid? Did he not realise that his actions would have the potential to cost thousands of lives, both Roman and Parthian?"

The two men's eyes met, Vasilis thought there may be room for some degree of compromise. He chose his next words very carefully. "King Nambed, for many years I have been privileged to be your most trusted advisor. Together, we have chosen the correct paths facing us. Now, I must strongly advise you to allow the Romans to return to Palmyra. To do otherwise will result in this problem escalating into a full-scale war. We cannot afford to lose so many men so early in this campaign.

Nambed's voice raised several octaves, and he slammed his balled fist into the bedcovers.

"If the Romans leave Parthia's protecting walls my calvary will charge from the east and west and crush them to shreds in a pincer movement. No army can match my armed archers. My Generals have their troops positioned and are ready to strike."

Vasilis sighed, for once he was not winning the debate. "Sir, there is no doubt our forces are numerically superior, but the Romans have two battle-hardened legions. They will be incensed at what they perceive to be your betrayal and will fight to the very last man; in doing so we will suffer grievous losses."

Now it was clear that the King was on the verge of losing his temper. It was only his long friendship and sense of indebtedness to Vasilis that he had allowed the man to speak so freely.

"Vasilis, what would you have me do? Would you have me release a rapist who carried out this vile act against my daughter in my own home? To do so would convey cowardice to the enemy and put us on our back foot. That I will never permit."

A long silence ensued before Vasilis replied, his voice conveyed his nervousness by trembling.

"Good King, I do not for one moment suggest that Aquillas goes unpunished. Have the man flogged to within an inch of his life before his mutilated body goes back to Palmyra with his Generals. After a cooling off period of several days it may be possible for talks to reconvene."

Nambed could no longer restrain himself and his shouts echoed the length of his quarters. Servants seemed to slip into the shadows.

"When that Roman raped my daughter, you were relieved of your oath of protection. The sentence of death stands. Governor Flaccus can return with what remains of Aquillas after sentence is carried out. You are now dismissed. Go now!"

Vasilis could see that further argument was pointless and may result in his own imprisonment for contempt. Having been summarily dismissed Vasilis decided it was best to brief the Roman captives; men who were here because he swore to protect them. Their small cell was protected by Parthians with long lances. Recognising Vasilis, they moved aside, and he faced the men who now despised him. Governor Flaccus simply ignored him. General Gratus was brusque.

"Well, what have you to say man? We were extremely foolish to accept your word that you could afford us protection.

Should harm come to one Roman head, our two Legions will attack! We may die as your prisoners, but your army will be routed and broken! Hail mighty Ceasar, hail mighty Rome. It's time for the scourge of Parthia to be removed from the face of the earth!"

Vasilis took a moment to recover his composure after the General's tirade. It was clear that the Greek was in a state of distress.

"Not all fault lies with Parthia, your stupid Tribune was unable to keep his dick in his kit. He fell into a trap set by that Vixen Nazanin and her power-crazy brother Haman. But I am not here to apportion blame. I must tell you that Nambed has refused my plea for clemency. I am going to go to General Titus in Palmyra to offer myself as a counter hostage, if you will, a balance of power in prisoners. I accept that should harm come to you then I also will die. There is no more that I can do to atone for my share in this shame."

I was amazed at Vasilis's courage, especially as it looked as Aquillas was going to meet his end. I said, "Well if you are determined to go to Palmyra, there is one more thing that you can do. Please deliver a scroll to General Titus. I found parchment and pen and wrote the following:

"General Titus, please ensure that no harm comes to messenger Vasilis despite any wrongdoing by Parthians. Under no circumstances are you to attack the Parthian positions. In this matter you must trust me."

Signed Senior Tribune Ezekiel Ben David. Countersigned by General Gratus. Governor Flaccus refused to sign but continued to scowl. Stupid bugger!

Now, how in the name of Hades was I going to extract ourselves out of this mess?

Chapter 45. The Mare of Steel

The Roman guards on the walls of Palmyra knew that the coming day was going to be very different to those previously. During the hours before dawn came the sounds of much activity from the Parthian positions. General Titus was alerted and was on the ramparts with his men as the first streaks of sunshine came into the eastern sky. The Parthians had erected posts holding small circular targets, these were positioned in a line from east to west. Another line of posts ran from north to south, but this time they held human full-size dummies complete with straw heads. General Titus knew that this morning the Parthians would provide more than the usual show of strength and intimidation. A lone horseman came from the Parthian camp approaching the gates at a gallop.

"My God, it's the Greek," said Titus to his second in command. Vasilis was escorted to Titus; he passed the scroll to the General before relating the whole sorry story of the previous day.

Titus was shocked, "I thought Aquillas was dim, even for a Patrician, but this act of stupidity plunges us all into dire danger and the fool faces execution! How and when will they kill him?"

Vasilis avoided answering, Titus was about to find out and soon.

Trumpets sounded and two contingents of Parthian cavalry assembled just out of the range of arrows, beyond the walls. The riders wore bright robes as though they were about to provide a military show, which indeed they were. They cheered and jeered and shouted at their Roman audience. Their language was Aramaic, but their hand gestures left their meaning in no doubt.

The two groups of riders separated. The first group rode like the wind along the east-west target line. Parthian calvary, armed with bows and arrows are beyond compare. Generation after generation practiced and excelled at this method of warfare which their forefathers developed in the Asian steppe. They rode without holding reins and whilst standing high in their stirrups fired a barrage of arrows into the centre of their targets. Their accuracy was astonishing, especially at the speed at which they travelled. Whooping with exuberance they left the field.

General Titus gave a grim smile to his subordinates. "The bastards are trying to put the wind up us and they are succeeding!" The second group of riders took to the display field. After delivering the mandatory insults they galloped to the dummies. These warriors held large, curved swords known as scimitars with a single convex blade honed to razor sharpness. The swords were beautifully balanced and did not need much force to inflict severe damage. The cavalry attacked the line of 'dummy men.' Straw heads were sent spinning in the air, the riders behind sliced the spinning heads whilst they were still airborne. The dummies were decapitated, their severed heads sliced in two and left lying in the sand. Show completed; the riders gave a perfunctory bow to the Romans. Titus turned to Vasilis, "We've had the warming-up acts, what's the main feature?"

Vasilis pointed to a large grey elephant which plodded out onto the plain. But it was not the beast that caused hearts to skip a beat, the elephant drew a device perhaps twenty feet in length and of similar height at its highest point. A curving steel blade shone brightly in the sun. The cold steel swept down at an angle of about 45 degrees before curling upwards at the bottom resembling the horn of a rhinoceros. This was a mobile edifice of execution. The machine had steel sides with runnels to drain off blood and gore. The mahout guided his elephant with soft words until a predetermined place had been reached. To his horror, General Titus realized that this is how Tribune Corius Aquillas would die, his body sliced asunder. Vasilis looked downcast, "The Parthians call this the mare of steel. This is the last ride any man will ever take."

Every nerve end in Titus's brain urged him to attack and stop this infamy. Attack and be damned! He would have done so immediately but for my command in the scroll.

We the prisoners followed the mare of steel. Our tumbril was enclosed, and our feet were bound. There was no possibility of escape from the horror to come. The tumbril came to a stop and Governor Flaccus cursed both me and General Gratus.

"You stupid Jew you convinced me against my better judgement to accept an offer of truce. You Gratus are incompetent and should never have had high command! To make matters even worse you have instructed General Titus not to attack. Now we are about to die like craven dogs instead of soldiers with a sword in our hands!"

I had nothing left to lose so I gripped Flaccus by his collar and shook him until his remaining teeth rattled.

"Flaccus it always amazes me that Rome promotes morons like you to positions above their ability. To Rome family name and privilege counts for everything. Patricians must rule to the exclusion of the plebs who could and would do a better job. For this reason, the edifice of Rome will surely fall and not too far into the future!"

Flaccus was shaken by my brazen insubordination. No one, not even the most senior officers dared speak to him like this never mind man handle him as though he was a mere soldier in the rank and file.

"If we survive this Jew, I will have you crucified, just like your supposed Messiah!"

I threw him against the back of the tumbril. "It would be an honour to die in the same manner as my Lord." General Gratus struggled to stifle his laughter for he too had no time for the obnoxious Governor. A trumpet call announced the arrival of King Nambed. He was accompanied by Princes Haman and Ramn. Princess Nazanin followed slightly behind; she had coyly covered her face with a black mask as though she was in mourning. The mask hid an ugly smirk of self-satisfaction. Once again, the King was troubled, and he turned to Prince Haman.

"My son, I cannot do this. I cannot give the order to the executioner for should I do so the Romans will kill my friend and confidant Vasilis."

Haman's face betrayed his contempt for what he perceived to be his father's weakness.

"Father, you have no need to give the order for I will do so now! Vasilis has grown old and weak, we no longer have need of his council, in fact we are stronger without him! Did he not advise you against this campaign against Syria? Look at what we have achieved; we have entered Syria unopposed. We have trapped two Roman Legions and have them at our mercy. When we slaughter them, nothing will stop our march through the countries of the Levant. All the riches of Damascus and eventually Egypt will be ours."

Without further ado and without his father's permission Haman signalled the executioner to come forward. The killer's face was enclosed in a black leather mask which had tiny slits for eye pierces. The ears had pointed fabric giving him the appearance of a vicious dog. No man had ever looked more macabre and gruesome. Haman ordered, "Take him!" He pointed to Aquillas. To his credit, Tribune Carius Aquillas stood and squared his shoulders. His ankle bonds were removed, and he stepped down from the tumbril prepared to meet his fate.

The executioner plainly enjoyed his occupation, sadistic bastard as he was. He ordered Aquillas to stand and look at the curved steel blade. "I thought you would like to know what is about to happen to your body. A criminal, who stole from his master is going to ride the mare immediately before you. I'm afraid that you must watch and wait your turn!" A man, stripped to his loin cloth was dragged forward. The executioner proclaimed in a loud voice, "This fool, this enslaved Syrian, stole from his master's purse. His name is Esam and Esam has forfeited his life for being a fool. Esam was prodded up a ladder which led to a small platform atop the death machine. He was offered a blindfold which he duly accepted. His feet were put into ankle clamps in the platform's base. Esam's wrists were bound behind him and attached by a line to a supporting strut. The executioner turned a wheel and the platform pivoted forward until Esam's body was suspended at 45 degrees to the sloping steel below him. A drum rolled and the executioner pulled a lever. To our horror the clamps and supporting line opened simultaneously.

Esam hit the steel with a loud smack, his body slithered down the blade which bit deep into his carcass. His legs fell to their respective sides, and he parted company with his groin and intestines which dropped to the sand. Finally, his head opened on the steel horn at the blade's end. Esam's grey brain matter fell in a glutinous mess from his cleaved skull. Even the hardened Parthian infantry looked away from the horror. I could feel the bile rise in my throat as slaves gathered the body parts in bloodied baskets. Accustomed as I was to brutal and gory death in the arena I vomited without control.

The executioner threw his head back and cackled with laughter which reminded me of the grey back crows prolific in Ireland. I watched with fascinated horror as Carius Aquillas was forced to climb the ladder to his death. Aquillas declined the blindfold, and his feet were inserted into the clamps and his wrists were attached to the line. The wheel turned and the platform pivoted to the required angle. The executioner's hand gripped the handle, death was a second away.

"Stop!" "Stop immediately!" I yelled at the top of my voice. "Take me instead, I am his commanding officer and as such am responsible for his actions!" You could hear a pin drop in the ensuing silence. For me it felt as though time was standing still. Men asked who is this fool who would volunteer to die in such a manner as this. All eyes looked to the king.

Nambed was smiling, I could see that some form of plan was hatching in his devious mind.

"Exchange the prisoners," Nambed ordered. Aquillas was reeled in unharmed. As we met at the bottom of the ladder the Roman who had been my devout enemy clasped my arm in a silent salute. Now I faced looking down at the cold steel still soiled with Esam's blood and body matter. As the platform pivoted, I felt my bladder release and hot urine ran down my leg. Not even in the arena had I felt such fear. Despite my distress I recognised a figure in black robes in the watching crowd. Worse, I could smell his disgusting evil scent, it was none other than Ammar (Satan). The vile creature yelled, "Kill him!" "Kill him!" The executioner moved his hand towards his handle.

In Palmyra the Roman cavalry prepared to charge. Contrary to my orders, General Titus was not prepared to allow the Parthians to escape punishment for their crimes. Horses stomped and riders withdrew swords from scabbards. Lances were held at the ready. The horses' hooves caused the ground to tremble, and the city gates began to rumble open.

King Nambed assessed the situation in a glance. He was not prepared for a full-on assault; his men were not in formation. For once he was at a severe disadvantage. It was a case of fight or flight! Well, perhaps not flight but he ordered that I be reeled into relative safety. Prince Haman was livid and stomped away in a sulk. No doubt Titus in his disobedience had helped to save me. Seeing that I was saved General Titus gave the order for the Romans to stand down.

But it was not fear of the Romans that had motivated the King. He had not had such a long unchallenged reign without developing much guile and cunning. Now the last piece of Nambed's plan was about to be put into place. Whatever the outcome he would be in a win/win position. Both his domestic and political problems would be put behind him and Vasilis would be saved. Yes, things were looking much better for King Nambed.

Chapter 46. Diplomacy but it ends in death

My bonds were removed, and I was escorted into the King's private quarters. Nambed had been impressed by my bravery on the mare of steel. "Tell me, "why would you choose to die such a gruesome death? Why would you a Jew die in the place of a Roman? These people rule your land by fear and inflict tyranny. Do you not despise and hate them as we do?" I looked the King straight in the eye. "I believe in the God of my fathers and in his son who teaches us a better way to conduct our lives. It is love, not hate which will prevail at the end of days." Nambed chose his words with care.

"You put great faith in this invisible God, this Yahweh, yet six hundred years before our time he allowed King Nebuchadnezzar to sack Jerusalem. Worse still, his chosen people were dragged off into bondage in Babylon, never to recover. He allowed his son to die on a Roman cross, why did you think he would save you?"

"I am here now, that is testament enough for me. It is foolish to attempt to try to interpret God's intentions, for all will be revealed to mankind at a time of God's choosing." Nambed gave a loud harumph.

"I trust in the God of my people, Zoroaster, who has guided Parthia to much greatness. We are the only people whom Rome has been unable to conquer. Even the Roman General Mark Antony and his slut Cleopatra failed against us. Then why should I fear Rome?"

My reply was simple and direct. "It is not Rome you should fear, but a power that is much greater than either Rome, Parthia or Israel for that matter." It was then that I saw a look of such cruel cunning on Nambed's face. He had decided to declare his hand. King Nambed looked at me quizzically, watching for my reaction to the proposal about to be made.

"Ok Jew, we both profess to be men of faith, but I don't think either of us are particularly religious men, we worship our

Gods when we want something!" I felt like telling him that he should speak for himself, but I held fast with my rebuke.

Nambed continued, "I propose that this stalemate be decided by a battle between our respective champions. Call it the battle between deities if you wish. You will choose a champion to fight alongside you against my two chosen warriors. This will be a battle to the death with no quarter asked or given. Should I win Rome must cede joint authority of Damascus to Parthia. In the unlikely event of you winning, we Parthians will abandon Syria and decrease our tax demands on the Silk Road. If you agree I will have my scribe draw up a legally binding treaty for signature by me and your senior commander."

I was stunned. Nambed's plan was audacious in the extreme, but it just might save thousands of lives, thereby completing the task with which I had been entrusted. It was way beyond my pay grade, such a treaty was not even within the remit of Governor Flaccus. Only the Emperor himself could make such a treaty, but Nambed was not to know that. I asked Nambed, "Who will you nominate as your champions?"

"My son Haman and General Zayin Krass!"

I was now fully aware of what this crafty bugger was up to. Somehow, both Nambed and I knew that both his champions would die. Nambed bore a sardonic smile, for he could see a way to remove his problem son and his quarrel with Rome. This man, this King was more than capable of fratricide. Nambed always believed the end justified whatever means he deemed necessary.

We were then joined by General Gratus who looked at me with incredulity when the plan was revealed. We were allowed to converse briefly in private.

"Governor Flaccus would never dare sign such an agreement, it would take the authority of the emperor to ratify this. If I sign and you lose, not only will I die but my family will forever be in disgrace. In any event Rome will claim it was signed under duress and will send Legions in force, Nambed is not as crafty as he thinks."

I asked, "General please trust me, I will win!"

Gratus was puzzled, "I trust you but perhaps you are wrong!"

My astonishing confidence changed his mind. "Ezekiel Ben David, we have no option, so you may fight, and I will sign."

It was my turn to ask a question, "But how do we bypass Flaccus?"

"Let's just say that Flaccus is about to go on a little opiate journey, from which he will remember very little!"

I was amazed at the risk Gratus was taking. "I have great faith in you Ezekiel Ben David, bring the document to me and I will sign it forthwith. Please choose your fellow gladiator well!"

Palmyra has a natural amphitheatre formed by small sloping hills. Roman engineers constructed seats from local stone and the arena had hosted many games over the years. But none had ever had such significance as the one about to be staged. The signed treaty provided for the Parthian soldiers to enter the city but only without weapons. Roman weapons would also be put away under lock and key. I almost drooled at the prospect of killing Zarin Krass.

The morning of the games dawned bright and clear, my comrades and I watched the Parthians stroll through the city gates, for them this was a day to be enjoyed, a day when they would neither kill nor be killed. Both armies began to mingle freely; hands were shaken, bets were placed. Against my better judgement the vendors were permitted to sell beer. The atmosphere took the feel as though this was a carnival of celebration; perhaps it would be a celebration of many lives saved.

I choose Hacerlo to be my fellow fighter in the arena. I had dubbed him the sprightly Spaniard and the little man jumped with joy when I announced my decision. Longinus and Fasil both protested, but neither had ever taken part in a fight to the death in the arena. Bugles summoned us, the combatants, to the sand. The Royal Box stood high with a commanding view of the proceedings. King Nambed sat with Governor Flaccus who was propped up by two Roman guards. Flaccus's eyes swam in his head, drugged he was not compos mentis and he waved drunkenly to the mob. Behind sat General Gratus together with Prince Ramn and General Titus. Gratus muttered to Titus, "Stupid bugger thinks he's at the games in Rome. Let's hope the effects of the opiate don't wear off too soon or we both will die!" Princess Nazanin set slightly to one side, she ran her seductive eyes towards Flaccus, unable to resist the urge to flirt with anyone in power, even though her brother faced death.

Vasilis was appointed referee as he was deemed to be neutral, being neither Parthian nor Roman. His workload would be light as in a death contest there were few rules. Hacerlo and I entered the sand from the southern side and the stadium erupted with Roman cheers. Zarin Krass and Prince Haman entered through the northern gate. Once again, the stadium erupted in noise. The Germans howled their approval for Krass. There was so much commotion that the guards had trouble handling their dogs stationed at either end of the Royal Box. Vasilis dropped a flag, and the contest was on.

Both sides took a moment to size up the opposition and their arms. Krass was a fearsome brute of a man. Standing at over six foot five inches his height was exacerbated by his bronze helmet which was topped by a small crescent-shaped blade. This helmet swept down protecting his jaws and nose but restricted his vision to two small eye slots. He wielded a curved Thracian sword which could cleave a man in two. His jet-black hair was fashioned in dreadlocks which hung out over a scarlet robe. The sadistic Syrian gave me 'the bird' as he cleaved the air with his weapon. Prince Haman was tall and well-muscled, and he also carried a Thracian sword. The prince had chosen to fight in the style of a Thraex gladiator adorned with a broad-brimmed helmet.

I addressed Hacerlo, "Remember our training under Abdo and all will be well. I will take the big bastard as I have a score to settle with him. I know that you can handle Haman, but never turn your back to him." Hacerlo may be small, but he is deadly fast. As such he choose to fight as a net man, known to the Romans as a retiarius gladiator. His weapons were a trident and a pugio, a throwing dagger. His net casting arm was protected by a Manica. He wore no other armour. His life depended upon his reflexes and agility. Hacerlo beamed his boyish smile from beneath his black, short curly hair. He looked as young as when we had fought together with Alketas in our troupe Familia at the ludus of Caeso Collina. We clasped arms in a brief salute before we got down to the business of the day.

Krass advanced towards me, swinging and swiping his sword before him. As he approached, I made the sign of the cross and it was then that he knew where we had met before. He was taken aback; he knew that I was seeking vengeance. If running had been an option, he would have taken it, coward and bully as he was. All of his huge sword slashes were well telegraphed, I had no trouble side-stepping them, they found only fresh air. The German troops looked despondent; they began to regret having backed their brute. Vasilis, watched them in the stands, again he muttered, "Bloody bastards!"

It was now obvious to me that Zayin Krass had never fought in the arena. True, in the field of battle his size and strength would have been formidable in the front rank where his pushing and slicing would have dominated, but this was not the field of battle, this was the arena. Here everything was very different. Gladiators, no matter their size, must learn to move quickly, feint and duck and divert to live. As it is in boxing, footwork is all important in moving quickly from defence to attack. Slashing for show kills a gladiator. Precision, well-timed thrusts are the route to survival. This brute had none of these vital attributes.

Call me sadistic, call me sad, if you must, but I was beginning to thoroughly enjoy myself. My hatred had begun to burn off and I was laughing. It was like a cat playing with a mouse before destroying it. I lowered my arms to my sides, I feinted, I ducked, I even dived and rolled and then stuck my tongue out at him. Even the Germans began to laugh. I got a hefty kick into his balls and Krass staggered and gasped. Now all the audience was enjoying his humiliation. It was too much fun to bring this to its climax, but it was time to draw a little blood. As Krass swiped I stepped inside the arc of his scimitar and the sword of Rhesus drew blood from his upper arm, his scarlet robe was rented and turned crimson with his blood. Now in a rage, Krass charged like a bull after a matador, his head lowered and hoping to hit me. At the last moment I stepped aside and with a flick of the wrist the sword of Rhesus pushed his helmet off his head. Krass bellowed, the crowd laughed, he puffed and panted, and his chest heaved with exertion. The brute had ugly spiral tattoos on his pock-marked cheeks making them even more heinous.

I ran pall mall for the arena side wall. It looked as though I had panicked. The crowd were bemused, what in hell is the Jew doing? As Krass charged he dropped his guard, his nose was an easy target, so I lopped it off. Blinded by his own blood he once again staggered forward. I remembered the wise words of my old trainer Abdo. "The gladiator who gets too cocky dies."

It was time to end this, but I was unable to resist one last piece of theatre to bring about his total humiliation. I moved to meet him and in an act of supplication bowed one knee to the arena floor. Krass wiped his blood away and now his vision cleared he could not believe what he saw. He raised his scimitar to strike, and I scooped up a fist full of arena sand which had been warmed by the hot sun. My aim was good, and the sand scalded his eyes and what remained of his bloody nasal passage. The scimitar fell and I hooked my knee behind his leg. A good push from me and aided by his own bulk Zarin Krass crashed to the ground. My bronze sword found the nape of his neck, one good push and it would be done, but I had a problem, I could not do it! I stood as though transfixed. I knew he must die, but how?

My fight was over, so the attention of the crowd switched to the struggle between Hacerlo and Haman. This was a much closer contest; the little Spaniard was not having everything his own way. Several times he had cast his net and several times he failed to entangle his opponent. Haman launched a fierce counterattack and Hacerlo had to fend him off with his trident. He received a serious arm wound when doing so. The rules of the contest, or rather the lack of them would permit me to assist him. But Hacerlo would not want that. He would want to win fairly, or he would die.

Haman could smell blood and he became far too anxious to end the duel. He had temporarily forgotten that he would also have to face me. One last desperate throw came from Hacerlo. Success: Haman's sword arm was entangled with his torso; he was briefly helpless for the more he struggled the more trapped he became. With a hook of his heel around his opponent's leg Hacerlo crashed Haman to the sand. A cry of despair came from the Parthian section of the audience. Haman's helmet fell from his head, and he saw the wicked prongs of the trident inches from his eyes. Like myself, Hacerlo had just to give one final little push. But he saw me standing undecided on what to do.

My indecisiveness almost cost the Spaniard his life, for he started walking towards me, forgetting the cardinal rule never to turn your back on a downed opponent unless you are sure he is dead. Now free of his tormentor, Haman was able to untangle himself, he took a throwing dagger from his belt.

"Hacerlo, behind you!" But for my frantic yell the Parthian dagger would have taken him in the back of his neck. Hacerlo was at his best when his reflexes were called for. In one fluid motion he ducked and spun and threw his pugio. Both daggers flashed as they crossed in flight. Haman's found sand, but Hacerlo's blade embedded itself between Haman's eyes and pierced his brain.

Below me Krass began to sob and beg for his life. We all had failed to notice how rapidly the storm clouds had assembled. Suddenly there came a deafening peal of thunder and forked lighting came to earth. The bolt of electricity grounded itself in Krass's head causing him to convulse wildly as his flesh dripped away like candle wax. To my amazement I was unharmed.

A panicked Princess Nazanin ran from the Royal Box to be with her dying brother. Boom! Another peal of thunder, louder than the first caused one of the guards to lose control of his vicious dog. It broke free of its leash and sprang catching the Princess by the throat. The brute snarled and snapped; the yellow fangs closed on her windpipe crushing it beyond repair. In life her beauty had been beyond compare; in death she metamorphosed into a true reflection of her real self. In the rictus of death, she was truly ugly.

All was over. The crowds began to disperse, and the disappointed Parthians with shoulders slumped went back to their tents. Governor Flaccus, still waving to all and sundry was assisted back to his quarters.

King Nambed was well pleased. By contriving to choose Haman as his champion, one simple act of fratricide had released him from a family power struggle and a political impasse with Rome. The King was clever, he had me do his dirty work for him.

Chapter 47. The fatuousness of Governor Flaccus

(It's the stupidity of men which enables them to snatch defeat from the jaws of victory.)

The morning after the games I stood on the city walls watching the Parthian engineers dismantle their vast encampment. It was King Nambed's quarters that was last to be dismantled. The bodies of Prince Haman and Princess Nazanin had been passed into the care of the embalmers. They would be interred in the Royal Mausoleum when the army returned to Ctesiphon, the Capital located on the banks of the River Tigris. In keeping with tradition there had been a brief period of mourning but neither Nambed nor his son Prince Ramn appeared to be unduly upset. Still, appearance is everything for any Royal family.

Tribune Fasil joined me. He told me that Governor Flaccus was back in the land of the living, albeit suffering from a major hangover. I hoped, for all our sakes, that he did not recall too much of what had occurred. Perhaps it would have been best if the opiate dose had been increased to a fatal level! Too late for that now! As these treacherous thoughts passed through me, I saw a of group of officers heading towards us. Governor Flaccus was out to see what the Persians were up to.

Flaccus, despite his aching head, took up his usual attitude of outrageous arrogance and autocracy. He began, "You see, I told you that the Parthian heathens have no backbone when it comes to a battle!" No one spoke, it was obvious that the Governor had not grasped what had happened when he was on his 'trip'. A common problem with stupid people is they think that they are clever. Flaccus strutted along the wall for five minutes as though he was a conquering hero before commanding. "All senior officers assemble in my quarters in five minutes."

I suspected a blunder of immense proportions was about to be made. Flaccus sat at the top table flanked by Generals

Gratus and Titus. The doctor had given Flaccus a potion to help him recover and now he seemed to be filled with a new vitality and vigour, such was his enthusiasm to vanquish the enemy. "Gentlemen, what a party we had last night at the expense of the Parthians. Why, I even dreamed I was at the games in Rome, seated in my usual place beside Emperor Tiberius. A beautiful girl, impressed by my status and power endeavoured to seduce me!" There was a ripple of sycophantic laughter.

Governor Flaccus continued, "But do not be fooled, not everyone here in this room is our friend." He pointed an accusatory finger in my face, "This man, this Jew, I do not trust."

The officers shuffled in their seats with embarrassment. Things took an ominous turn, they had all heard how I had shaken Flaccus in the manner of a terrier breaking a rat's neck. The rant continued, "You Jew have served your purpose, I hereby relieve you of your command and are dismissed. Go back to your own people before I change my mind and have you put to death!"

The air could have been cleaved with a knife. From the corner of my eye, I caught Longinus signalling that I should not make an angry retort. Accordingly, I bit my tongue and remained silent, but it was General Gratus who came to my aid.

"Governor Flaccus, Sir, please consider that it was Tribune Ben David who successfully negotiated this peace pact with Parthia, successfully completing the task which I assigned to him. I cannot and will not turn my back on him now!"

Governor Flaccus was not used to being spoken to like this by any soldier, no matter how high his status. "General Gratus, you and your men will carry out my orders or I will relieve you of your command. A full report will be sent to the Emperor telling of how you failed to take the opportunity to annihilate our sworn enemy."

We knew that this was not an idle threat, and once again, the officers shuffled in their seats. All knew the man was a moron, but no one wanted to lose his command and suffer the ignominy of being sent home in disgrace. All eyes looked at Gratus and then reverted to me. I spoke up, "Governor Flaccus, as I am such an irritation to you Sir, I gladly step down. I therefore bear no responsibility for what happens next between you and Parthia."

There was silence once again until Gratus who had had enough brought things to a head.

"Sir, Ezekiel Ben David has served Rome and me well. He is an honourable and trustworthy man whom I greatly respect. Furthermore, we are not yet out of the woods, the Parthians are still at our gates, they are an undefeated enemy and we do not know if they intend treachery. But we do possess one advantage, the Greek Vasilis has a good relationship with Tribune Ben David. I am confident that if treachery is afoot Vasilis will warn us via Ben David. It would be a wise commander who retains Ben David until we have made good our withdrawal."

Flaccus gave his customary harumph, "Very well, I concede your point, the Jew stays until we route the enemy!"

A murmur of disbelief from the men passed through the room. This time it was General Titus who spoke up. "Governor, we have made an international agreement with Parthia. We are honour bound to keep it."

Flaccus exploded, "Soldier, do you not realise that I am the Commander in Chief of Syria and Israel and that no pact or treaty can be made unless I am a signatory. I made no such pact and as such you will disregard any stupid concessions you may have made. Have your men prepare to attack within the hour. The enemy are focused on dismantling their camp and not even Mark Anthony had an opportunity such as this!"

The Roman officers had no choice, they must obey even though this order was the folly of a stupid fool. I made a final plea for reason. "Sir, we have an opportunity to withdraw and save two Legions. We will still retain a small garrison unit in Palmyra and maintain control of the city. The Silk Road will remain open and both sides will maintain face. Even if you manage to kill King Nambed, the seeds of war will be sown with Parthia, to be fought by future generations. There will be no safe trade on the Silk Road. This is an act of futile utter stupidity!"

Flaccus ran at me and slapped me hard. "Take the Jew and have him crucified to the nearest tree!"

Carius Aquillas stepped forward, dagger in hand. Momentarily, I thought myself to be his target and Aquillas was going to take the opportunity for vengeance. But no, he passed me by: his pugio cut deep into the Governor's throat slicing his carotid, blood spurted upwards in a high arc. Flaccus's eyes bulged, and his hands gripped the wound in a vain attempt to stop the bleeding. Then with arms flailing wildly he fell dead across his desk. Aquillas dropped the dagger.

One crisis was now replaced with another. Tribune Carius Aquillas had just committed the murder of a Roman Governor in front of a room full of witnesses. Even though Flaccus was detested by one and all, he occupied one of Rome's highest offices. For this crime no pardon could or would be forthcoming. Gratus had no choice, he must sentence Aquillas to death and his family to disgrace. General Gratus was stunned; we were all badly shaken, horror had been heaped upon horror. Gratus held neither love nor respect for Tribune Aquillas but to have to pass the death sentence on an officer was appalling to him. But there was one option: in Roman elite society suicide was an acceptable way out of an untenable situation.

General Gratus chose his next words extremely carefully. "Tribune Carius Aquillas, although your act this morning undoubtedly saved the lives of your men, it is impossible that you go unpunished for the murder of a Roman Governor. The death sentence is mandatory and is passed upon you! We have had many differences, but I take no pleasure in doing this and inflicting disgrace upon one of Rome's most noble families. But the option of suicide is open to you. All in this room, including myself, will be sworn to secrecy. Your family will be told that you died a valiant death as a soldier of Rome defending your country. Your body will be cremated in Palmyra's central plaza with full military honours. Carius Aquillas weighed up his options: it was a no brainer, suicide or disgrace; no contest.

Tribune Carius Aquillas stood before me. He spoke clearly and without emotion. "Tribune Ezekiel Ben David, there has long been enmity between us. I admit that in times past I have done much wrong both to you and to your wife Batya. Now, I need your help and indeed your forgiveness. I do not wish to die by my own hand, I request that I be allowed to die as a soldier and that you assist me. Will you help me?"

I felt that I had no choice but to accede to his wish, after all, he had saved Batya at the river. I asked him, "Why me?" A flicker of a smile passed over his face, "I'm being purely pragmatic, you have killed in this manner many times. You have great skill in these matters and my death will not be botched."

Carius Aquillas bowed on one knee and lowered his head exposing the nape of his neck. Tribune Fasil fetched me the sword of Rhesus. I hesitated but for a moment and in my mind, I heard the words of my mentor in the British army, Sergeant Major Michael Maguire,

"Young Sir, if you are to be a leader of men you must act and be decisive, especially in matters unpleasant!"

I thrust downwards, the blade split Aquillas's spinal column and ruptured his heart. The man who had been my enemy toppled forward and did not move. It had been quick and clean, and I hoped that in death he would find the peace that he missed in his life.

The funeral pyres were built and made ready for the bodies of Governor Flaccus and Tribune Carius Aquillas. Their biers were borne with great solemnity by officers of the Praetorian guard dressed in black. A Cornelius sounded and burning brands pushed into the pyres. As the bodies were consumed by the hungry flames, I reflected on the man Carius Aquillas. No doubt he had been a rogue, a rapist and a villain of the highest order. But he had shown bravery and virtue when he saved his men from carnage. He knew by killing Flaccus he would sign his own death warrant but he gave his life so that others may live.

In Rome there was much mourning. Whereas Tribune Aquillas was remembered as a fallen hero, Governor Flaccus's death was less noble, simply he died the victim of a flat-headed desert serpent! Such is the hypocrisy of Rome!

Chapter 48. Purple Haze

(No one last forever – or do they?)

It was decided that General Titus remain in Palmyra in charge of the small Roman garrison until such time as normality was restored. Even in the aftermath of difficult times food was still plentiful in Palmyra. The crops had continued to be tended and the bakers had continued to bake, even in the darkest of days. The city victuallers were able to provide the city inhabitants with staple foods.

The soldiers of Legio X Fretensis and Legio XV1 Flavia Firma were already regretting to have to leave this green and pleasant place where water from the aqueduct sparkled and gushed in the city fountains. Now the Roman cavalry made ready their mounts, pennants were unfurled, and Legionaries formed up in their marching order. Slaves replenished the supply wagons with food, all was ready for the return march.

Before we left, I saluted General Titus in the Roman fashion of clasping arms. I said, "It has been a pleasure to serve with you Sir." The thought occurred to me that I may be becoming more Roman than the Romans themselves! God forbid! The remains of the funeral pyres had been cleared from the plaza. The remains of Governor Flaccus and Tribune Aquillas were placed in urns for return to Rome. Eventually they would be interred in their respective family mausoleums.

Batya, an accomplished horse rider, requested that she be allowed to ride alongside me. She emerged from her wagon to take her mount and my mouth dropped open with delight and surprise. She wore a long flowing white dress which she had packed in case such an occasion arose. Her dress allowed free movement of her legs thereby allowing her to ride as well as any man. This lady would never ride side saddle! She turned all the soldiers' heads, including General Gratus to look and marvel at her transformation from servant to a beautiful lady. My heart filled with pride for this woman was mine. But something ominous hung in the air; we all felt that this day would not end well for Batya and me.

The advance party led the exit from the city. The Aqualifier hoisted the Legion eagle high, and the marching pace was set by Centurion Longinus. All seemed to be normal. But I knew it was not so. We Romans set our course south west on a heading leading to Damascus. The Parthians turned east bound for their capital city on the Tigris, the city of Ctesiphon. Then to our surprise three riders approached from the Parthians.

It was King Nambed accompanied by Prince Ramn and Vasilis. The King rode with the agility of a much younger man. Back in the day he would have been a formidable warrior. General Gratis and I moved forward to meet them, we all stopped, and the horses snorted as though in greeting. King Nambed was first to speak. "Greetings General Gratus, Ben David, please allow me to express remorse for the loss of your beloved Governor Flaccus." There was a look of devilment in the face of the King,

"He died a tragic death, at the hands of a viper I hear! And of course, the loss of Tribune Aquillas, apparently died valiantly in a skirmish with my men. I do admit to being slightly puzzled, as I am not aware that any fighting took place between our forces! However, this is of no real concern to me. I wish you and your men and that beautiful woman safe home." He pointed to Batya who was watching.

General Gratus raised his arm in salute. "May I express my remorse at the loss of both your son and your daughter, I wish that things could have been different." King Nambed exchanged a glance at his remaining son.

"General, I also wish things could have been different, but the lives of men on both sides have been saved. I know you to be a man of honour, but one must provide for all contingencies. Nambed raised his arm and a cacophony of trumpets rang out. Immediately a regiment of horse archers appeared from behind an eastern set of sand dunes. A second regiment appeared in the west. Nambed continued, "A mere precaution and of course these men are now stood down!" A nefarious look was exchanged between Gratus and me. The King noticed and smiled. But for the sacrifice made by Aquillas the slaughter would have been widespread. How fitting it was that Governor Flaccus was going home in a jar! We all knew that disaster had been narrowly averted.

"My friend and advisor Vasilis has requested a leave of absence from my service, which I have granted to him. Vasilis will explain."

The Greek, whom I now regarded as my friend rode alongside me. "Ezekiel Ben David, I do not believe that you are from this time and this place. I think that you and Batya are about to experience great sadness and I wish to be present and to try to help you both in a time of need."

I was amazed at the man's prescience. Vasilis continued, "King Nambed has given me permission to do so. If you and General Gratus allow, I wish to come with you."

General Gratus nodded his acceptance, and we rode south in silence.

The humidity increased, sweat appeared on both men and animals. The sky began to darken, and the horses whickered with fear, for they sensed thunder was approaching. General Gratus warned, "Sandstorm!"

Vasilis spoke as he scanned the sky, "This is like no sandstorm I have known, look!"

There came a peel of thunder, and the clouds began to rotate in a vortex heading directly towards us. But it was the colour of the clouds; they were a deep purple, the colour of royalty. The command party dismounted and encouraged our mounts to lie down to afford men and animals shelter. Longinus ordered the rank and file to kneel in expectation of an onslaught of driven sand. Strangely and without any comprehension as to why the sand remained settled. The swirling clouds enveloped us all and we were in the eye of the storm. Here it was extraordinarily peaceful and serene. It was as though the laws of physics were suspended. I thought I could hear joyous singing, but it did nothing to quell my fear; I clasped Batya's hand tightly. Then he appeared, the man known to me as Gabriel, the messenger of God.

Gabriel offered his outstretched hand and gestured that I should join him. No! I would not, for I had done as requested, would God please allow me time to pursue my new life with Batya? I did not want to return to the problems I would face in the future! It also shocked me to realise that I did not want to desert Batya and go back to Libertad. But God does not always grant what you want. As though some magnetic force was in action I was pulled inexorably towards Gabriel. Simultaneously Batya was drawn steadily back into the arms of my friend Vasilis. Our entwined fingers gently separated until only our fingertips touched. Then she was gone, our time together in Israel and Syria was finished, I requested Vasilis that he take good care of her. He nodded, tears flooding from his eyes.

Gabriel smiled as he escorted me into the swirling purple haze. "Patrick Doyle do not worry. Each man has a purpose, you are blessed to have been chosen to have many."

I did not understand, and I did not care. I mourned for the loss of my Batya.

Part 3. A New Beginning

(One must finish this life before entry is gained to the next.)

Chapter 49. Melancholy at the museum

I awoke in the recovery suite at Cromwell Hospital. My vital signs were now fully stable, and I appeared none the worse for my hypnosis at Harley Street. Liber and our two boys, Miguel and Peter, together with Chaplain Jamie Dougan sat by my bedside. Jamie was the first to speak. "Paddy, you gave us all quite a fright, I thought Doctor Aldermatt was going to take a turn for the worse!" My friend laughed with relief before continuing, "No doubt the good doctor could see litigation for malpractice coming his way. We all know how much the Swiss love their francs."

Liber and the boys enveloped me in a group hug. I sipped some water, "How long was I away for?"

Libertad looked at the bedside clock, "Only three hours, but it seemed like a lifetime."

I was amazed, how could events in Israel and Syria have happened in only three hours. Jamie sensed my unease, "Paddy, remember that time is relevant, when you are well you will tell us of your experiences."

The doctors suggested that I spend the night for observation, but I had never felt better. "Bring me my discharge papers please." I was determined to return to our rented London home.

And so, the days turned to weeks, the weeks to months and I became bored. I confided my tale to my family and to Jamie. I could see that Libertad flinched at the mere mention of Batya's name. One morning she brought it to a head. "You must have loved this woman very much. Every night you cry out her name in your sleep. I thought that hypnosis may cure you of your problems. Now I feel that a ghost of a woman is sharing our marriage and I do not know if I can cope with that!" Our relationship, once warm and loving was taking a downward slide and I did not know how to fix it. So much for the doctors!

It was with much reluctance that I resigned my commission from the army. I was accepted as an intelligence operative in MI5 based in London. Libertad and the boys could live with me in relative safety in the capital. As head of army intelligence in Ulster, life had been fraught with tension and danger daily. I would never tell Liber, but I had loved it!

Although we lived together as a family, we were not happy. What had begun as a downward drift had turned into a downward spiral. And now I had more time in which to brood. Liber and I snapped at each other without provocation, and each of us could not extend either patience or understanding. Our mutual bad behaviour was affecting the boys who strived not to take sides.

I had never been a person who frequented museums but come Saturday morning I decided I would take my sons, Miguel and Peter, to the British Museum. The museum, located in Gt. Russell Street is very impressive. The colonnaded façade reminded me of St. Peter's Basilica in Rome. Miguel and Peter took delight in investigating and exploring, no doubt glad to be away from the squabbling of their parents. I found myself to be drawn to the department of ancient middle east which has exhibits from ancient Syria together with all the countries of the Levant.

There at the far wall stood a large glass fronted case, and I felt inexorably pulled towards it. What I witnessed threw my fragile emotions into turmoil. There before me was the bronze sword of Rhesus. The blade gleamed in the museum's overhead lights and the precious stones inlaid in its handle sparkled like stars in the darkest sky. This artefact was both beautiful and deadly. I had used it to deadly effect many times. Beside the sword on a stand hung the uniform of a Senior Roman Tribune, a soldier who reported directly to the Legion General. An engraved caption read, 'Although of very different origins both sword and uniform had been excavated from the same location in the sands of Syria. The sword had been carefully wrapped in the uniform and upon a piece of parchment had been inscribed: placed here in loving memory of Ezekiel Ben David, a soldier of God. Signed by his friend Vasilis and his loving wife Batya.'

    My tears flowed freely as memories of times good and bad came rushing back. Batya the beautiful woman with whom I had shared a short life. Precious friends such as Alketas, Longinus and Hacerlo, with whom I had risked life and limb. And of course, the enigma of Carius Aquillas. How I longed for the heat of Israel and the warm embrace of Batya. I was still crying when Miguel and Peter found me; nothing was asked and nothing was said, I could not hurt them by telling them of my love for a ghost.

Chapter 50. Libertad springs a horrible surprise

My work at MI5 was intelligence gathering. I sifted through reports which arrived on my desk from various agencies. I no longer had a senior position, and my workload was far from onerous. I was now a civilian after spending most of my adult life in the army, but I still had a permit for my personal protection weapon, a Walther .32 PPK. Everyone in MI5 is bound by the Official Secrets Act and employees are charged with maintaining the security of the United Kingdom. The service motto is Regnum Defende (defend the realm).

I shared an office in Millbrook House, a grade II listed building at Lambeth. I had a pleasant view of the river, an ideal work location in London. I was on good terms with all my colleagues; life should have been good, but there was a problem, I was bored at work. The hustle and bustle of city life was beginning to irritate me, I was not designed to live in a place like this.

As usual, I arrived home from work at about 7pm but something was absent, the usual delicious aroma of a prepared dinner did not come from the kitchen. I entered our small lounge to find Libertad sat beside a stranger. My first thought was P.I.R.A. have found us. My hand found the butt of my Walther and the weapon glided from my shoulder holster.

Libertad shouted, "No Patrick! All is ok. This is Luis!"

Adrenalin coursed through me. "And who the hell is Luis?"

The swarthy stranger stood. He did not extend his hand in greeting. "My name is Luis Sanchez, I am Spanish from the city of Malaga, the home of your wife. Libertad and I know each other from when were children and we met, quite by accident, here in London where I have been managing a tapas bar." Luis Sanchez was well built and looked to be fit, but he stood at only five feet eight inches. He had to crane his neck to meet my gaze.

It was Libertad who told me the worst. "Patrick you and I have not been happy for some time. I found solace in my friendship with Luis and then from being friends we became lovers. I am returning to Malaga to live with Luis and taking the boys with me. I was in shock and sweat broke upon my brow. Thankfully, I had returned the Walther to my holster.

Luis Sanchez watched my every move, as did Liber. Ripping his head off would have given me great pleasure, but in the end only more pain would come from it. I looked at Libertad; it took two to tango. I left the room and did not look back.

Chapter 51. Palace Barracks Hollywood Co Down

News of my separation from Libertad spread fast, bad news always does. The director of MI5 expedited my request for a transfer to Northern Ireland. Soon I was on a plane to Belfast. I landed at Aldergrove International and sought a taxi. Gone were the days of a government car, driver and bodyguard. A wise man once said, 'humble yourself or life will do it for you.'

Palace Barracks is home to MI5 in the province. It is in the small town of Hollywood, North Down, just outside Belfast. Palace Barracks is a place well known to me having been there many times when I had the role of G2 in charge of army intelligence in Ulster. I was warmly welcomed by the staff, some of whom insisted on addressing me as 'Sir' even though I no longer had the Queen's commission. One of the first to come and greet me was Colonel Robert Conway, a man whom I had detested but was now a firm friend.

'Basildon Bond' Conway pumped my hand as though his life depended upon it. "Welcome back old boy. I always knew that you would come home. Back for me to save your life one more time!"

Nothing had changed with Bob's demeanour. I said, "Great to see you Bob, been doing any boxing?"

"Heard about you and Liber; damn sorry. Still here you are surrounded by friends and of course the old enemy P.I.R.A. They haven't gone away you know!"

I took up residence in the barracks until such time that I could find suitable accommodation and a car. I had some free time and decided to explore some old boyhood haunts, I even went to see the old family home on the Shankill. I walked along the Falls past the Holy Cross Boxing Club but did not venture in, too many painful memories. It would be best to get back to work and not to dwell too much on a painful past. My wish for work was about to be granted.

Chapter 52. Synthesis – Provos and Prods united

(A very unholy alliance)

A high level meeting was called at Palace Barracks. Present were Colonel Bob Conway, Commander Thomas Heron, R.U.C. Special branch, my replacement as G2 Colonel William Walters, and old faithful, James Carter, now working for Walters.

Conway's authoritative tones brought the meeting to order. "Gentlemen, as we feared, the provos and prods have formed an alliance formed in hell. This is not about orange or green, the politicians continue to squabble, but these people have found a common denominator: money. These bastards have merged resources and skills to exploit youth on both sides of society. Drug dealing is taking place on an industrial scale. Shipments of heroin, cocaine and amphetamines are finding their way into the province. Increased searches and surveillance have not stopped this plague arriving onto our streets. We must find a way to put an end to it!"

I asked, "Do we have suspects?"

Commander Heron replied, "Yes, Roger 'Hacker' Hamilton is known to us for his L.V.F. activities. Bosco 'Bloody' McLernon is a known P.I.R.A. drug dealer. We believe these two are the brains behind this, but we have not been able to prove it. Its too dangerous for anyone to inform, if they dared to do so their end would be swift and painful."

"Has anyone any ideas?" G2 put the question to the room.

Before I realized it, I had raised my hand. "Could we mount a sting operation. We send an agent to pose as a dealer and set a trap. All perfectly legal except in the Philippines, but that is of no concern to us."

There was a short ripple of laughter before Bob said, "Yes, of course we have thought of that; legal aspects aside it would be fraught with danger for our man. These evil bastards would kill him at the slightest sniff of suspicion."

"Do we have an agent who could set up a meet with these gangsters?"

Conway looked directly at me; I think he knew what I was about to propose. "We have a low-level informant, but he's not very effective, in fact quite the reverse."

My voice was calm, "Tell your informant that a new buyer has arrived in town and has one million dollars to spend."

"And who may that be?"

I did not hesitate, "Why me of course!"

All in the room looked at me as though I had taken leave of my senses. Perhaps they were correct; life without Liberty and the boys was empty; I needed a purpose to live for.

Chapter 53. The Sting

The wheels of MI5 and special branch rolled into motion. A new identity, a new persona, was created for me. William John Lavery, a man with a criminal record was born. He was a suspected killer and drug dealer, but the problem was lack of proof. William was a man who wanted money; lots of it and did not care how he got it. I enjoyed getting into my new role, I let my hair grow lank and long and unwashed, my chin sported several days stubble. I made sure that my old Belfast accent was as strong as in the days before I left for England and the army. One morning Basildon Bond Conway came to see me. He wrinkled his nose in disapproval. "Would you look at you! I always thought you looked like a criminal, and you have proven me correct!"

I gave him the bird.

Basildon laughed, "We have just had the most amazing piece of good fortune! One of my best agents, code-named 'brave heart' has just been accepted by these gangsters as a genuine player. She will make sure they have a full dossier on William John Lavery and in doing so will sow the seeds of their destruction.

One week later the 'meet' was on. I was contacted by our agent and told to be outside Malcolm's jewellers' shop in Chichester Street at midday. I was to be unaccompanied and carry a copy of the Belfast Telegraph under one arm and the Irish Times under the other. How appropriate! I stood at the jewellers thinking that all that glitters is not gold. I caught sight of my reflection in the window; I looked and felt like a complete bad ass villain. A car pulled over at the kerb, two occupants in the front and a third in the back. The guy in the back summoned me over and I got in; we sped off in the direction of Victoria Street. I was given a rough search and instructed to put on a blindfold. "He's clean Sean!"

We did not travel far, and I knew we were in the docks area as I could hear the sirens of ships. We stopped; the door was opened. A pair of strong hands guided me into a building.

"Ah, William John, may I call you that? Sean take off his blindfold." I tried to appear stoic and remained silent. Facing me was a squat guy, perhaps five feet eight inches in height but built like a barrel. His hair was snow white and barbered in a crew cut. The eyes were soulless and round like a rat. When God had made this albino, he had not skimped with his ugly stick. For some reason I decided I would refer to him as 'pink' perhaps sarcastically referring to his lack of pigmentation. Pink did not offer a handshake but continued to talk. "My name is Roger Hamilton; some people refer to me as 'hacker' but you should know that I find that most offensive! This is my business partner Bosco McLernon, he does not mind being referred to as bloody Bosco! I don't understand his moniker." Pink guffawed with pleasure. This guy was much bigger, dark greasy and evil. I had killed this type many times in the past.

'Pink' was the talkative of the two. "Well William John, we've got the low down on you. You have quite a reputation, it would seem that you are a very naughty man!

I affected a very cocky smile, "Well Roger, I can assure you that I am much worse than my reputation! I'm seeking a business partner, someone who can supply me with the goods I require. I have an established business, but I need an importer to get the product to me."

Tall, dark and ugly sauntered over, he bore an air of menace. "And what and how much would the like of you be needing?"

It was time for me to put my cards on the table. "Cocaine, 1 million dollars worth, now can you get it, or do I need to go elsewhere? Perhaps my business is too big for you guys to handle?"

Pink was about to go ballistic! He was struggling to control his temper and the veins at the corner of his eyes twitched and jumped! I had gone too far, but the thing was I didn't give a damn for my safety. Pink swallowed and I think he bit his tongue. After a full two minutes he said, "Nothing happens until your money is in our Zurich bank by electronic transfer. We will not do business until we have further checked your Bonafede!" When we have the money, and we are happy then we may proceed. That is our terms, you can take it or leave it!"

"How do I know you will not simply bank my money and then disappear?"

Pink was regaining his composure and confidence, "And where would we go to William? Belfast is our home as it is yours. Perhaps if we default you could get the L.V.F. to pay us a visit!" Pink thought this to be very funny.

I would get no further, so I agreed. Bosco, dark and ugly said, "You will be contacted with our bank details, do not attempt to contact us, we will contact you. Now I will replace your blindfold, your chauffeur awaits you. Now get the fuck out of my face!"

I gave him my most charming smile, "I love you too."

The Synthesis Bank details were duly received. The bank was contacted by Interpol and immediately agreed to cooperate. The gnomes of Zurich would not mess with Interpol, especially when drugs were involved. Our electronic wizards would make it appear to the account holder that one million dollars had been deposited even though not a dime had been sent. A month passed without any contact; I suspected that I had been rumbled. Then William John Lavery received a telegram.

It read, 'Be at Warrenpoint port, November 17th 6:15pm. Your goods arriving on vessel Darwin's Dream. One man, one van. We have many eyes and ears.

I exclaimed, "We have hit the jackpot!"

Agent Braveheart reported all roads leading to the port will be watched and at the sniff of anything suspicious Darwin's Dream will not dock and will make haste for international waters. The roads may be watched but there is more than one way to skin a terrorist. The motor vessel, 'Prince of Wales' was a frequent visitor to Warrenpoint, but on the night of November 17th she would be manned by a very different crew.

Warrenpoint port is the province's largest port by tonnage, it is strategically located close to the town of Newry in Co. Down. It is in the Dublin to Belfast economic corridor and is about an hour from each capital city. Darwin's dream docked on time in the dark and drizzle. The Prince of Wales was moored just 100 metres away, she showed no sign of lights or life.

My battered Renault van was parked on the dockside, side lights on. My wipers cleared the mist and rain from the screen, and I peered out into the dark. A hooded figure left the Darwin and walked towards where I was parked. I flashed my headlights for him to join me. The stranger and I walked on the dockside partly illuminated by overhead gantry lights. As I stepped onto the Darwin's gangplank adrenaline surged through my body, a feeling very familiar to me. Strangely, I felt no fear; had I acquired a death wish, was this my time to die?

I decided to maintain the persona of William John Lavery for as long as possible. Roger 'Hacker' Hamilton, known to me as 'Pink' and Bosco 'Bloody' McLernon awaited me. This time 'Pink' did extend his hand, "Ah William John, you see that I am a man of my word. Your money is in my account and your story checks out. My men will help transfer your goods to your van. I could see the sacks being unloaded onto the quayside as I left the Darwin.

A double click on my radio transmitter was the agreed signal which lit the night with flames. S.A.S. soldiers and black-clad special branch officers tossed thunder flashes which stunned all of us on the dock. My ears rang and I was temporarily blinded but I did not have to draw my weapon. Hands were raised in surrender, all except one. Bosco 'Bloody' McLernon chose to fight instead of imprisonment and sent a burst of automatic fire towards his assailants. Bullets ricocheted sending sparks from the quayside and the black-clad soldiers dived, all except one. Sergeant Les Cooper stood and calmly took aim, Bloody Bosco's head burst open, and his body tumbled into the oily waters. What a fitting end to a dirty man.

The gangsters were rounded up, all except one. 'Pink' had managed to slip through our net. It was a mistake which almost proved to be fatal.

Chapter 54. Boxing amongst the drumlins

Autumn passed into winter and the annual murmuration of starlings took flight above Belfast City Hall. Millions of the little birds were joined by their Scandinavian cousins escaping colder climes and they created beautiful and fluid shapes in the crepuscular light of dusk. The phenomenon was enjoyed by young and old as they went about their Christmas shopping.

After the excitement of 'the sting,' my work at MI5 became much more routine and less dangerous. Whilst living in Belfast did not appeal to me, a home in the mountainous area of the Dromana hills most certainly held appeal. I secured a tenure for a small cottage in the small village of Ballycroob, which offered the serenity of a rural setting but was within easy commuting distance of my Hollywood base. After living amongst the chaos of London my home seemed like heaven. Ballycroob is at the foot of Slieve Croob, the mountain is only 1,752 feet above sea level but is still an impressive peak. To the north of the Mountains of Mourne, in Irish it is called Sliabh Cruibe (mountain of the hoof). The mountain is the source of the River Lagan which flows deep and wide through Belfast before joining the sea at Belfast Lough.

The problem which bedevils my home province is the people's inability to separate religion and politics. It is not the worship of God, which is the problem, but the competing political ideologies which align themselves to the two main faiths. Roman Catholics who, in the main, look towards Dublin and protestants who profess to be British. In this respect Ballycroob was no different; here most people would define themselves as being nationalist. But here I was at home with my neighbours, no one asked about either my religion or my employment, they simply did not care. However, Colonel Bob Conway, Basildon Bond, was concerned that should my past come to light my choice of location would make me an easy target for P.I.R.A. or L.V.F. terrorists. I must be doing something right as both lots hated me! Bob would have much preferred me to live and lose myself in the anonymity of the capital city. But I was having none of it.

It was my friend and colleague Chaplain Jamie Dougan who told me about the Father John Feeny Memorial Boxing Club. Jamie has a keen interest in amateur boxing, and we had sparred together many times. He had many contacts within the sport, one of whom was Martin Feeny, Father John's brother. The club operated from a converted barn in which the young athletes trained. Guys punched heavy bags and speed balls, muscles and reflexes were being toned for competition. In the ring two guys sparred under the watchful eye of trainer Martin. The atmosphere prevailed of sweat and effort and reminded me of boxing at Holy Cross where Father John had been my mentor.

Martin called a stop to the sparring. The two boxers were told to finish off their session by punching heavy sandbags. Martin was a tough task master. He stepped down from the canvas. "And so, you fought at Holy Cross under the tutelage of my brother John?"

"Yes," I replied, "Father John taught me everything I know."

That brought a smile to Martin's face. "You're a wee bit long in the tooth to box but Jamie says you would be interested in doing some coaching here!"

Obviously Martin was not a man to pull his punches, please excuse the pun.

It was Jamie who laughed, "Paddy, I did warn you this bugger is very direct!"

Martin tossed a pair of gloves to me. "Would you care to show me what you know?"

I could never resist a challenge.

I stepped through the ropes onto the firm canvas floor of the boxing ring. Immediately I felt at home. Martin held up his gloves palms outwards. "Now give me some jabs!"

I duly obliged; these were followed by hooks and uppercuts.

"Good," he grunted, "Now give me some right and left hooks and put some bloody piff into it!"

The hook is the power punch and when delivered properly can put your opponent's lights out! It was well that Martin's gloves were my target and not his body for my hooks rocked him back on his heels.

"Jeasus!" Was all he said. We finished after a short sparring session. Martin, although a good boxer did not have the finesse of his brother John. He telegraphed a lot of his punches and even at the age of forty-seven my footwork was sufficiently fast to lead him a merry dance. He knew that I could have laid him out cold if I had chosen to do so.

After five minutes he said, "Enough, when do you want to start? We train on Monday, Wednesday and Friday evenings; but don't expect to be paid."

I replied, "If my work permits, I'll do all three; money is not my motive."

Martin asked no more questions.

Chapter 55. A star is born

Perhaps once in every generation a person is born with a God-given gift enabling him or her to excel in their chosen endeavour. For some it's art, literature or music. I found my star in the sport of boxing. His name is Sean Goldmann, and he has been boxing at the Feeny club since he was five. Now, in his early twenties, Sean stands at six feet two inches, weighs just under fourteen stone which puts him at the top of the weight range for cruiserweight. Everyone knew he had the potential to turn professional in the fight game. There was no other boxer comparable in the Feeny club and Sean's list of trophies filled the club's cupboard. The Irish amateur championships were fast approaching, and Martin asked me to take charge of his preparations, which I gladly did.

I intensified Sean's training regime daily; it reminded me of the gladiators of old. My trainer in the arena, Abdo, would have approved. Weights, sandbags, punch balls and skipping, Sean endured all without complaint. No pain, no gain, became our mantra. As we sparred, he reminded me of the boxing style of someone I had fought with. Sean's footwork, body shape, and fighting ability were very familiar but I was unable to join up the dots. The name Goldmann was obviously Jewish, but to my knowledge I had never boxed with anyone of that name.

One evening, training completed I arrived home at the cottage to find an unexpected visitor. Colonel Robert Conway, the one and only Basildon Bond, stood in my porch. "Good evening old boy," his posh tones sang out, "And would there be any chance of a gin and tonic for an old friend?"

Small talk completed we sipped at my bottle of Cork Gin, a drink I had formed an attachment to over many years. "Now Bob tell me why you're here?"

Bob sighed, as though he was slightly uncomfortable. "You will be aware that Her Majesty pays me a considerable sum of money to investigate people and problems, so I do so to the best of my ability. Tell me what you know about Sean Goldmann."

I replied, "Very little other than he's a fantastic fighter, and is destinated to become one of Ireland's best."

Bob looked at me intensely, "Do you find anything familiar about him?"

"Yes, but I cannot fathom it out."

Bob said, I'm not surprised, now listen because I'm going to tell you a little story. Goldmann is his adoptive parent's name. He was christened as Sean Gallagher, called after his father."

Sean Gallagher! The name hit me like a hammer blow. Sean Gallagher, all those years ago when we were in our twenties, had been my best friend and my sparring partner. To my great regret Sean had chosen the wrong road and had joined the provisional I.R.A. Those of you who have read 'Combatant' will be aware of the tragic history between us. I had saved the life of a wounded British soldier and Gallagher had been ordered to kill me. It was during his attempted assassination of me that he died at my hand, it was the reason I had to leave Belfast. No wonder this boy and his boxing style was so familiar to me. I asked Bob, "Do you think he knows who I am?"

Bob said, "We are not sure, Sean junior was born shortly after his father's demise. His mother, Deidre, was unable to cope with the loss of her husband and the birth of a baby boy. Deidre agreed to Sean's adoption by the Jewish Goldmann family. She had been sickened by the troubles between the protagonists, but Goldmanns being Jewish were not aligned to any of the feuding factions. The family were filthy rich and would give the boy the best possible start in life. We don't think young Sean to be a threat, but we had to give you the heads up."

The shock was beginning to wear off and I poured a second gin for both of us. Bob continued with his litany of trouble. "Of more concern to me is the fact we have been unable to find Roger Hamilton the guy whom you refer to as 'pink.' He has disappeared, none of my agents can get a handle on his whereabouts. He's an evil bastard and will be intent on revenge. Until we catch him, I will be a regular visitor to Ballycroob, I might have to save your life yet again!"

That called for a third gin!

If young Sean knew about my past and the fact I had killed his father, he never said, nor did he ask any questions. Life continued as before, the strenuous training for the championships was maintained. My total concentration was on the boy's future and the championships, not to dwell upon the past. In fact, working with Sean had been a blessing, it helped me to stop maudlin over the loss of Liberty.

Training had finished for the evening and as often was the case I stayed behind to clear up and lock up after the boxers had left. Sean was the last boxer to leave, "Good night, Sean." My protégé stepped out into the darkness. I had switched off most of the fluorescent lights when I heard the click of a round being chambered into a pistol. A flash of fear caused the hairs on the back of my neck to stand. I turned slowly to stare into the soulless eyes of pink. A small calibre .22 pistol was levelled at my head.

"Ah good evening, William John, or should I address you as Patrick Doyle? I do hope that you didn't think I would forget you or your treachery. That would never do!"

Pink's gun was about three feet from my grasp, perhaps I could taunt him into making a mistake.

"Good evening, Pink, you fucker!"

"Why do you call me that?"

The nerve at the corner of his eye was beginning to twitch. So far, so good.

I delivered my next line. "Perhaps it's because you're a colourless, soulless, spiteful piece of shit!"

Come on, I thought, just one more step forward and I'll spring. Better to die than meekly submit. Pink's face was livid with rage, but he did not make the mistake of coming forward.

My taunts continued, "Why Pink, that's just a peashooter you're using, perhaps you're not man enough to hold a real gun!"

The barrel wavered but his finger was curled around the trigger. One squeeze and I was dead.

Pink's voice was laden with hatred, "This little gun is ideal for what I'm about to do. It will send a bullet through your brain without much noise. I've despatched many 'taigs' with this little toy. You might say that I'm a pragmatic prod."

I spat on the floor at his feet. "Pink, taig is not a nice term. Do you call your partner Bosco a taig? You do surprise me using the word pragmatic. I thought you were still reading the Dick and Dora primary school stories."

Pink was now twitching all over; come on you bastard, just one foot forward. He commanded, "Get on your knees!" Gone was the chance to spring, but I had to keep him talking, anything to delay the inevitable. I slowly lowered onto bended knees and asked, "Do I get the chance to say my prayers?"

The longest prayer known to me is the Lord's prayer and I began to recite it aloud. I found solace in the words, if I had to meet Yeshua again before my time, this was a good way to prepare. I reached the words 'and deliver us from evil' – Bang! The converted barn reverberated with the crack of a single shot. I looked up to see the top of Pink's head spinning towards the overhead lights. His eyes rolled up into their sockets as his brains and blood rolled down. The gangster pirouetted elegantly before collapsing in a heap, splattering me with his blood and brains. Sean Goldmann stepped from the shadows of the small kitchen. Luckily for me I had not yet locked the outside door.

Sean held a Glock 17, a 9mm pistol. It was steady in his right hand and smoke curled lazily from the barrel; an ejected cartridge lay on the floor. He said, "This gun belonged to my father, he hoped that I would never have to use it."

I took the weapon and wiped it clean of prints. "How did you come to possess it?"

"About four years ago, my mother Denise found me. We met in secret, and she passed the gun to me. Other than my Christian name, it was the only legacy I received from my father. It remained hidden until tonight, I had a real feeling that something bad was about to happen, hence my return to the club. I'm very glad that I did."

So was I!

The latch on the kitchen door clicked and I pointed the Glock at the intruder. In from the cold walked Basildon Bond. He smiled when he saw Pink's remains. "Looks as though I was a tad late to save you tonight, Patrick! Thankfully, the boy did it. It does take all of us to look after you. Now pass the Glock to me, this is my legitimate kill, we can't have young Sean involved in this sorry mess. My friends in the constabulary will be delighted that we got Roger."

For once Pink's face had colour, for his life blood drained copiously down his cheeks.

"Gotcha!" Basildon gave the corpse a hefty kick, "Now go and rest in hell!"

In the distance police sirens wailed. Basildon laughed, "Here they come late as usual. There's never a policeman when you need one."

Chapter 56. Timeless love

Sean Goldmann's talents extended beyond boxing. He had recognised my name Paddy Doyle and had done a little bit of sleuthing. He found out about my history and that of his dad. One evening after our training, he approached me. "My father put you in an impossible situation. He put an ideology before everything else, including you and my mother. I know that you regret having killed him, but you had no choice. I bear you no malice. By killing Pink, I am paying back a debt my family owes to you."

My eyes filled with tears, and I hugged him.

Sean continued, before we leave for Dublin for the championships, please join me for dinner with the Goldmanns. My adoptive parents would like to meet you."

And so, it was arranged.

Ari and Nina Goldmann were jovial hosts. They were good company and exuded warmth and hospitality. Ari and I discussed his son's prospects over a good wine; Nina prepared the meal, assisted by Sean. We were expecting a special guest, the Goldmann's niece who had recently returned from Israel. There was an atmosphere of joyful expectation. Sean answered the doorbell. The woman who entered was startling in her beauty. Although her dark hair was beginning to have some grey tips, it was long and luscious sweeping down to her shoulders. Her oval face was complemented by almond-shaped eyes, bright blue in their intensity. Her hourglass figure was augmented by a full bosom. Ari rose and kissed his niece on both cheeks. "Paddy, may I introduce you to Batya Rosenshine!"

Batya's face flushed with recognition. Her eyes had been opened; God was no longer keeping secrets from us. Batya crossed the room and kissed me full on the lips and took me in a warm embrace. "Ezekiel Ben David, I knew we would meet again someday. I have waited a long time to be reunited with you, my soulmate."

All the angels in heaven must have been singing for I could hear their voices raised in praise. The Goldmanns and Sean looked puzzled; how could we possibly know each other, who was this guy, Ezekiel Ben David?

Dinner was a traditional Jewish recipe. Shakshuka was served in cast iron pots. Poached eggs, tomatoes, chilli peppers, and onions were mixed with other spices which I could not identify. It transpired that Batya had recently been widowed. Her husband, Aron, had been killed in the ongoing conflict with the Palestinians. Batya decided she would come and live in Belfast for a time with her aunt and uncle. Out of the frying pan into the fire! Some things never change.

For the remainder of the evening Batya and I conversed to the exclusion of the others. We sat with our hands clasped together. Our behaviour bordered on being rude, but Ari and Nina just smiled; their beloved niece was happy and that was good enough for them. Sean hit me a playful punch as he and I cleared the dishes. At long last there was light at the end of a very dark tunnel.

Epilogue

Sean Goldmann won the Irish championship welterweight division and changed to become a professional boxer shortly after. His father would have been very proud of him. Despite the risks, Batya moved into my cottage at Ballycroob. She told me that Romans and Parthians had failed to separate us. Provos and Prods would not do it either. When my divorce from Libertad was finalised Batya and I married in the Belfast synagogue.

Eventually we took our leave of Ballycroob. The Father Feeny Memorial boxing club gave us a rousing send off. There was much hugging and tears when we took our leave of the Goldmanns. We swopped Belfast drizzle for the sun and warmth of Israel. My application for Israeli citizenship was approved and I established a successful security business in Tel Aviv. Batya was not surprised when I named it 'Ezekiel Ben Doyle Security Solutions.' The name reflected times both past and present.

An official-looking letter arrived in the morning mail. It read, "Patrick Doyle, your country needs your specialist services regarding dealing with terrorists. Please confirm that you can be in my office at your earliest opportunity. Signed by the director of Mossad."

Bloody hell! Here we go again. Would fate ever hold anything different for Patrick Doyle?

The end (Or is it?)

Coming Soon – Paddy Doyle, Mossad and the Mad Mullahs